Berkley Sensation titles by Lucy Monroe

TOUCH ME
TEMPT ME
TAKE ME
MOON AWAKENING
MOON CRAVING

Moon Awakening

continued . . .

Moon Craving

A CHILDREN OF THE MOON NOVEL

Lucy Monroe

BERKLEY SENSATION, NEW YORK

THE BERKLEY PUBLISHING GROUP
Published by the Penguin Group
Penguin Group (USA) Inc.
375 Hudson Street, New York, New York 10014, USA
Penguin Group (Canada), 90 Eglinton Avenue East, Suite 700, Toronto, Ontario M4P 2Y3, Canada
(a division of Pearson Penguin Canada Inc.)
Penguin Books Ltd., 80 Strand, London WC2R 0RL, England
Penguin Group Ireland, 25 St. Stephen's Green, Dublin 2, Ireland (a division of Penguin Books Ltd.)
Penguin Group (Australia), 250 Camberwell Road, Camberwell, Victoria 3124, Australia
(a division of Pearson Australia Group Pty. Ltd.)
Penguin Books India Pvt. Ltd., 11 Community Centre, Panchsheel Park, New Delhi—110 017, India
Penguin Group (NZ), 67 Apollo Drive, Rosedale, North Shore 0632, New Zealand
(a division of Pearson New Zealand Ltd.)
Penguin Books (South Africa) (Pty.) Ltd., 24 Sturdee Avenue, Rosebank, Johannesburg 2196,
South Africa

Penguin Books Ltd., Registered Offices: 80 Strand, London WC2R 0RL, England

This is a work of fiction. Names, characters, places, and incidents either are the product of the author's imagination or are used fictitiously, and any resemblance to actual persons, living or dead, business establishments, events, or locales is entirely coincidental. The publisher does not have any control over and does not assume any responsibility for author or third-party websites or their content.

MOON CRAVING

A Berkley Sensation Book / published by arrangement with the author

PRINTING HISTORY
Berkley Sensation mass-market edition / February 2010

ISBN: 978-0-425-23304-7

BERKLEY® SENSATION
Berkley Sensation Books are published by The Berkley Publishing Group,
a division of Penguin Group (USA) Inc.,
375 Hudson Street, New York, New York 10014.
BERKLEY® SENSATION and the "B" design are trademarks of Penguin Group (USA) Inc.

PRINTED IN THE UNITED STATES OF AMERICA

10 9 8 7 6 5 4 3 2 1

For all of the readers who asked and e-mailed about this book. Your enthusiasm for this world and desire to read the next story blessed me so much. Hearing from you helped me to keep working on it even when so many other things were vying for my attention. And I thank you! I sincerely hope Talorc and Abigail's story is worth the wait. It was a very special story for me to write and one that I hope connects with all your hearts!

Hugs and blessings,
Lucy

Prologue

Millennia ago God created a race of people so fierce even their women were feared in battle. These people were warlike in every way, refusing to submit to the rule of any but their own . . . no matter how large the forces sent to subdue them. Their enemies said they fought like animals. Their vanquished foes said nothing, for they were dead.

They were considered a primitive and barbaric people because they marred their skin with tattoos of blue ink. The designs were usually simple. A single beast was depicted in unadorned outline, though some clan members had more markings, which rivaled the Celts for artistic intricacy. These were the leaders of the clan and their enemies were never able to discover the meanings of any of the blue-tinted tattoos.

Some surmised they were symbols of their warlike nature, and in that they would be partially right. For the beasts represented a part of themselves these fierce and independent people kept secret at the pain of death. It was a secret they had kept for the centuries of their existence while most migrated across the European landscape to settle in the inhospitable north of Scotland.

Their Roman enemies called them Picts, a name accepted by the other peoples of their land and lands south . . . they called themselves the Chrechte.

Their animal-like affinity for fighting and conquest came from a part of their nature their fully human counterparts did not enjoy. For these fierce people were shape-changers and the bluish tattoos on their skin were markings given as a right of passage. When their first change took place, they were marked with the kind of animal they could change into. Some had control of that change. Some did not. And while the majority were wolves, there were large hunting cats and birds of prey as well.

None of the shape-shifters reproduced as quickly or prolifically as their fully human brothers and sisters. Although they were a fearsome race and their cunning was enhanced by an understanding of nature most humans do not possess, they were not foolhardy and were not ruled by their animal natures.

One warrior could kill a hundred of his foe, but should she or he die before having offspring, the death would lead to an inevitable shrinking of the clan. Some Pictish clans and those recognized by other names in other parts of the world had already died out rather than submit to the inferior but multitudinous humans around them.

Most of the shape-changers of the Scots Highlands were too smart to face the end of their race rather than blend with others. They saw the way of the future. In the ninth century AD, Keneth MacAlpin ascended to the Scottish throne. Of Chrechte descent through his mother, MacAlpin was the result of "mixed" marriage, and, his human nature had dominated. He was not capable of "the change," but that did not stop him from laying claim to the Pictish throne (as it was called then). In order to guarantee his kingship, he betrayed his Chrechte brethren at a dinner, killing all of the remaining royals of their people—and forever entrenched a distrust of humans by their Chrechte counterparts.

Despite this distrust, the Chrechte realized that they could die out fighting an ever increasing and encroaching race of humanity, or they could join the Celtic clans.

They joined.

As far as the rest of the world knew—though much existed to attest to their former existence—what had been considered the Pictish people were no more.

Because it was not in their nature to be ruled by any but their own, within two generations, the Celtic clans that had assimilated the Chrechte were ruled by shape-changing clan chiefs, though most of the fully human among them did not know it—only a sparse few were trusted with the secrets of their kinsmen. Those who knew were aware that to betray the code of silence meant certain and immediate death.

That code of silence was rarely broken.

Chapter 1

We, the most distant dwellers upon the earth, the last
of the free, have been shielded . . . by our remoteness
and by the obscurity which has shrouded our name . . .
Beyond us lies no nation, nothing but waves and rocks.
  —KING CALGACUS OF THE PICTS, THIRD CENTURY AD

"Is it war then?" the grizzled old Scot, Osgard, asked
his laird.

Barr, second-in-command to their powerful leader,
frowned. "On our own king?"

The temptation to say yes was great. Talorc, Laird of the
Sinclair clan and alpha to his Chrechte pack, had to clamp
his jaw tight to keep the word from coming out. It would
serve David right. Talorc had no doubt that if he ordered
them to, his clan would go to war against the king still disputed as ruler over all Scotland by many Highlanders.

In the Highlands, at least, first loyalty still went to the
clan leader, not the king. Where would that leave the "civilized" king then?

But the man raised by Normans in that hellhole to their
south was a friend. Despite the *Sassenach* influence, Talorc
respected King David, when few men earned that honor.

"Was it not enough he sent you one English bride, that

he now sends you another?" Osgard asked, his aged voice still strong enough to express his fury.

"He has no plans to send this one," Barr said.

As if Talorc didn't already know the details of the damn message. "No, he expects me to travel to England to wed this woman."

"'Tis an outrage," Osgard growled.

Barr nodded. "An offense you canna take lightly."

"According to the messenger, 'twas both King David and England's king who took offense you did not marry the first Englishwoman," Guaire, Talorc's seneschal, quietly inserted, earning himself a sulfuric glare from Osgard.

The old man, who had stood in Talorc's father's stead as advisor since his death, deliberately turned so Guaire was no longer in his line of sight. "Some might care about offense to the *Sassenach* king, but there are those of us that know better than to trust the English. Especially one who seeks to be wife to our laird."

"I am concerned about neither king's displeasure, but merely point out that they were offended first and that might explain our own king's unpleasant request." Guaire stood his ground, but it was clear the young soldier was bothered by Osgard's comment.

Osgard harrumphed and Barr kept his own council, but Talorc nodded. "No doubt. I had no intention of marrying the Englishwoman Emily, and 'tis clear my overlord realized that after the fact."

"You did not go to war when the Balmoral took and kept her," Barr said.

"A Chrechte does not go to war over the loss of a *Sassenach*," Osgard spit out, disgust lacing every word.

Guaire frowned. "The Balmoral would."

Talorc's seneschal was right. The leader of the Balmoral

clan, now married to the Englishwoman his king had first bid him wed, would no doubt go to war over her. As impossible as it might be for Talorc to understand, all indications led him to believe the other Chrechte laird *loved* his outspoken wife.

Osgard spun to face the younger warrior and would have knocked him to the ground, but another warrior's hand stayed him. The big, battle-scarred Chrechte stared impassively at the old man. As big as Talorc's second-in-command, Barr's twin, Niall, could intimidate without effort. His hard features were made more imposing by the scars that marred the left side of his face.

Killing a Chrechte was no easy task, but Niall had almost died in the same battle that had claimed his older brother Sean, Talorc's former second-in-command and brother-in-law.

Osgard flinched, even though no threat had been spoken from the massive warrior.

Talorc had to bite back amusement. Little intimidated the old Scot, but Niall did it without effort. In fact, besides himself, the only other member of the Sinclair clan that did not tremble in Niall's presence was his twin, Barr.

Opening and closing his mouth like a fish, Guaire stared with wide eyes at Niall and Osgard.

"I see you decided to join us," Barr said to his twin.

"I heard a messenger from the king had arrived."

"You heard correctly," Talorc replied.

"What did he want this time?" Niall asked, as if demands from Scotland's monarch came frequently.

"You can release my arm," Osgard groused.

"You will not hit the boy."

"He insulted our laird," Osgard said.

"I am not a boy," Guaire said at the same time, and then

when he realized what Osgard had said, he puffed up with offense. "I did no such thing."

Niall released Osgard's arm but stepped between the old man and the young redheaded warrior. "Our Guaire would no more insult our laird than betray him."

"He said our leader was not as strong as the Balmoral."

"I didn't!" Guaire's face flushed with his own fury.

Niall looked inquiringly at Talorc. "Were you offended, laird?"

"Nay."

"There. See?" Guaire crossed his arms, edging away from Niall toward Barr.

The lines around Niall's mouth tightened, but he said nothing at the telling action.

Guaire said, "I merely referred to the fact that the Balmoral had found benefit in his English wife and our laird could as well. After all, she is Emily's sister."

Aye, the Balmoral had found a mate to his wolf in the English human. She had recently given birth to their first child. A daughter. Talorc actually felt pleasure for them, though he could not imagine why. The Balmoral was a pain in the ass. But a strong Chrechte warrior all the same.

"Our laird will not be stepping foot onto English soil to be wed," Osgard said with pure conviction.

"Nay, I won't." Talorc turned to Guaire. "You will write a message to the king for me."

"Yes, laird."

"Tell him I will wed the *Sassenach* as requested, but will do so on the soil of our homeland. I will travel south through MacDonald land; they are our allies."

"Yes, laird. Anything else?"

"I will accept the land bordering the Donegal clan that has been in dispute these years past and the other dowry items he offered to provide, but will require an additional twenty drums of mead and twenty shields, twenty helmets, ten swords, and ten poleaxes in payment for taking the English bride."

"What need have we of shields and helmets?" Osgard asked, though it was clear he approved of Talorc requiring a bigger dowry of his king to marry the *Sassenach*.

"Not all our warriors are Chrechte," Talorc reminded his aged advisor.

Some, indeed the majority of their clan, were human. They did not have the power of the wolf to protect them in battle, or the ability to change into the beast.

Only the Chrechte had those abilities, and their dual nature was a closely guarded secret. Though they made no secret of the truth, they saw themselves as superior warriors.

Human treachery could undermine Chrechte strength though. MacAlpin's betrayal of the Chrechte people was still fresh in most of their minds, though it had taken place in the last century. Other wounds were more fresh, like the treachery of Talorc's stepmother, the human Tamara. She had betrayed his father and the entire Sinclair clan. Her machinations had resulted in many deaths, both human and Chrechte alike, Talorc's father and brother among them.

The fact that she had brought about her own death as well did not assuage Talorc's fury or his grief.

'Twas not a thing Talorc was likely to forget. Ever.

He could almost pity the human Englishwoman chosen as his bride because of it.

Abigail snuck into the room her stepfather used mostly for meetings with his steward and the captain of his guard. It was also where he stored written correspondence and kept the few books that comprised the Hamilton library. No one but Sir Reuben and his lady, Abigail's mother, were allowed in the room without an invitation.

Abigail's clenched hands perspired with nerves at the prospect of being discovered, but she had no choice.

Not after the argument she had witnessed between her lady mother and her younger sister, Jolenta. She wasn't supposed to have seen that, either, but needs must.

And she needed to know more than others about what occurred in the keep. If for no other reason than to protect her own secret.

So, without hesitation, she had watched her mother and sister's disagreement from her hiding place on the other side of the bailey. She had seen only her sister's face so knew only one side of the argument, but Jolenta's words had caused deep disquiet within Abigail, and she had come looking for answers.

Among other, more alarming things, Jolenta had mentioned a message from the king. She had accused their mother, Sybil, of favoritism toward Abigail. Which had been so absurd, Abigail had laughed with silent, bitter mirth even as the argument continued.

Her watching had resulted in more questions than answers. Abigail was hoping the message from the king had been written and that she would find it here.

Before going to the Highlands to marry a laird there, her stepsister, Emily, had once said that she would never know what was going on if she did not eavesdrop. Abigail did not have the option of listening in on conversations, but she had her own methods of discovering that which her mother would keep hidden.

Like reading her sister's lips from a distance.

Abigail had lost her hearing and her mother's love six years ago to a fever that had almost taken her life. When she'd woken from the fever and her affliction was discovered, her mother had refused to return to Abigail's sickroom. It was left to Emily, her stepsister only a couple of years older than she, to nurse Abigail back to health.

It had taken only one visit with her mother and stepfather after Abigail was well enough to leave her room for the girls to realize Abigail no longer held status as a precious daughter. Indeed, Sir and Lady Hamilton did their best to pretend Abigail did not exist at all.

Once the girls realized the effect her deafness had on their parents' affections, they had known they could not let others know about it.

Emily had been worried Abigail would not only be rejected, but be seen as cursed. The older girl had taken on the task of helping Abigail hide her burden from the rest of the keep. She had worked tirelessly with Abigail, teaching her to read lips and to continue to speak in a well-modulated voice.

Emily had been a strict taskmaster, but Abigail knew her sister's insistence on practice to the point of exhaustion had been motivated by love. Nevertheless, there had been times Abigail had wondered if waking from her fever had been for the best. Out of her own love for Emily, Abigail had never given voice to her doubts.

She had not wanted to hurt the stepsister who loved her and treated her more kindly than her blood sister ever would. Abigail missed Emily so much.

And without her there to help, Abigail's voice had dropped to what she knew was a near whisper. Speaking was difficult enough; speaking normally was almost impossible without Emily's constant covert instruction. It was a testament to how well Emily had trained Abigail to speak that none of the servants had discovered her secret in more than two years since her sister had gone to Scotland, however.

Abigail lived for the day she would join her sister and be able to escape the Hamilton Keep.

Sir Reuben's attitude had softened toward her once he had seen that she would not embarrass him by making her affliction known, but her mother made it clear that she considered Abigail a stone around her neck. She pinned all her hopes of a progressive marriage match on Jolenta.

Yet Sybil had refused Emily's initial petition to send Abigail to the Highlands for an extended visit.

Abigail did not understand why. Unless her mother simply hated her so much that Sybil could not stand the idea of Abigail happy, as she surely would be, reunited with the one person in the world who loved her and truly desired her presence.

Abigail spent most of her days in her own company. Thankfully, Emily had taught her to read letters as well as lips. Though few and far between, letters from her sister had been her only link to Emily since going north to marry her Highlander. Abigail studied the books Sir Reuben allowed her to read and the letters Emily had left behind from her friend, the abbess. In the past six months, Abigail had begun her own correspondence with the learned woman as well. Her inability to hear had no power to tarnish a friendship carried out in writing.

Their housekeeper, Anna, was kind, but she was a busy woman, and Abigail did not like to be a bother. She only continued to work on improving her Gaelic with the old woman born in Scotland because she refused to give up hope. Eventually Sybil would allow the daughter she considered useless to join Emily in the Highlands. She had to.

Indeed, Abigail had been sure that time had come when Sybil had taken her aside these seven days past and told her that she would be leaving the keep with Sir Reuben and Sybil on a trip. Abigail believed Sybil had finally acceded to Emily's entreaties and thrown herself into preparations for the trip with excitement she had not felt since her sister had been taken from her.

Of course, Abigail had experienced some trepidation at the prospect that she was being taken to a nunnery. But surely the abbess would have said something in her last letter if that were to be the case. Abigail had asked her mother if she would be seeing Emily.

Sybil had replied that it was possible. Abigail had thought she was just being coy. Now, she feared the older woman had meant exactly that. It was possible, not probable.

Finally, Abigail found the letter from the king and read it with growing panic.

It could not be possible. Her mother would not be so cruel. But the missive from the king said otherwise. Sybil, damn her avaricious soul, had said nothing of the true reason for the upcoming journey, but the letter laid out her mother's greed and treachery in ink, sealed by the king himself.

How could a mother plan something so nefarious for her blood offspring? Worse, how could she do so without warning Abigail of what was to come?

A hand grabbed her shoulder, fingers that felt like claws digging into her. Her heart stopped and then began beating faster than a rabbit's.

She was spun violently around and came face-to-face with her livid mother.

Sybil demanded, "What do you think you are doing?"

She could not hear the words, but Abigail had no trouble reading the anger or the question coming from her mother's lips.

At first, shock and fear at being discovered paralyzed Abigail's thoughts. She tried to speak, but could tell no sound had made it past her throat from the disgusted expression twisting her mother's features.

That disgust sliced through Abigail, leaving a bloody trail of inner pain behind. However, instead of the shame she usually felt at her inabilities, fury at her mother's betrayal boiled up inside Abigail.

More than two years had passed since the first edict from the king that had torn Abigail's world apart for the second time. Because of Sir Reuben's miserly response to the king's call for soldiers from his landed knights, the king had demanded his vassal provide a marriageable daughter. He and Scotland's monarch wanted to intermarry English nobility with the hard-to-control Highland nobles.

Emily had been sent to Scotland to marry Talorc, Laird of the Sinclairs. Only she had ended up kidnapped and wed to his rival, the laird of the Balmoral clan.

When Abigail had learned of this situation, she had assumed that would be the end of it. Scotland's king should be happy one of his Highland lairds had taken an English wife. Naïve as that thought might have been, she was certain she had been right.

According to the king's letter, *Abigail's* planned upcoming marriage to the original Highland laird was the result of Sybil's petition for redress, not the Scottish king's. Her mother had petitioned her king, knowing the outcome would be that her deaf daughter would be given in marriage to a stranger in a foreign land.

Abigail put every bit of loathing she felt at her mother's perfidy in her glare. "I was looking for the truth; something difficult to come by in your company."

Sybil dismissed the insult with a sneer. "You have no business in here."

"By your action, you believe I have no place in this keep at all."

A silent stare answered her accusation, but it spoke more loudly than words could have. Sybil wanted Abigail gone. Pain tore through her, the years of rejection coming together in one moment to pierce her heart with a mortal blow.

"When were you going to tell me?" Abigail asked, making no effort to modulate her voice.

"When I felt it necessary," Sybil replied with dismissive venom.

"At the altar? When I stood before a priest to say vows?"

Her mother's expression was all the answer Abigail needed. Sybil had had no intention of preparing Abigail for the wedding that was to take place across the Scottish border. Abigail didn't think anything could hurt worse than the betrayal she found between the lines of the king's missive. She had been wrong.

Knowing not only that had Sybil arranged for this marriage, but that she intended Abigail to go into it not only deaf, but blind as well, destroyed the last vestiges of hope of her mother's love to which she had stubbornly clung all this time.

"How could you be so cruel?" How could any mother set her daughter up so foully?

"It is not cruel to secure your future."

Abigail didn't believe the benevolent justification for a second. "There is no security in subterfuge."

She should know. She lived in daily fear of being revealed as deaf. Many considered such an affliction the result of demon possession. The Church's answer to such a circumstance was enough to give Abigail nightmares. Many, many nightmares since her sister left at their king's edict to marry a Highland laird.

"You should be grateful. What chance would you have to marry without my machinations?" Her mother had the gall to look self-righteous, but Abigail knew better.

"Emily wanted me to live with her. I would have been out of your way then." Abigail forced the words out, knowing her mother had no patience for her affliction.

"Not permanently. Once her husband realized you were cursed, he would send you back to us." Sybil spoke as if the words were not daggers to the heart of her eldest daughter. "This is a better solution."

"Emily's laird knows of my affliction. She told him."

"Of course she didn't. If she had, he would never have allowed her to extend the invitation for your visit."

Abigail felt herself shaking. "Do you hate me so much?"

"I am showing a mother's concern in securing your future. Jolenta is jealous of the good match you are making," Sybil had the gall to point out, confirming she had told Abigail's younger sister of the wedding plans.

The truth that the slight had been on purpose could not have been more obvious.

Abigail had to swallow back bile as she became physically ill at this additional evidence of her mother's hatred. "The only future you are securing is your own."

"Think what you like." Sybil shrugged. "You clearly place no importance on my motherly wisdom. Thankfully, I still have a daughter who listens to my advice."

The unjustness of the accusations took Abigail's breath.

Sybil had withheld both motherly affection and advice ever since her eldest child had become an abomination to her. Saying as much would carry no weight with her lady mother, though, so Abigail did not try. "I think the Sinclair laird will be furious when he realizes he has been deceived."

"Then you had better make sure he never finds out."

"How can I do that? We will be married." She didn't have Emily to nudge her when others spoke to her or cover for her when she missed something.

"You need spend little time with him. He is after all, a barbaric Scot."

According to Emily's rare letters, Talorc of the Sinclairs was both barbarian and proud. What would such a proud laird do when he learned of the deceit? Would he kill her? Declare war on her father? Sending her to a nunnery or back to her family was the best possible scenario, but not one she could rely on.

And the sad truth was, Abigail's mother obviously didn't care what the outcome would be, so long as she was rid of her cursed daughter.

"He will be my husband regardless. What if he seeks out my company?" she asked, with little hope of reasoning with Sybil.

Her mother's expression revealed what she thought of that possibility. "He hates the English. He is acceding to the marriage because of the dowry his king has offered him."

The king's missive had said as much, outlining a very generous dowry that sounded more like a bribe from monarch to laird to ensure the Highlander's cooperation.

"What of *my* dowry?"

"You think I would provide such when your sister ended

up married to the wrong laird? I insisted that the dowry provided with Emily be returned to the Sinclair laird or for him to do without."

Cold certainty settled in Abigail's heart. "You want to rid yourself of me and had no intention of paying a nunnery a proper dowry to do so." That was supposing a nunnery would take her, even with the right monetary incentive. "So, you have orchestrated this bargain made in hell."

Sybil slapped Abigail, knocking her backward. "Do not dare speak to me thus."

"Why not? It is the truth." Abigail put her hand over her throbbing cheek, screaming in her head, but unable to express the pain through her voice.

"The truth is, you will no longer be my problem."

Abigail staggered under the verbal blow so much more painful than the slap. "What if I tell him before he is bound to me? What will you do then?"

She could stop the madness before it began.

Those words were the last Abigail was able to utter as Sybil lifted the stick that hung by a thong from her girdle— the one she used to pound on the table for attention or as a weapon to punish servants. Realizing what her mother intended to do, Abigail turned to run, but tripped on her gown.

The first blow fell across her shoulders as she tried to regain her footing. The second came swiftly after, and soon Abigail gave up on trying to get away, but merely curled into a ball, her only protection in making a smaller target for the enraged woman to hit.

The blows stopped abruptly and Abigail sensed a scuffle above her, but she refused to uncover her head to see what was happening. Gentle hands lifted her as a familiar scent told her who held her. It was her stepfather. She raised her head to discover Sir Reuben looked furious. He yelled something at her mother, but Abigail could not read his lips from her position. She could tell the words were strained and angry from the taught muscles in Sir Reuben's neck though.

Her mother opened her mouth, but he spoke again, shaking his head. Abigail could feel the vibrations in his chest.

Sybil's eyes widened in shock and then narrowed in anger, but she left. And at that moment, Abigail craved nothing more.

Sir Reuben said something but clearly was not attempting to communicate with Abigail as he tucked her more firmly against his broad chest. He carried her through the keep to her small bedroom and laid her on the bed.

"I have called for Anna to come tend you." He spoke carefully so Abigail could read his lips without effort.

"Thank you." She was too distraught to be sure her words had voice, but she hoped he understood.

He sighed, looking guilty—which surprised her. "I should have realized she would not tell you of the wedding."

Not knowing what to say, unsure if she was capable of speech at all, Abigail looked away.

Sir Reuben turned her head back. "Listen to me, child." She gave him a look.

He smiled. He actually smiled. "Then read my lips."

She nodded grudgingly, barely moving her head up and down once.

"At first, I thought your mother's idea mad, but then we got the first letter from Emily."

Abigail sucked in a betrayed breath. So, her mother had planned this as soon as the rumors had reached them that Emily had wed not the Sinclair, but the Balmoral laird? She had long suspected Sybil wanted to send Abigail, rather than Emily—the stepdaughter she relied on to help her run the keep—in response to the king's initial marriage edict.

Only Emily had refused to confirm Abigail's fears. She had even acted excited about the prospect of going north. She had promised to send for Abigail as soon as she could.

Now Abigail knew for certain that it had not been Sybil's choice to send Emily. She did not know how her stepsister had managed, but Abigail was certain Emily had arranged to be sent in order to protect her from the very outcome she now faced.

"Emily . . ." It was the only word she could get out.

Chapter 2

Sir Reuben sighed. "Your mother never intended to allow you to go to Emily. She saw that solution as too tenuous."

"She hates me," Abigail whispered, the words burning like acid in her throat and heart.

"Sybil is a perfectionist. She put great store in your looks and the probability you would make a good match and advance her aspirations. The fever that took your hearing stole her dreams as well."

Abigail glared, trying to move back from her stepfather, causing pain enough to make her wish she had stayed still.

His shoulders sagged and an expression of deep sadness lurked in his usually commanding eyes. "Her behavior was not justified, but none of us are perfect. We often hurt those we love the most when our disappointment is too great to overcome."

Emily had told Abigail a story of when she was little, before her father and Sybil had married. Abigail wondered if he spoke of that time now. It did not matter though. No matter what her mother's reasoning behind her cruelty, it left Abigail in a horrible circumstance.

"He will kill me," she said, giving voice to her worst fear.

Sir Reuben's shoulders drew back and his pride settled on him like a mantle. "I would not allow it if I thought there was even a remote chance of such a thing."

"You cannot know."

"I can. There is a far more likely outcome."

She doubted him but felt far too disheartened to argue the point. "Why?"

"Why did I allow it?"

She nodded the tiniest bit.

"Your sister found happiness with her highland laird; perhaps you will, too."

Abigail could not make all the words come. She finally managed to say, "Hates."

"Your mother has heard he hates the English, but Emily said in her letters that he was now allied with her husband. He cannot be that filled with hatred, or he would not have allied himself with a man married to an Englishwoman."

Abigail just stared at Sir Reuben, tears burning tracks down her temples.

"You have hidden your affliction from the keep, surely you will be able to do so in his castle."

She shook her head vehemently, pain rolling through her at the movement. But it was impossible. She knew the keep and its people. It would be different somewhere else. Much, much too hard.

Sir Reuben caressed her cheek and smiled sadly. "Perhaps he will find out, but if he does, do you not think he will find it more convenient to return you to your closest family, rather than send you all the way back to England?"

For the first time since reading the king's missive, a tiny glimmer of hope came to light in Abigail's heart. Was it possible this situation would reunite her with Emily after all?

Sir Reuben must have read the hope in her eyes because he nodded. "I considered all the possibilities before I allowed your mother to petition the king for redress on what she saw as a grievous offense, that of her stepdaughter being married to the wrong laird."

Abigail shook her head again, bringing on another wave of pain in her shoulders. But it was a lie. Her mother was full of them.

"Whatever her true reasons, this was the only way you could leave her influence forever. Had you gone as a guest to the Highlands, she could have called you home at any time. I love your mother, but I know she has a vindictive streak."

Abigail's tears had been drying, but at the reminder of the hatred her mother had for her, they spilled over her eyelids once again.

Sir Reuben brushed them away with his thumbs. "Here now. It will be all right. If you wish me to tell the laird the truth of your affliction, I will."

She stared at him, her tears drying in her absolute shock.

"I give you my word."

Her stepfather was a hard man, a man she had never gone to for comfort or solace, but one thing she knew: he kept his word.

Anna arrived at the door then, clucking and looking as

upset as she had the time her own little granddaughter had fallen too close to the cooking fire and burned herself.

"Think about what I have said. We are to leave for the border tomorrow. You can give me your answer once you have looked in the eyes of the man you are intended to marry."

The words stunned Abigail all over again. Only the most besotted parent took their child's opinion into account when arranging marriage. It was a boon she could not have expected, for she was not cherished at all.

Sir Reuben's offer was beyond a boon even; it might be enough to give her the courage to face what the journey tomorrow would bring.

"Thank you," she whispered, forcing sound she could not hear, only feel in her throat.

His face twisted in a grimace. "I owe you far more, child."

Then he left Abigail to Anna's ministrations.

The trip to the MacDonald holding took two days.

Abigail had spent both days in pain and avoiding looking at or responding to her mother in any way.

Ever since her fall from grace, she had hoped to again earn her mother's approval and love. She now knew that to be more a fairy tale than any of those Anna had told her and Emily about werewolves in the Scottish Highlands. It would never happen.

And she would not care.

Her mother did not love her, but Emily still did. Her stepsister had never stopped caring for her. Abigail intended to be reunited with the only family that mattered to her. Somehow. Some way. She would see Emily again, and Abigail would tell the other woman how important her devotion had been.

She now knew Emily had truly saved her life, in more ways than one.

It was easy to ignore her mother in the journey as fear and pain vied for Abigail's attention. She could not think about her future without great trepidation mitigated only somewhat by her hope.

And while Anna had treated Abigail's injuries with an herbal mixture better than anything the leech could have achieved, no herbs could remove all the discomfort from Abigail's many bruises. The maid Sir Reuben had insisted travel with her had helped Abigail apply the concoction each night and morning, leaving her smelling strongly of rosemary and witch hazel. Not an unpleasant fragrance, she consoled herself.

It was late afternoon of the second day when they reached the MacDonald keep. It was nothing like her step-father's home. There was no moat, no tower, just a house about four times the size of the surrounding cottages and a timber fence that would burn all too easily in battle.

Nevertheless, the people seemed unworried by the presence of an English baron and his complement of soldiers.

The MacDonald plaid was a deep red-orange and forest green. Abigail searched for a different set of colors, trying to identify her intended husband or one of his people. Only there was no other clan present. No other plaid than the one they had first seen after coming onto MacDonald land.

An old man and two burly but young warriors approached their entourage as Sir Reuben pulled his horse to a halt outside the keep. "Welcome to MacDonald's holding," he said in careful English.

Abigail slipped into her well-practiced method of

reading lips, watching first the Scotsman speak and then Sir Reuben.

Sir Reuben swung down off his horse, followed by the most senior soldier and two others. The rest remained mounted. "You are the laird?"

"Nay, he is out hunting with the Sinclair."

Her stepfather was clearly taken aback. "My daughter's intended is out hunting?"

"Aye."

"And your laird went with him?"

From the look on the old man's face, something in the way Sir Reuben spoke alarmed him. "Ye dinna gainsay the Sinclair, my lord."

"Perhaps he wanted to provide the meat for the wedding feast himself?" Sir Reuben asked.

The old man nodded his head quickly. "Aye, I'm sure that was it."

"I see." Sir Reuben looked around him. "Your laird has made arrangements for our comfort?"

The MacDonald man pointed to a cottage separate from the others and near another building. "Aye. The cottage yonder, near the chapel, is clean and ready for your occupation."

"And my soldiers?"

"Are they not accustomed to sleeping outside like a Scottish warrior?" the old man asked, a wicked twinkle in his eye.

Abigail found herself almost smiling.

"We have tents for them to pitch around the cottage. I can provide for all my people in a civilized fashion," her stepfather said with what she was sure was arrogance. It was in his eyes and the way he held himself.

Sir Reuben was a powerful lord, which was why his

only sanction upon sending a miserly number of soldiers as tithe to his king when he had a bevy of them had been the loss of a daughter.

Abigail knew her mother was speaking as well because the old man's eyes strayed in Sybil's direction a couple of times, though he did not seem to ever speak directly to her as he and her stepfather worked out arrangements for where to pitch the soldier's tents.

For once Abigail was grateful she could not hear. She could not be forced to listen to her mother's words and she chose not to watch Sybil's lips.

The decision to pitch the tents for the English soldiers on the west side of the cottage, farthest from the keep, made little difference to Abigail.

She wanted a chance to see the man she had been commanded to wed, the laird she had to deceive about her affliction.

At least until they reached the Highlands.

Later that night, Abigail willed herself to sleep as she lay in the small bed in the corner of the cottage. Only it was to no avail. Her mind was whirling with questions and possibilities.

Why had her intended groom been out hunting when she and her family had arrived? Surely he had known the date of their arrival; it had been dictated by him through his king to hers.

He had yet to return to the keep, having missed the evening meal.

Was this his way of showing his unhappiness with the prospect of marriage to an Englishwoman? Was he delivering a slap at her stepfather's consequence? His dislike of the English was no secret, but he had agreed to the marriage and all the stipulations surrounding it.

Stipulations that scared the tiredness right out of Abigail and filled her with worry on top of the apprehensions already plaguing her. His king had required the marriage be consummated before they left the Lowlands. Abigail had no idea why Scotland's sovereign would demand such a thing, but the prospect leant additional discomfort to a situation that already had the power to terrify her completely.

None of those fears were soothed in any way by the fact that she had yet to even see her groom from a distance.

When she looked into his eyes, would she see cruelty? Hatred to rival her mother's? Would he recognize her affliction despite her best efforts to hide it?

Tonight's dinner had been a trial unlike anything she had experienced since first losing her hearing. It was hard enough to keep track of several people speaking at once; the unfamiliar surroundings only made it worse. She had received help from an unexpected source. Sir Reuben had done his best to help Abigail maintain the threads of the conversations happening around her.

None of the MacDonald clan spoke directly to her. She got the impression this was out of respect to the Sinclair laird.

Even without being directly involved in discussions, she had made several mistakes because she had not realized she was being spoken to.

The old warrior who had filled the laird's position as host had believed Abigail's faulty Gaelic to be the cause, when in fact, Abigail understood and spoke Gaelic quite well now. As convenient as the excuse, how long would it serve to cover the fact she simply didn't always know when someone was speaking to her?

And what would Talorc, Laird of the Sinclair, do when he found out?

Emily had made it clear in her first letter that she and Talorc had not suited at all. Abigail's older sister had written that the man hated the English. He had not wanted what he called a *Sassenach* bride under any circumstances. He must be seething with fury over the second order from his king to that effect.

Would that work in Abigail's favor or against her? Certainly, if she wanted a powerful Scottish laird for a husband as her younger sister Jolenta seemed to, the knowledge that Talorc of the Sinclairs despised the English would wound her hopes. But Abigail had given up hope of ever having her own family when her blood kin rejected her because of her affliction. No man, be he Scottish barbarian or English knight would want a wife cursed by deafness.

The possibility that Talorc's dislike of the English, and naturally subsequent desire to be rid of her, would be great enough for him to see her deception as a gift rather than an offense over which he would declare war, was her one slim hope.

Sir Reuben seemed unconcerned with the idea Laird Sinclair might declare war over such a thing. However, from what Emily had said in her letters regarding the pride of the Highlanders and Talorc especially, Abigail had her doubts. In addition, if Talorc was as hard a man as Emily had implied in her letters, he might very well exact a personal revenge from a deceptive bride.

The prospect terrified her almost as much as her first lucid moments after her world had gone silent.

At this moment, there were altogether too many prospects to cause her concern, and Abigail envied her maid the oblivion of sleep. She craved escape from her thoughts, but not enough to wish she'd joined her parents. Sybil and Sir Reuben were in the keep, along with the soldiers on duty and those that had not chosen an early night.

Abigail had not been invited to join them, and she had not requested to do so. Supper had been difficult enough with her struggle to read unfamiliar lips and features. Added to that had been the nerve-racking condition of being the center of all eyes, a condition she had no experience with.

Abigail was used to being ignored among her stepfather's people. Only here, she was the future wife of a powerful Highland laird obviously respected and admired by the MacDonald clan—and perhaps even a little feared. Everyone had stared at her, and she felt their judgment even if she could not hear the whispers going on around her.

Sadly, *none* of her experiences since reaching Scotland had served to quiet the anxiety screaming inside her soundless world.

The dirt floor of the cottage vibrated. Emily had taught Abigail that she had to use her other senses to compensate for her lack of hearing. Otherwise, she would be found out and become an outcast even in her family's own keep. She had learned to "hear" a great deal through what she felt around her. Dropping her hand to the floor, she let it settle against the compacted earth. The vibrations were in no way subtle and indicated a party of warhorses riding past the cottage. Her soon-to-be groom and the MacDonald laird must have returned.

They had certainly taken their time about it. It was full dark, and the two lairds had missed the evening meal by more than two hours.

Careful not to wake the sleeping maid, Abigail climbed

from her bed. She could not miss this opportunity to get a glimpse of the Sinclair laird.

She snuck quietly to the cottage window facing the front, but when she pulled back the covering, she saw no horses or men. She hurried across the one-room dwelling and pulled the covering aside on the window facing the chapel.

The nearly full, waxing moon illuminated a large group of warriors. Nine men in all. Five were on huge warhorses and held themselves with greater confidence than the others. Or perhaps it was simply that they exuded dominance over everything around them. They were all big men, though two were near giants. They all wore a plaid different from the MacDonalds, though the colors were hard to distinguish at this distance in the moonlight.

The Sinclairs. They had to be.

The four remaining men wore the MacDonald plaid. Watching the interplay among them, it was easy to determine who the MacDonald laird was.

The Sinclairs were not so uncomplicated to read. The other four warriors, including the MacDonald laird, deferred to all five of the Sinclairs in subtle but unmistakable ways. At least they were evident to a woman who had spent as much time deciphering the language of body movement as Abigail.

And while it was clear someone among the Sinclairs had given the order to dismount, she could not tell who had done it. The giant with hair the color of a raven that brushed his shoulders, or the one with light-colored hair that glowed almost silver in the moonlight?

Neither wore a shirt with their plaid, which she had been told was common when a Scottish warrior hunted or

fought in battle. At least among the Highlanders. The Mac-
Donalds all wore shirts, even if they still displayed their
naked legs with a total lack of civilized modesty. Abigail
had spent so much time blushing over that Gaelic ward-
robe idiosyncrasy, she was sure her cheeks were tinged a
permanent pink.

The raven-haired man had an intricate, dark tattoo cir-
cling his left bicep. She had heard there were tribes in the
Highlands that practiced the barbaric custom of permanently marking their skin with blue ink, but it had never
occurred to her that the Sinclairs might be one of them.
The dark swirls moved as the warrior's muscles bunched
when he swung down from his horse.

She experienced the most perplexing desire to follow those lines of dark ink with her fingertips. The urge
shocked her to her very core. Abigail was far more innocent than her younger sister, Jolenta, who had spent several
months every year for the last four at Court. Jolenta had
boasted of flirting with numerous men in attendance.

She had told Abigail that she had gone so far as to
allow a few of those men to kiss her. When Abigail had
expressed dismay at such wanton behavior, Jolenta had
merely laughed.

Since her sister was rarely willing to spend time in Abigail's company, she did not plague Jolenta about it further.
Only she had wondered if her sister's forward ways had
been the reason Jolenta had returned early this year from
Court.

Unlike her wayward, if courageous sister, Abigail rarely
spoke to the opposite sex. She had never touched a man or
even wanted to. She had been touched for the first time in
memory by a male when her stepfather carried her to her
chambers after her mother beat her.

The truth was she hardly ever made physical contact with *anyone*.

To want to reach out and caress someone was a feeling so new and disturbing it benumbed her thoughts as well as her person for several seconds.

As she grappled with this unexpected sensation, the raven-haired man turned so she could see his face. Abigail's breath seized in her chest. A day's growth of beard outlined a strong jaw and firmly set lips on the most handsome face she had ever seen.

And the most frightening.

Because she knew with inexplicable certainty that this was the man she was to marry. Power surrounded him like a mist that would never dissipate. No one but he could be leader of the Sinclairs.

He turned his head, and she would have sworn he looked directly at her, if it were possible. It was as if he knew she was watching him, but that could not be. The urge to duck fully behind the curtain was strong, but she was still feeling the paralyzing effects of her desire to touch him. And surely he could not see her in the dark of the cottage?

Was that cruelty or strength in his glittering eyes? There *was* knowledge. Logic notwithstanding, he knew she was there. But how?

Unlike him, she did not stand in a clearing with no hindrance to the revelations of bright moonlight. She was hidden almost completely by the window covering, and what wasn't hidden should not have been distinguishable in the dim light, made darker by the shadow of the cottage's roof.

If circumstances were not odd enough, the pale-haired giant warrior turned his attention on her as well, though she had seen nothing to indicate the other man had apprised him of her presence. This warrior's eyes were dark, though she did not think they were brown. He was maybe even bigger than the dark-haired man, but she did not assume that made him laird.

While might would be important in determining leadership among the war-bent clans in the north, size was not the only determining factor in strength. The blond giant looked strong enough, but he did not look toward her with quite the intensity of the other man.

He did not have a tattoo on his arm either, and she was guessing that was significant. His left cheek was marred by a battle scar; even so, he was almost as handsome as the other man.

Abigail felt an instant rapport with the marked soldier. It was too easy for others to judge a person's worth on a physical affliction. This warrior could do no more about his scar than she could her deafness.

The raven-haired man came toward her with purposeful strides. The other giant warrior followed him, a strange half smile on his face. The puckered flesh gave him a sinister look that the amusement in his eyes belied.

At that moment, Abigail definitely should have ducked behind the window covering. She couldn't. The tattooed warrior held her attention as firmly as she held on to the hope of seeing her sister again one day.

His silent command to stay still was unmistakable.

Even if the command *was* only in her imagination, it would not let her go. Her body felt strangely heavy, but her head felt light. Fear and exhilaration coursed through her as her fingers curled around the window covering in a stranglehold.

As he came closer, the pace of her breathing increased until she was panting as if she had been chasing her sister through the meadow near her stepfather's keep like she had when they were children.

He did not stop once he reached the cottage as she expected, but continued around to the front. She stared after him, confused and painfully disappointed when she should never have wanted to speak to the man alone in the first place.

Her gaze swung back to the light-haired soldier where he had stopped a few feet from the window. He looked at her, but if he was curious about her like the MacDonald clan, he did not show it. His scarred face and gray eyes were devoid of emotion, his square jaw set as if words would not leave his mouth anytime soon.

She stared back, uncertain if she should do or say anything.

The lack of communication stretched between them until the dark-haired man returned, a scowl of anger twisting his masculine lips. His blue gaze seared her, his eyes darker than the daytime sky, but nothing like the dark blue velvet of night.

Her heart beat more quickly in her chest, and she laid her hand against her throat to ensure she was not making sounds she was unaware of.

"Why are you angry?" she felt herself asking without first thinking to do so. She spoke in Gaelic, not so halting as it had been when she had been learning with Emily, but at a lower volume.

She should not have spoken at all. It was forward behavior Sybil would have scolded her severely for with a certainty.

"No one guards you."

"There are soldiers in their tents on the west side." Surely he had noticed.

"They sleep."

"They would come if I called for aid." Though honestly, she did not know if she was capable of yelling any longer.

It had been over two years since her sister had left and equally as long since she had someone to help her determine the height of her voice.

The man's scowl only deepened. "Where is the guard for your door?"

She so wished she could hear his voice. The pain of her loss pricked at her in a way she had not let it do in many years. Everything else about him was the stuff dreams were made of. No doubt his voice would be the perfect pitch for such a powerful man.

"There is none." She knew the answer was not what the man wanted to hear the moment she'd uttered the words.

He said a word she could not interpret and glared over his shoulder, barking out an order she could not hear. She didn't need to though, because one of his other soldier's was making his way rapidly around to the front of the cottage. Abigail knew it was to take up a guard's position at the door.

She would have gone to check but could not make herself leave the dark-haired warrior's company.

"Where are your father's soldiers? Surely they do not all sleep?"

"Those on duty, or who wished to visit with the Mac-Donald soldiers, are inside the keep. With him." She kept her hand against her throat to make sure it vibrated with sound, monitoring her tone as Emily had made her learn to do.

"He is not on his own land. All of his soldiers are on duty at all times," the Sinclair warrior bit out, his jaw clamping between words.

Abigail looked toward the keep where her parents entertained themselves with no thought to a deaf daughter's terror on the night before her forced wedding. "It is not for me to say."

"You are Emily's sister. The woman I am to wed."

She nodded and brushed her curls back in a nervous gesture Sybil would have harped at her for. "You are Talorc, Laird of the Sinclair. I knew it the moment you faced me. You carry yourself like a lord."

Talorc's eyes narrowed dangerously, and she thought she had offended him with her out-of-turn comment. He reached toward her, and she wanted to flinch back, but she would not let herself.

She must face this man with strength or forever lose herself to the fierce terrors plaguing her.

Perhaps he would think her wanton for not attempting to avoid the shockingly gentle brush of fingers against her cheek, but she would not move. The most amazing sensation of shivering pleasure spread throughout her body at that one small caress.

She would question her sanity on the morrow, she was sure, but she felt as if in that moment she had been touched by a piece of her soul that had been missing. How could that be?

"Who hit you?" His fingertip rested gently on the least painful of Abigail's bruises. The one Sybil's slap had left on her cheek.

"It is nothing."

He did not respond, nor did he take his hand away. It was as if he was willing her to answer him.

And she could not stand against that will.

She sighed. "My mother was not happy with my response to her."

"Your mother? Not your father?"

"No. Sir Reuben has never raised a hand to me."

"Never?"

"Never."

Talorc nodded and then frowned again before pushing the loose neck of her sleeping gown aside. "There is another bruise. This one uglier."

The word broke her trance as nothing else could have. No, Abigail could not claim beauty. She could not claim anything that would make her the right wife for this powerful laird.

Her only hope was that he did not discover that truth before taking her to the Highlands.

She jerked back, stepping out of his reach yet still holding the covering back from the window. "I am sorry my looks displease you."

"That is not what I said."

"Nay, he remarked on your bruise, lass. Ye'd best tell him who gave it to you." The other giant soldier said.

Abigail only caught the words because her movement had reminded her they were not alone and she needed to watch the other soldier as well, lest she be caught in her subterfuge before the wedding.

She held back a sigh of frustration with herself. For all she knew, he had spoken before this. She must be more careful.

"My mother," she said again, making sure she could see both warrior's faces.

Talorc's darkened with fury. "She beat you. Why?"

Abigail spent her life lying by omission about her affliction, but she had promised herself long ago not to lie about anything else. Ever. "I would rather not say."

"You will tell me."

Chapter 3

"Perhaps she was no more reconciled to this marriage than you, Talorc." The pale-haired giant seemed amused by the possibility.

"You find this entertaining, Niall?" Talorc demanded of the other soldier.

"A bit," Niall replied, clearly not frightened of his laird.

"Is this true?" Talorc asked her.

As close as she could get to it. "Yes."

"You were beaten until you agreed?" Talorc asked, disgust clear in his features.

"I did not submit."

"And yet you are here."

"Sir Reuben told me I could choose once I had looked you in the eye."

Something like respect crossed Talorc's features. "You have now looked me in the eye."

"Yes."

"Well?"

"What would you have done if it had been my father who beat me?" she asked rather than answer.

"Kill him."

"You would not beat a woman?"

His lips twisted in an animalistic snarl. "I am not English."

Abigail felt laughter well up for the first time since Emily had left Sir Reuben's keep. Talorc really did despise the English, and instead of it frightening her further, she found that assurance far too amusing in the current situation.

And he could not conceive of a Highlander male beating a woman. That knowledge comforted her as nothing else had.

"You find that humorous?" the other soldier asked.

"I find your laird's arrogance amusing," she whispered, covering herself. "His assumption that only an Englishman would beat a woman relieves some of my fear of what is to come."

She hadn't meant to make the admission, but she needn't have worried. Neither warrior seemed particularly moved or impressed by it.

Niall said, "He is your laird as well."

"If I marry him, he will be."

"You will marry me." She could not hear his tone, but the certainty in his eyes left no room for doubt. In either of them.

"Surely you would be pleased if Sir Reuben refused the match," she could not help saying.

"I would be insulted and forced to kill him." He didn't look particularly bothered by that possibility, nor did he appear to be making a joke.

She, on the other hand, felt another clammy hand of fear take hold of her heart. The probability Talorc would declare war on her stepfather when he discovered her deception— as he was sure eventually to do—only increased in her mind.

"Why be insulted? You hate the English."

"Aye."

Her stomach dropped, her concern for her stepfather forgotten for the moment. "Then you hate me."

"No."

"No?"

"Nay."

"He does not hate the innocent," Niall clarified.

Talorc looked over his shoulder at his warrior and then back to Abigail. He shrugged. "I do not hate the innocent."

There was something about the way he said it, something in his expression that implied he thought English and innocent antithetical to each other. And yet he had said he did not hate her.

She searched his gaze for the truth. She knew hatred. She'd lived with her own mother's for years now. Talorc's stance was not combative, nor was it, or his demeanor, dismissive. He stood ready for action, but not with an attitude of boredom or any indication he had better things to do than converse with his English bride-to-be.

Even if he had made no effort to be in attendance upon her arrival. Suddenly, she considered the possibility that slight was meant for her parents, not necessarily for her.

When he looked at her, Talorc's expression showed wariness. There was also distrust, even frustration, though from what, she did not know, but he did not look at her with hate.

She knew that once he learned of her inability to hear, he would reject her as his wife. He might even hate her then, but her choices were meager. If she thwarted the marriage, Sybil would find a way to punish Abigail much more severely than with a single beating. Her only chance at seeing Emily again lay in marriage to this man.

Who might hate the English but did not hate her. "I will marry you."

He nodded as if it had never been in question. No doubt in his mind, it hadn't. He seemed the type of man to get what he wanted and who allowed nothing to stand in the way.

"The Sinclairs do not beat women, but we do kill traitors."

As her mind translated Talorc's words, Abigail felt herself flinch. "I will never betray your clan."

"You give me your word?"

"On my soul." Hiding her affliction was not a betrayal of his people. Indeed, from their lack of welcome to her sister, Abigail was certain the Sinclairs would be only too happy to be rid of her once her defect was revealed. But she would never put the clan at risk or reveal Talorc's secrets, as her mother sometimes did her stepfather's in gossip and in search of admiration from her peers.

He scoured Abigail's gaze as carefully as she had his. Finally, satisfaction gleamed in his amazing blue eyes. "Your mother deserves death for what she did to what is mine."

He was completely serious. He was not posturing. This was no idle threat to impress the English with his might. He meant it.

She shook her head, glad her muscles no longer ached with the slightest movement. "No, please. She believes it is her right to dictate my life and force my will to bend to hers." Abigail was sure it was the same for most parents among the nobility. "Regardless, my stepfather does not deserve death. He stopped her. He promised to protect me from a marriage that terrified me."

Abigail's throat muscles hurt from all this talking. Sometimes, days and days would go by without her uttering a single word and now she was forced to converse as she once had with Emily. Only she knew Talorc made no effort to read her lips, so she had to modulate her voice to be heard. Even if it was a whisper, it was there.

"He would challenge me over the vicious bitch you call mother?"

Abigail's gasp was not audible to her, but she could feel the expulsion of her shocked breath. "Yes," was all she said though.

"They will never be welcome on Sinclair land. She hurt you. He should have done a better job of protecting you."

"Okay." She did not care if she ever saw her parents again. Emily was another matter entirely. She swallowed for courage. "But Emily, she is welcome on your land?"

"The Balmoral is an ally. His wife is welcome."

"I am glad. I have missed her."

Talorc nodded and then spun on his heel and started walking away. Niall didn't leave, however. He took up a guard's stance a few feet from the cottage. When she looked over at him, he winked.

She smiled back and mouthed a thank-you.

He jerked, as if surprised, but then grinned back before turning to face the front, his expression gone serious, scary even. A few minutes later, two of her father's soldiers joined him, but the big soldier did not leave.

When she checked out the front window, sure enough, she had both a Hamilton guard as well as one of Sinclair's soldiers.

Abigail went to sleep, feeling safer than she had in a very long time.

$\mathcal{T}$alore stood before the English priest in the small chapel. The MacDonald warriors and most of the English baron's soldiers had to remain outside. His own warriors, the MacDonald and five of his men, his bride's family and a few English soldiers were the only witnesses for the wedding to come.

There were no flowers, no pomp and ceremony for this royally dictated marriage. That should not have bothered him, but the soft-spoken woman he had met the night before seemed to deserve more. Even if she was English. She had been so vulnerable, and yet when he had demanded to know if she planned to marry him, she had taken her time replying.

She had weighed him. He could feel her doing it, and she hadn't been adding up the size of his lands in her head. She'd been judging him personally, and something inside him had refused to be found wanting.

She was nothing like Emily, which was both good and bad. He did not relish the prospect of being likened to a goat by another Englishwoman, but he had no desire to see Abigail Hamilton eaten up and spit out by his clan. Emily had come to the Highlands to protect this very sister from such a fate. He could not help believing her fears had been justified.

Abigail spoke in whispers, seemed oblivious to her beauty and had a nervous habit of holding her hand over her throat when she talked. As if she was preventing the wrong words from coming out. His wolf felt protective toward her like he did no other besides family. Since the only one left, his younger sister, Caitriona, was now mated to the Balmoral's second-in-command, it had been a long time since Talorc had felt those instincts stir so restlessly.

He wanted to believe it was only because the woman was slated to be his wife, but his wolf had shown no such concern for her sister when King David had originally instructed Talorc to marry Emily. The wolf had wanted to howl at the evidence of bruising on Abigail's pale skin.

And then hunt.

Talorc spent his time waiting for his bride's arrival glaring at the woman's mother and forcing down the wolf's threatening growls.

Lady Hamilton had that same greedy, unreasonable look to her that his stepmother, Tamara, had had. As if she expected the world to do her bidding, and woe betide anyone who refused. At first, the bitch had attempted a smile, but Talorc merely warned her with his eyes how close to death she had come by mistreating the woman that was his.

The fact that he had not wanted an English bride made no difference. The kings had dictated that Abigail was to be his, and no one dared to mistreat a Sinclair. He was still tempted to kill Lady Hamilton, despite his bride's pleas to the contrary. His wolf clamored for retribution, if not death.

Eventually, the English *lady* began to squirm under his hostile regard.

Good. She had no place in Abigail's life and he meant her to know it.

Niall cleared his throat, but Talorc did not need the prompting. He had picked up Abigail's scent the moment she entered the chapel. Fragrant herbs, known to heal, mixed with her own unique perfume, created a heady fragrance that called to his beast. It was all Talorc could do not to turn to watch his bride walk up the aisle.

It would not do to show such interest though. The English baron might take it as a courtesy. Not that his wolf seemed to care that Abigail herself was English. The beast never took notice of women, but he certainly noticed Abigail.

And wanted her.

With a ferocity that forced Talorc to keep strict control of the semi-stiff member under his kilt.

The wolf fought to get out and make itself known to the woman about to marry the man. Talorc had to concentrate harder than he ever had on keeping his wolf inside while he waited for Abigail to make her silent trek up the aisle on the arm of the baron.

Finally, he turned, if only to appease the wolf.

Abigail was not smiling, but she did not hesitate in her slow procession toward him. She looked scared but determined, and he respected that.

It was easy to face battle without fear; much harder to face it with uncertainty of the outcome. Eyes the color of rich earth reflected fear but not terror. That was something. He should not care, but he did not like the idea that marriage to him would terrify her. It was natural for her to be somewhat worried about her future.

She was leaving England for the Highlands. Her life would never be the same.

Nor would his, a low voice inside him insisted. One that sounded suspiciously like his wolf.

Her long ringlets, the color of pure, sweet honey, swayed just above her hips with each step she took. Talorc experienced an unfamiliar desire, nay *need*, to reach out and run his fingers through the silky strands.

He bit back a curse. Where had that thought come from? He had never wanted to touch Emily. Or any other woman. Not since the years during which his body had transitioned from boy to man. His sexual urges had run rampant then, but he had not acted on them.

He had not been ready for a wife and had not found a mate. He would never dishonor his family by not following through on the promises of the flesh either.

Unlike the Balmoral, the Chrechte among the Sinclairs believed sex a binding act. The Balmoral held more lax standards so their warriors could gain control of their ability to shift at will at a younger age.

Luckily for Talorc, his father had had the good sense to mate a white wolf who passed that ability at birth on to their children.

That control over the beast within him had never been truly tested until now.

The wolf wanted Talorc to claim Abigail in the way of his people, but he had no intention of doing that in front of a chapel full of people. Nor did he intend to mate her on anyone's land but his own.

It was bloody frustrating, but for an Englishwoman, Abigail was beautiful and all too alluring. She had perfect bow-shaped lips on a feminine, oval face. Her nose was small and straight, and her brown eyes were big and expressive. She'd tried to hide her body's allure in the English clothes she had donned that morning.

She wore her father's colors for the last time. The female tunic over the long dress covered every inch of her skin from her neck to her dainty feet. At least she wasn't wearing the awful cowl thing her mother had donned. He thought the English women called them wimples. Tamara had insisted on wearing one with the Sinclair, constantly reminding the clan she would not relinquish her English ways.

If Abigail thought to dress so, she would soon learn her mistake.

He would not allow it.

A question came over her lovely features, and the baron blanched beside her. Talorc realized he was scowling. He smoothed his features into expressionless repose and put his hand out to take her from her stepfather.

The priest cleared his throat. "We are not yet to that part of the ceremony, my lord."

Since the man spoke English, Talorc chose to ignore him.

He lifted a brow to his bride, asking why she had not complied with his request.

In a move that surprised him and clearly Sir Reuben as well, she dropped her stepfather's arm, stepped around him and took Talorc's hand.

He nodded, grasping her hand firmly and turned to face the priest.

The man looked flustered and took several moments to collect himself before beginning the service. In Gaelic, after only one false start.

Talorc spoke the vows of his people in Chrechte when the time came, ignoring the murmurs around him. When his bride's turn came, he moved her so they saw only each other, not the rest of the congregation gathered as witnesses. He told her the vows to speak, speaking slowly so she would not stumble on the unfamiliar words.

Her expression puzzled, but accepting, she whispered

them back to him, making lifetime promises he was determined she would keep.

Her mother had a fit then, demanding their vows be
repeated in English. Talorc ignored her until the priest
intervened.

"I have married her in the way of my people," Talorc
said in Gaelic.

The priest nodded. However, when he told Lady Hamilton in English what Talorc had said, the older woman
refused to be appeased.

Talorc did not care. The vicious bitch's opinion was
of no importance to him. Bored with the argument and
unwilling to stay in the company of the English any longer,
he swung his new wife into his arms and carried her out
of the chapel.

Abigail's arms flew around his neck, but she did not
fight him. Nor did she make so much as a peep in surprise.
He looked down at her only to find her gazing at him with
an expression bordering on panic in her dark brown eyes.

"You are mine now."

"I know."

"You have no need to worry."

"Was the wedding over? The priest did not say the final
blessing."

"We spoke the blessing ourselves as befits my people."

"I did not think the Scottish were so different from the
English."

"I am from the north. We have not taken on your *civilized* ways."

"A priest's blessing is civilized?"

"It is unnecessary. He spoke the words that made us
man and wife and we said our vows."

"All right."

He should have been glad she gave up so easily, but again he worried about her spirit when faced with the people of his clan. They were not cruel usually, but they respected strength and abhorred weakness.

Sir Reuben shouted something behind them, but Talorc ignored the baron just as he had the man's wife.

His warriors had followed him out of the chapel and were already mounting their horses, clearly as eager as he to get out of the Lowlands. He went straight to his horse, but when he went to toss Abigail on its back, she squirmed from his arms faster than he would have thought possible for a human.

He grabbed her arm before she could dart to the cottage.

She frowned up at him. "I need my things."

"No."

She shook her head and twisted from his grasp with shocking agility.

He went to grab her again, but she backed up. "Please. I have gifts for Emily."

"She needs nothing from England."

"Thank you for your opinion on the matter, but I must disagree." She spun and headed toward the cottage.

She had disobeyed him. The shock kept him from going after her at first.

"What is she doing?" Niall asked.

"Getting her gifts for her sister."

"The Balmoral will not like his wife receiving tokens from our enemy's land."

"I know. 'Tis why I have chosen to allow Abigail to get the things."

Niall laughed. "His wife will be grateful."

"'Tis another reason to allow Abigail leeway in this."

"Aye."

The Balmoral might now be his ally, but Talorc did enjoy needling the man.

Just when Talorc was considering the possibility Abigail had taken refuge in the cottage rather than merely gathering her belongings, she came out. She was carrying one large and two small bundles.

He glared. "You'll not wear English clothes as my wife."

"I left all but what I wear now behind," she said, showing more sense than he thought one born a *Sassenach* might have. "These are the gifts, my sewing and other personal things, and herbs for healing."

The English baron and his wife had come out of the chapel and had spent the last few moments haranguing the priest. But even a holy man knew better than to question the will of the Sinclair. He had refused to demand further concession on the wedding vows.

So, now they were shouting at Talorc, demanding to be heard.

Talorc derived marginal pleasure from ignoring them. He looked at the MacDonald. "Do you have a woman who can help my wife don my colors?"

The laird of the Lowland clan nodded. "Aye, indeed."

He waved his wife over and told her what Talorc wanted. The redheaded woman gave Talorc an approving nod before going to Abigail and guiding her back into the cottage, after handing her bundles to Talorc's warriors.

The English baron had given up on the wedding and was now demanding Talorc share the nooning meal with them like a civilized man. As if Talorc desired to be such. Idiots.

"Surely you wish to partake of the game you hunted yesterday for just this occasion."

He had hunted to avoid spending more time than necessary with the English. He had given his game to the Mac-Donald as thanks for the use of the clan's holding to host the wedding demanded by their king's edict.

When the other man did not seem to know he was supposed to shut up, Talorc turned to the baron with the full force of his displeasure. "I am neither civilized nor am I English. We leave as soon as my wife is garbed appropriately."

"There was nothing wrong with her dress. Her clothes are the height of fashion." Lady Hamilton looked mortally offended.

"Niall, inform this woman who thinks nothing of beating her daughter into submission how close to death she came."

Niall said the appropriate words in English.

The woman started shrieking at her husband to take exception to such an insult.

Talorc turned to the baron. "You allowed her to harm what belongs to me. You live only because your daughter pled for your life."

Niall started to translate into English, but the baron waved the words away. "I speak your language," he said in English. "I was led to believe you speak English as well."

"Our laird does not allow the language of traitors to pass his lips," Niall said with harsh anger.

Instead of getting angry, as Talorc would have expected, Sir Reuben merely looked thoughtful. "Your father married Lady Tamara of Oborek."

Talorc nodded.

"I would not wish such a match on my worst enemy."

It was Talorc's turn to be shocked, but he did not allow his surprise to show on his face.

"Sybil can be a grasping shrew, but she would not betray her house," the baron said in Gaelic.

"That shrew will never see her daughter again."

"I supposed as much."

The woman in question was still complaining, but no one paid her any heed, not even her husband. She moved from complaint to wheedling, trying to talk Talorc into staying so Abigail could share a last meal with her family.

Since she continued to utter the profanity to his ears that was English, he made no attempt to answer. Or even acknowledge she was speaking.

A few minutes later, Talorc's attention was drawn to Abigail coming from the cottage.

She wore a pale yellow blouse under his plaid. She looked worried, her lower lip caught between her teeth and her gaze flitting from one person to another so quickly it was like a butterfly lighting.

He put his hand out again and she seemed to relax a bit. She started walking toward him with a faster gait.

Her mother went to grab her arm rather than let her pass.

Talorc let out a subvocal growl, and the only thing that saved the abusive witch from his wolf was the MacDonald's wife slapping the Englishwoman's hand aside.

"No one touches a laird's wife without his permission," she spit out in heavily accented English. The glare she gave the Englishwoman indicated she had seen Abigail's bruises and either guessed their cause or had asked Abigail and learned the truth.

"Sybil," the baron barked. "Come here, now."

"You would let him deny me my final good-bye to my daughter?" Lady Hamilton asked with furiously offended dignity.

"If she touches what is mine, she dies," Talorc said in a tone that promised he made no threats, only promises.

"I deny it," the baron said furiously. "You reneged your rights as her mother on too many occasions to count. She is no longer your daughter. She is a Sinclair."

His willingness to marry such a viper put his wisdom in question, but Talorc thought the Englishman might actually have some marginal intelligence after all.

"His king promised proof of the consummation," the woman shrieked. "How are we to get that if he leaves with her now?"

"He can send the bloodied sheet by messenger."

"What if he doesn't?" She scooted around her husband and stood in front of Talorc. "You promised your king. Are you a man of honor or not?"

Talorc's fury burned so bright, his wolf literally itched under his skin to get out and tear out the bitch's throat. "You dare question my honor?"

He didn't wait for the baron to translate Talorc's words for the stupid woman. His king *had* made the requirement, and Talorc had no intention of wasting a messenger on sending bloodied sheets to the grasping Englishwoman.

He marched forward, grabbed his bride and dragged her to the cottage. He went inside and slammed the door so hard the walls rattled.

Chapter 4

Talorc turned to face his bride. "Your mother is a bitch."

"She is no longer my mother," Abigail said in a bare whisper, terror coming off her in waves. "Sir Reuben said I am a Sinclair now. You did not deny it."

"One barrier stands between you and that truth."

"My maidenhead." There was no sound to the words, merely a breath of air as she mouthed them.

"Aye."

Abigail's hand flew to her throat and she looked wildly around her. "You would take me now?"

Not likely. He would not be dictated to by his king, much less an English lady in this matter. But before he got a chance to say so, his bride simply crumpled.

Using the preternatural speed of his wolf, he caught her before she landed on the floor. Damn, she was vulnerable. Not like her sister. Emily would have called him a goat and told him to go to hell before having her maidenhead breached within minutes of her wedding.

Talorc should have been disgusted by his new wife's weakness, but instead he felt regret to have caused her such distress.

The feeling shocked him, but even more astonishing was the way it echoed in his wolf's heart. Neither of them wanted her hurt. He gently laid her on the smaller of the two beds in the cottage. The other stank of the baron and his wife. The narrow bed Abigail had slept on smelled only of her and fresh air.

Her eyes fluttered open, her body going immediately taut with wariness.

Their gazes met. Her eyes flared and then filled with sadness. "This is it, then."

"You are so bothered by the prospect of sharing my bed?"

"Frightened. I know nothing of the ways of men."

"That is to be expected."

"You do not understand. My mother, my maid, no one has told me *anything*." And clearly, the unknown scared her out of her wits.

"Do you want me to tell you what is going to happen?"

Her dark eyes widened with surprise, but they glowed with hope. "Would you?" Again her words came out silently, but he had no trouble reading her meaning.

"Aye."

Though her skin was the color of a dark rose in bloom, she nodded and swallowed. "Please."

"I will. Please you, I mean." It was a matter of pride for both him and the wolf that lived in him. "I will begin by kissing you. Have you ever been kissed, Abigail?"

He doubted it and might have to kill someone if she had, but he needed to ask.

She shook her head.

"That is good. I do not want to have to go hunting in England."

Her eyes widened farther and stayed that way as he described in minute detail how he would touch her before, during and after her deflowering. He left nothing out of how it would feel for her or how he expected to feel.

He laced their fingers while he spoke and was in no way surprised when her hold on him grew so tight he would almost think she had the strength of the Chrechte in her. But she never balked at his description or turned away from the words he spoke, her gaze fixed on him with desperate intensity.

When he finished, she stared at him for several seconds.

"Truly?" she finally asked in a whisper. "You will do all that?" Her cheeks were so crimson, the bruise from her mother's slap was almost hidden.

"I will."

"You will be careful."

"I told you I would. It may hurt, but I will prevent as much pain as possible. It is my duty as your husband."

"Are English husbands so considerate?"

He shrugged. "They are English."

"I am English."

"You are mine."

"I suppose I am." She looked surprised by her own acknowledgment.

"Do you still fear?"

"A little."

He nodded. "That is to be expected in your innocence, but I will take care of you. Starting now."

She flinched but said nothing. And then nodded resolutely.

"Stand up."

She gave him a questioning look but obeyed.

He pulled the knife from his boot. It was sharper than the one he kept on his belt.

She took a step back, but confusion rather than fear showed in her eyes.

He put his hand out over the right spot on the sheet and then cut a thin, short line down his palm. Her mouth was open, but no sound escaped as she stared in uncomprehending fascination as drops of his blood decorated the sheet.

"Your mother wants the blood proof. I will give it to her, but I will not claim you on the land of another."

Abigail nodded as understanding, and then relief, settled over her lovely features. She gave him an intense look and stuck her hand out. "Cut me, too."

Very little had the power to shock him, but her offer slammed into him like a blow from Niall. "It is not necessary."

"It is."

He shook his head.

She stubbornly put her hand right over his, palm up. "We share in this as we will share in the other. Later."

His entire body reacted to her touch and the unexpected words coming from between her innocent lips. A growl of approval came from the wolf, and Talorc acquiesced with a jerk of his head.

He laid his knife against her small, white palm. "You are sure?"

She nodded.

"So be it." He cut her, just a prick, but enough to let her drops of blood mingle with his on the sheet.

When there was sufficient blood to indicate a bedding, he ran a hand across the drops to make streaks as if there truly had been a sex act. Then he raised her palm to his mouth, and allowing his wolf's saliva to mix with his own, he licked her cut. The bleeding stopped immediately, but he did not release her hand. The flavor of her skin and the few drops of blood on his tongue was unlike anything he had ever known. And yet like something he would never have expected—the satisfaction his wolf felt after a successful hunt.

The beast inside him howled in exaltation Talorc did not understand. It was that sense of victory he felt that gave him the impetus to let go of her hand. She was human and English. She stood between him and ever having a true mate. His wolf should be whimpering, not howling.

Her expression one of guileless certainty, she took his palm and returned the favor. Even though she did not have the wolf, his wound had been close to closing anyway and the blood stopped. But the feel of her lips was addictive, and he had to bite back an instinctive denial as she pulled her lips away.

They stood there in silence for several seconds, neither looking away, neither appearing ready to speak. Heat suffused his body. It was like a fever, but he was not ill. Her eyes reflected confusion and wonder. He did not know what had just happened, but it was profound.

Unable to stop himself, he pulled her closer, until their scents commingled and their bodies were aligned.

Then, he kissed her. Because he could. Because he couldn't *not*.

As soon as his lips touched hers, another wave of heat suffused his body and he heard what sounded like the barest of sighs in his head. Was his wolf that affected that the beast sounded so unlike himself?

The prospect was not a pleasant one on any count. It felt too much like weakness.

An anathema.

Refusing to give in to the sweetness of her lips, he stepped back from her.

She looked up with an expression he had no idea how to decipher. And he refused to allow himself time trying.

He deliberately turned away from the connection he felt to her and ripped the sheet from the bed. "Your mother will have nothing to harp about now."

He stormed from the cottage, tossing the bloodied sheet at the feet of the baron. Lady Hamilton bent and grabbed it, examining it even as Talorc leapt to the back of his horse and looked to see if his wife had followed. She had. He bent to grab her. She settled in front of him without a murmur of protest.

He gave the signal and he and his warriors set their horses galloping north . . . toward home.

Abigail concentrated on not falling off Talorc's great beast of a horse. Until she realized the stone band around her middle that was his arm wasn't about to let her go anywhere. The horses were galloping so quickly, the green beauty around her was naught but a blur to her dazed eyes.

She had never ridden at such a pace in her life. It was most exhilarating.

Despite the trauma of her wedding and near bedding, Abigail felt a smile of pure pleasure steal across her face and laughter welled up inside her. She realized it had not been silent when the body so close behind her stiffened as if in surprise.

She cocked her head back and turned it so she could see

Talorc's face. Sure enough, he had a questioning look on his darkly handsome features.

"What?" she asked.

"What has you laughing?"

"I believe I enjoy riding Scottish horses, my laird."

"This is no mere horse; 'tis a beast worthy of a Chrechte warrior."

His arrogance made her laugh again. "No doubt."

To have his confidence would be a wonderful thing. Abigail spent so much time in fear of revealing her true self, she rarely felt confidence in the company of others. But right at this moment, she knew unadulterated joy as they rode away from a life and family that had caused her pain and pain again.

"You surprise me, lass."

"Perhaps that is a good thing." She could not believe her own temerity, but Abigail felt freer than she had since waking to a silent world as a terrified young girl.

"Aye." He looked quite serious. "I believe it is. I would not have you eaten, lass."

"The Highlanders are cannibals, then?" she asked with undisguised humor, knowing they were no such thing.

He stared at her as if seeing her for the first time. "Nay, but my clanspeople have little tolerance for weakness."

"You think I am weak?" She did not know why his judgment should surprise her so. She worked hard not to be noticed; it would be a true shock should he realize the woman under the exterior. So, rather than be offended by his assessment, she found in it her own private joke.

Though in this case, she did not let him see that.

"There is much fear in you."

She could not deny that. She lived in daily terror. "I am not afraid right now."

"I can see that."

"I was afraid when I thought you would bed me with brutal expediency," she admitted, still grateful he had not done so.

"Aye. You were terrified." No worry at that truth showed on his features, yet he had protected her.

"You alleviated my fear."

He shrugged, causing her body to move against his.

Quite unsettled, she gasped. "I have not been this close to another person since my sister left our home."

"No one else will hold you thus."

No, really? She was no wanton to allow another man to touch her. She rolled her eyes at him, but then had a thought. "I will hug Emily when I see her again."

"You dare to defy me?" Was that a twitch at the corner of his lips?

"In this instance, yes."

"If you think to let another man touch you . . ." He let the rest of his clear threat remain unsaid, but a fury completely unjustified by their current talk glowed in his blue gaze.

"Do not be daft. I'm not fully reconciled to *you* touching me."

"You will grow used to my touch." There was that amazing confidence again.

"It is your responsibility to make it so." Had she truly said such a thing aloud to him? But it was no more than he had claimed when explaining what the marriage bed would be like for her.

"Aye."

"What is Chrechte?"

He did not answer but stared into her eyes with an

expression she could not read, no matter the time she'd spent learning how to do so.

"You said the horse was worthy of a Chrechte warrior. Is that another word for a Highlander?"

He shook his head.

"Then what does it mean? Chief? Laird?"

"Do you always ask so many questions?"

"In truth?"

"I will always expect the truth from you."

Her heart twinged at his words. She determined right then that though she could not tell him her secret, she would never lie to him. "I often wish to know things I do not ask about."

"Yet you do not hesitate to query me."

"Should I?"

He did not answer immediately.

"Well?" He could not know how important his answer was to her, but it would say much about her place in his esteem.

"Nay."

"That is good to know."

"The Chrechte are an ancient tribe of people who live among the Highland clans now."

She smiled at this confirmation of his willingness to appease her curiosity. "You mean the Picts?"

"That is what the Romans called us, aye."

"Like the Normans among the English?"

He shrugged again, but there was no mistaking the moue of distaste on his lips at the mention of the English.

Abigail turned to face the front of the horse again, her pleasure draining from her. Talorc hated the English. That would never change.

No matter how considerate he was this day, the fact that he claimed not to hate her would not last indefinitely. If for no other reason than that she was not the innocent he and his warrior Niall believed her to be. She *was* lying to them by pretending to be something she was not. A whole woman, worthy of being a laird's wife.

For the first time, Abigail felt grief at the inevitability of her future. Talorc was not the monster she feared him, nor was he the barbaric animal her mother had claimed.

He had assigned his warriors to watch over her the night before, showing she had more value to him than she had to her parents. Even if she *was* English. He had also protected her from a soulless bedding Sybil had been only too happy to demand.

Abigail did not know what had led her to insist on adding her blood to his on that sheet. She only knew that something inside her had told her it was the right thing to do.

And he had respected the gesture. She had seen it in his eyes. Their incredible blue warming with approval, however brief. One day, probably sooner than later, that same blue would grow icy with distaste when he discovered her secret.

And there was naught she could do about it.

Talorc did not know what caused his new bride to draw back into herself, but he admitted, if only to himself, he did not like it.

He had enjoyed her pleasure in the ride, her laughter a truly beautiful sound. He shook his head. He was going as daft as she claimed him to be if he thought an English-woman's laughter beautiful.

But she was not English any longer, was she? She was *his*.

Or so his wolf and his king claimed.

The beast had never laid such certain claim to another, not the members of his pack, not even of his family. The wolf howled for the moment when they reached Sinclair lands so they could claim Abigail in the most basic and irrevocable of ways. Words could be dismissed, but joining his body to hers could not be undone.

When Talorc called a halt to his men for the night, Abigail's joy in the ride had given way to numb exhaustion. They had stopped only twice to water the horses, and only one of those times had they dismounted. They had eaten bread and cheese then, but that had been hours ago. Yet, as hungry as Abigail was, she was too tired to contemplate eating.

She stumbled into the forest to deal with her body's most pressing needs. When she returned to the men and horses, Niall and one of the other warriors were erecting a small tent of skins.

He noticed her when she came near and nodded, his frowning visage not changing, but there was an understanding in his gray eyes that nearly moved her to tears.

"I thought Highlanders slept under the stars," she found the energy to tease.

He smiled at that, pulling the scars on the left side of his face into a twisted grimace. "It's for you, English."

"Oh." She swallowed inexplicable tears. "Thank you."

He shrugged and she decided that was the Scottish warrior's answer when he did not want to be bothered with speaking.

When the other soldier finished putting furs inside the tent for her to sleep in, he left and only then did Abigail's tired brain tell her she had been rude not to ask Niall for an introduction. When she said so, the giant scarred warrior gave her an odd look.

"Talorc will make them known to you at the proper time."

"Oh." She did not know what that meant and was too fatigued to try to make sense of it.

She turned toward the tent and stumbled. Niall was there faster than she could have imagined possible, stopping her from falling on her face.

She looked up at him with gratitude. "Thank you."

He held her arm, obviously concerned she would stumble again. "Are you all right?"

When was the last time anyone had inquired after her with no more reason than basic human concern? These Chrechte warriors might not be civilized, but they showed more care for her well-being than her family.

She brought forth a smile, a weary effort at best. "Merely tired. It has been a . . . complicated . . . two weeks."

"Preparation for marriage is that way for women, I have heard." He dropped her arm but stayed close enough to be of assistance should she need it.

"I did not know I was preparing for marriage. I believed I was going to Scotland to visit my sister, Emily." She was not sure why she had admitted it; maybe it fell under being as honest as she could be. More likely it was simply that she trusted this big, scarred warrior as a friend. For no more reason than her heart told her she could.

"The Balmoral's wife?" he asked, confusion lurking in his gray eyes.

"Yes."

"I do not understand. Your father petitioned your English king for redress when she married the wrong laird.

Your marriage to our leader has been a foregone conclusion—at least to our monarchs—these past weeks."

"I did not know that."

Niall looked at her with pity and something else. Something that told her she was right to trust him as friend. *Understanding.* "When did you learn you were to be married?"

"The day before we left my stepfather's keep."

Looking properly furious, Niall nodded as if agreeing to something someone said, and his gaze fixed on something behind Abigail.

Chapter 5

She turned to find her new husband standing not a foot behind her. Normally, she was much more aware than this. It must be her exhaustion.

"Hello, Talorc."

"I will not apologize."

"I will not ask you to," she said, trying to figure out why he thought she expected it.

"It was her idea, wasn't it?"

Ah, he had overheard her conversation with his soldier and had correctly surmised her mother's machinations had been behind Abigail's ignorance. Maybe he had called Sybil an indelicate name?

Abigail did not care. "Yes. She did not think I needed to know the plans for my future."

Neither man asked Abigail why her mother would treat her so cruelly. Thank goodness. They probably attributed it to the fact Sybil was English.

Talorc winced. "When I arranged my sister's first wedding, I told her the moment the plans were finalized."

Emily used to remind Abigail that tone of voice held as much or more meaning than the words people spoke, but Abigail could not even remember what those tones might sound like. She only knew that when watched closely, a person's face told its own story. One that did not always agree with the spoken word either.

Talorc's expression was a mixture of chagrin and righteousness, both at odds with his claim.

"That was the same night he had her wed to his second-in-command," Niall said with a wink.

Ah, that explained it. Her husband had no wish to think he was like the Englishwoman he had called bitch.

"'Twas not the same. I had not arranged her mating with a stranger from a foreign land. Caitriona knew Sean from the time she was a babe, and they liked each other well enough." But something in Talorc's expression told Abigail he felt guilt for his actions all the same.

She liked him for that. He cared that he might have hurt his sister. It was something Abigail could cling to in regard to her own future. She hoped.

"The first time she wed?" she asked.

"Sean died in battle. Cait wed Drustan, second-in-command to the Balmoral, after."

"No wonder you are now allies."

Niall snorted. It was not words but an expression of disbelief that Abigail had seen far too many times not to recognize. Talorc gave his soldier a quelling glare—with little appreciable effect.

"Your sister and my own would have it no other way," Talorc said.

There was definitely more to it than he was saying, but

Abigail was caught by one truth above all others. "And you listened to them?" she asked in true shock.

Her stepfather never admitted to taking the advice of a woman, even Sybil's.

"It was a good alliance to make."

"Aye, it was." Niall inclined his head toward Abigail. "Your bride is so tired, she can barely stand."

"She needs to eat."

"Let her eat in the tent, where she can sleep after."

"You think to advise me how to treat my bride?" Talorc asked, looking dangerous.

"Why not?" Abigail asked. "He is your second-in-command, isn't he? Surely he is allowed to have an opinion." She wasn't trying to be rude but realized after speaking that her questions could be taken that way. She simply wanted to understand the Highlander's way of things.

Niall's smile might be considered frightening by some, but Abigail saw the honest amusement lurking in his gray eyes. "Your wife is feistier than I thought."

"She is."

"She does not flinch from me." He appeared both pleased and astounded by that fact.

"I noticed you held her arm."

"She would have fallen otherwise." Niall's head bowed in apology.

"She is right here." Abigail frowned at both big men. Really. She was accustomed to being ignored by her family, but this was getting out of hand.

For good or ill, Talorc gave her his full regard. "Niall is not my second-in-command. His brother holds that place."

"But . . ." She did not understand. "Which one is his brother?" She looked at the other warriors, not seeing any that looked like they could get away with ordering Niall about.

"Barr has command of the clan while I am away," Talorc replied.

"I see. So, Niall *is* your second-in-command at present." She nodded, satisfied by her ability to reason that out in her current state of exhaustion.

Talorc did not reply. No doubt because he did not wish to admit she was right.

"I will look forward to meeting him, then."

"Why?"

"Because he is your second, and I like his brother. I am bound to like him."

"You like Niall?" Talorc asked.

"You needn't be so incredulous. I do not hate the Scottish as you do the English."

"Most in our clan find Niall intimidating."

"Then they must find you positively terrifying."

That had Talorc looking pleased and Niall laughing, which from the shocked expressions of the other soldiers, must not happen often.

Abigail decided she had had enough of the discussion and attempting to be awake when all she wanted was to sleep. So, she curtsied and excused herself before ducking into the tent. Bright moonlight filtered between the edges of the plaids draped to make the walls of the tent and soon her eyes adjusted.

She had barely removed her shoes so she could settle on the furs when Talorc joined her, making the already small quarters feel overwhelmingly crowded. She scooted to the very edge of the tent to make room for him.

He handed her an apple. "Eat."

She thought of arguing, saying she just wanted to sleep.

Only it would probably take more effort to convince the big warrior than to eat.

She accepted the apple and took a bite. Crisp and juicy, the fruit's flavor exploded over her taste buds, reminding her body how long it had been since she'd last fed her stomach. When she finished with the apple, he handed her a skin of water to drink from. She drank and then found herself presented with a hunk of yellow cheese and a hard roll. She ate the cheese.

However, after one bite of the hard roll and chewing it for what seemed forever, she placed it aside. "I'll just save this for the morning."

"I will provide you with food to break your morning fast." He looked downright growly.

"I'm full."

He narrowed his eyes. "Are you sure?"

"I'm not a warrior. I don't need that much."

"I'll not have you wasting away, wife."

She felt a blush climb her cheeks at his verbal claim to her. "I won't."

"You are small."

"Are Highlander women so much larger, then?" Emily hadn't mentioned such a thing in her letters.

"Nay, but you are fragile." He said the last word with a twist of his mouth.

Ah, the weakness thing again. "Emily is no bigger than me, and she's doing just fine among your brethren."

"She lives among the Balmoral."

"Same thing."

"No, it is not." He frowned fiercely. "We are the Sinclair, they are Balmoral."

"Are there no Chrechte among them?" she asked, trying to understand her new husband's point.

Perhaps he thought the fiercer warriors a danger to her. Though that didn't make much sense to her either, but then much of the way men thought didn't.

"The Balmoral is Chrechte."

"Emily's husband?"

"Aye."

"There, you see? I will do fine." She might be afflicted, but that had only made her stronger, not encouraged weakness.

Though only Emily had ever acknowledged such.

"You think to compare me to the Balmoral?"

She decided she would be best served with one of the shrugs so popular with the Highland warriors.

He shook his head as if unable to believe her. "You are a Sinclair now, you will not forget that."

"Trust me, I'm not likely to." She was deaf, not daft.

"It is time to sleep."

"Finally," she muttered as she turned and attempted to find a spot to lie on that would not put her body into contact with his.

He had no such compunction. As he stripped his plaid and shirt from his body, he made no effort to avoid brushing her side with first an arm and then his leg.

"Are we on Sinclair land then?" she asked with a squeak she could not be sure had enough volume to be heard.

He turned to stare at her. "Nay."

"But . . ."

"Undress. You'll not sleep all twisted up in your plaid."

"I . . ."

He blew out an impatient breath. "You may remove your plaid under the furs to protect your modesty."

He should have thought of that before hopelessly compromising it by getting wholly naked in front of her. She'd never seen a man's body before, and she found it both frighteningly repelling and inexplicably fascinating.

He made no move to cover himself as she stared at him in helpless curiosity. In fact, the part he should have covered and that she should definitely not have been looking at began to grow. She remembered he'd mentioned such a phenomenon that morning, when explaining the marriage bed. But she had not understood what he meant. Now, she did.

Oh dear, *did she understand*. It was quite amazing and entirely mortifying. Especially since she could not seem to look away.

"That's . . ." She licked her lips and swallowed. "Does it get bigger?" She was unable to stop herself from asking.

"Keep looking at it like a kitten ready to lap up cream and it will."

She jolted at his words. "I . . . I wasn't. Not thinking of licking." *Licking?* Was he truly serious? He looked so, not a flicker of amusement anywhere in his expression. But *licking*?

He'd told her they might do that. Taste each other in such intimacy. She'd thought he must surely be exaggerating, playing on her ignorance. Clearly, he hadn't been. Oh, my.

Did he expect her to do *that* now?

He reached for her.

Surprisingly, she did not faint again. And showing a complete lack of self-preservation, she made no move to run screaming from the tent.

His face a mask over some emotion so fierce, the very blankness alluding to it, he untied her belt. She grabbed it and stared at him, unable to voice a question or complaint.

He said nothing. No words of comfort, no demand she not impede him.

Was the fire burning in his blue gaze lust? A man's desire for a woman was not something she had any experience with. Though Jolenta had told her stories, implying the whole time that Abigail would never have to worry about such a thing.

Isn't that what they'd *all* thought, Abigail herself included?

Sybil had not come right out and said she did not think Talorc would want Abigail, but she'd implied it well enough. And yet, isn't that what Abigail saw in his eyes right now?

"Do you want me?" she asked, once again showing her self-protection skills were at a very low ebb.

But she truly needed to know.

"Yes."

"But I'm English." *Shut up, Abigail.* She'd spoken more to her husband in the past day than she often did in a week. Surely she could stop talking. But words just kept popping out of her.

"I will not claim you now," he said, ignoring her last comment.

Then why did he wish to undress her? This question she managed to keep to herself. Barely.

He tugged at her belt and, of their own volition, her fingers released it. For surely she would not have done so on purpose. He pulled it away and began undoing the pleats of her plaid. Shock and a strange stirring in her belly held her immobile as he removed the blue, green and black fabric from her body.

When he finished, he knelt there, unmoving. Unsmiling. Silent, but his gaze spoke volumes could she interpret the messages there. Her blouse barely reached her thighs and her shift only a few inches beyond that, but at least she was not as naked as he. That was something. So, why did she feel as if he could see right through it?

Suddenly, she remembered that the furs they knelt on were for more than cushioning her body from the hard ground. They would afford protection from the incendiary heat of his gaze.

When she scooted to get under the furs, he stopped her with a hand on her naked calf. "Do the English sleep in their clothes, then?"

She shook her head mutely.

He began to tug at the hem of her blouse.

She grabbed it and held it in place. "You said I could undress under the furs."

He looked like he would argue, but after a few seconds he nodded. "Do it."

She clambered under the fur, forcefully keeping her eyes away from the stiff member between his legs. Flesh that had indeed grown to truly intimidating proportions. Within seconds, he had joined her, showing her supposed reprieve to be a false hope. She could even feel his naked leg touching her own under the soft furs.

She would have moved away, but he put that stone-hard arm that had kept her safely on his horse for so many hours around her waist and tugged her close to him. "Let's get rid of this now."

She was so lost in nerves she could barely read his lips as he spoke, much less make sense of the words.

His big hand grasping the hem of her blouse again explained to her senses what her brain refused to grasp. He didn't wait for her assent, just started tugging the blouse upward, and then it was gone, leaving her vulnerable in nothing but a too-thin shift. Seconds later that was gone as well, leaving her completely naked outside the bath for the first time in her adult life.

Yet as much as she feared the unknown, she did not fear *him*. He had said he would not take her until they were on Sinclair land. She trusted him to keep his word. Something deep inside her told her she could.

"You are mine," he said, a feral expression in his eyes.

She could do naught but nod.

He reached out and yanked the flap down on the tent, cutting off the light from the rapidly fading sky. There was barely enough light to see his form, much less read his lips.

She could tell he said something, but not what it was.

She reached out and placed her hand against his lips. "No talking."

She had no idea how he would receive the order, but nothing could have prepared her for the kiss that he gave her. His lips dominated hers, demanding entrance into her mouth, silently claiming his right to her.

She could do nothing but allow her lips to part. Inexplicably, she craved such intimacy. His tongue slipped between her parted lips, gliding past her teeth. He tasted like apples and the dry biscuit she had not eaten, but more than that. There was a wild, feral flavor to him that her woman's instincts told her was nothing but her husband.

And she who had been starved of any affection for the past two-plus years could not get enough. The truly intimate sensation of tasting him in a way no one else had a right to do was instantly addictive. She savored his tongue with her own. He allowed her untutored exploration for long patient moments. A jolt like lightning burned all the way to the most feminine part of her as his patience broke and he began to suck on her tongue.

She stopped caring that she was naked, stopped worrying that he was, too, and simply reveled in the amazing and blissful connection between them.

He rolled on top of her, his body hotter than the furs. Rather than feel frightened by being blanketed by the huge warrior, Abigail felt safety unlike anything she had ever known. His hard knee pressed her tender thighs apart and she did not resist.

That big, hard manhood rubbed against the apex of her thighs, and she thought she might expire from the pleasure of it. She knew they were not actually copulating; he was not inside her as he said he would be. But she could not imagine anything more personal. This was something she would never share with another.

Something he would give only to her. He'd told her that, too.

His mouth slid from her lips to move down her jaw and then onto her neck, where he stopped. She waited, her panting breaths sawing in and out of her. Finally, he broke the suspense of the moment.

He gently bit the join of her neck and shoulder, pressing down so she could feel his teeth in a circle of claiming. She did not think he would break her skin, but his teeth felt unusually sharp. Or perhaps her senses had simply been heightened.

To near-unbearable levels.

He began to suck hard enough she knew it would leave a mark. She could not make herself care. Instead, she arched her neck in silent invitation to continue the unexpected pleasure. Shocks and excitations shivered through her body, the wonderful feeling from his biting kiss almost too much.

His teeth slid from her skin and he laved the small sting, building pleasure upon pleasure.

Her body writhed against his, though she'd had no conscious thought of doing so. Their skin slid along each other. And it felt delicious. Incredible. How could any woman withstand such pleasure?

Her hips arched toward something she could not name.

Hard hands pressed down on her thighs, stilling her movements.

Then he was on his knees above her, his mouth burning a trail downward until he reached her breast. When he gave it the same series of kisses he had on her neck, she felt a keening cry leave her throat. But she could do nothing but let out a silent wail of indefinable pleasure when he moved to pay similar attention to her nipple. He played, first with his tongue and then with his teeth, until she thought she would die from the unfulfilled, nameless longing coursing through her.

But his mouth did not stop there; he moved farther down, stopping several times along the path he had set for himself. Each time, she thought she would reach some pinnacle of pleasure that might well kill her, but in each case, he moved on as her body verged on the precipice.

When his mouth covered her most intimate flesh, she was so far drowned in the pleasure he had given her she had no thought to protest. He licked at her and then stabbed inside her with his tongue, not far enough to breach her maidenhead, but deeply enough that she felt irrevocably marked as his.

They lay together in a tableau so unbelievable, her mind refused to picture it—his head between her legs, his intimate kissing so intense she could barely breathe. He reached up with both hands, first cupping her breasts as if weighing their small curves before pinching both her nipples at once. She screamed . . . did not know if it had been silently or not, and could not make herself care if his warriors had heard.

He changed the way his tongue moved on her. The cliff of pleasure she had felt over and over drew closer, and then she was going over, her body going rigid as convulsions rocked her. He took her through the pleasure and into a series of smaller inner explosions until her body fell limp against the furs below her.

He surged up between her legs and reached for her hand. He placed it over the burning heat of his erection. Her fingers curled around him convulsively. He wrapped his hand around hers and began to move them both over his male heat.

His hips snapped too and fro, his hand around hers so tight it bordered on painful. Then she felt him give a triumphant shout, the sound beating in the air around them even though she could not hear it. Hot liquid landed on her stomach and breasts, searing her with yet another act of his possession.

Talorc's wolf howled his triumph as the warrior shouted his pleasure and his seed shot out to land on the silken skin of his wife. The climax lasted longer than any orgasm he had ever had, each spurt of his come that landed against her skin giving his wolf feral pleasure Talorc could not begin to deny.

When he had finished climaxing, he leaned forward and

began to rub his seed into her skin, marking Abigail in an unmistakable way for all Chrechte warriors to recognize.

Unlike other women who might have objected to something so earthy, Abigail lay compliant below him as he caressed every last drop of his come into her skin, until she was so thoroughly marked with his scent his own wolf would have a hard time distinguishing between their bodies.

She was his and all would know it.

Chapter 6

~

Abigail woke alone.

After an initial pang of disappointment, relief flooded her. She did not know how to face Talorc after her wanton behavior the night before. It had felt so natural then, but in the first light of day, it seemed aberrant. She wished she could convince herself it had been a vivid dream. An amazing, if outrageous, dream.

Anything but the embarrassing reality that it was.

Did men and women really engage in such acts as a common occurrence in the marriage bed? Regardless if others did, she had a feeling she and her husband would. Talorc was not a man to deny himself what he saw as his, she thought. Add that to his assurance the morning of their wedding that he expected them both to find pleasure in their shared bed, and doing such again would be a definite matter of course.

At least until he learned the truth of her affliction.

She could only be grateful she would have experienced the mysteries of her own womanhood by then.

What had once terrified her had become a journey she was eager to take. And that, as much as what they had done last night, mortified her.

She was a true wanton.

Surely, she should not be so eager. Not that propriety mattered one way or the other. She spent too much time hiding her deafness, she had not subterfuge leftover to mask this newfound need. And no stomach for doing so either.

With that truth resounding in her conscience, she sat up and looked around her. No sign of Talorc. Again relief assailed her. The flap was down on the tent, but morning light filtered in from the outside. It looked like the cool light of early dawn. Knowing her laird, he would expect to return to their journey north soon.

She pulled back the fur covering her and reached for her shift, but stopped and wrinkled her nose. She smelled like him. *Like sex with him.*

It wasn't just her cheeks that blushed, but her whole body, as renewed embarrassment flooded her. She could only hope his soldiers would not notice the fragrance of lovemaking over the stench of horses and their own sweat.

She would give her entire stash of spices she had brought with her for a stream to wash in right now. Not because she disliked the scent of Talorc's seed on her, which caused yet another surge of shame. She should find it offensive rather than oddly satisfying, shouldn't she?

However, regardless of her odd reaction to the situation, she hardly wanted everyone else to know what she had been doing with her new husband the night before.

She felt the vibration of heavy steps outside the tent and

dove for the fur. She'd barely covered herself when the tent flap flipped back and Talorc scowled at her. "So, you are awake."

Familiar dread sank in her stomach like a lodestone. She had missed something. Again. "Were you calling me? I just woke."

The scowl diminished a tiny bit. "If you wish to eat before we break camp, you need to do so now."

"I would rather wash."

"There is no time." He looked like that fact pleased him for some reason.

"I smell um . . ."

"Like me."

"Yes."

"It is as it should be."

"You truly are uncivilized, aren't you?"

"Yes." He actually smiled, clearly unperturbed by the question.

At least she had not insulted him. Sometimes she spoke without thought, and she hadn't meant to offend. She herself was not sure whether she was appalled or charmed by her husband's primal views.

"Do you wish me to bring your food to you in here?"

"That won't be necessary. I'll get dressed right now." Well, as soon as he left to give her some privacy.

He showed no signs of doing so, however.

"I do not wish to dress in front of an open tent flap."

He let it fall closed behind him, moving fully inside the tent.

Nonplussed, she stared at him. "You wish me to dress in front of you."

"Do you know how to fasten your pleats already?"

"Um . . . no?"

He shrugged as if that was the only answer she needed.

She managed to get her shift and blouse on under the fur before climbing out to allow him to help her with the plaid. It was hard to get on in the small confines of the tent, but she managed it—with his help. When she was dressed and about to leave the tent, he put his hand on her arm.

She looked back at him over her shoulder.

"I will see all of you. Soon."

She didn't reply, just scrambled from the tent.

She rode her own horse this morning, a beautiful white mare his stallion seemed to have a fondness for. Talorc kept her horse positioned between his and Niall's for the long morning ride. When they stopped to water the horses and eat again, the sun was high in the sky. Summer days were long and she had no doubt they would spend most of the light riding.

While they kept a fast pace, it was not as blurring a speed as the day before. Abigail was glad. She was a good rider, but she would have been nervous riding so fast without his strong arm around her to keep her planted on the horse's back.

Their break was short and she forced herself to climb back onto her mare without complaint. She would not add to Talorc's belief she was weak.

They had been riding for an hour when he grabbed her reins and forced her to meet his eyes. "Agree, wife."

"Of course," she said, before she could think better of it.

"I will tell you when it is safe to speak again."

Ah, he had instructed her silence.

She nodded.

"Good." He nodded. "You are a unique woman."

Because she spoke little unless in a direct conversation of someone else's making? It was a trait by necessity only. She would spend more time talking if she could trust herself not to betray her secret doing so. As it was, her silence at the wrong time was damning enough.

They stopped to water the horses again but did not dismount, just like the day before. This time, she noted no one spoke though. The warriors were all alert, and Talorc looked grimmer than usual.

She met Niall's eyes and asked a question with her own.

"Enemy territory," he mouthed.

Her eyes widened. It had not occurred to her that they would have to cross enemy territory to get to Sinclair land. She did not remember mention of her stepfather's soldiers having to do so when they escorted Emily to the Highlands nearly three years ago.

Suddenly, Talorc was there and she was being swept from her horse to his. She landed against his chest with a silent gasp.

He looked down at her with a fierce expression, as if prepared for her to argue the change. She simply let herself go limp against him and closed her eyes for sleep.

She wasn't a warrior, and if he was going to give her an unexpected opportunity for a nap on this bone-jarring ride, she was going to take it.

She sensed his surprise but ignored it as his arm wrapped her close and secure against him. She was asleep a moment later.

Bemused, Talorc held his sleeping wife to him.

He was not sure what had prompted him to put her on his horse with him. She'd been tired, but his action had been an instinctive reaction to the silent exchange between his wife and his warrior at the water.

Talorc had had no idea that he and his wolf would become so possessive with a wife—particularly an English one. He had not reacted thus with Emily, but then three years ago, he had had no intention of marrying the Englishwoman sent to him by order of their kings.

That must be the difference this time. Abigail was indisputably his wife, not a woman he *was* supposed to marry.

Yes, that must be it.

She moved in her sleep but made no sound. Not that it would matter now. They were in safer territory now and would be until midday tomorrow when they would cross Donegal's holding. Donegal's people were not Talorc's enemies, but the other clan was not happy at the king's edict to cede the disputed boundary land to him.

"She is surprising."

Talorc felt a growl build in his chest at Niall's words, but he merely grunted in reply to Niall's comment.

There was no reason for the jealousy burning inside him. Niall had a mate, though the youth seemed oblivious to the connection between them. Humans could be funny about the natural way of things.

Regardless, Niall would never be untrue to his mate, even if the scarred Chrechte warrior never lay true claim. He was, in fact, the safest of companions for Talorc's wife. Even his wolf recognized that.

And yet, the jealousy remained.

If he had known taking a wife would come with such complications, Talorc would have put his king off, recommending his sovereign choose a different laird to bestow the *honor* on. Even as he had the thought his wolf growled viciously in response to the idea of Abigail married to another.

And Talorc knew his frustrated thinking for the lie it was.

"She is not afraid of me," Niall said, bringing Talorc's attention back to the soldier.

"I noticed."

"I think she *likes* me."

Talorc would shift to wolf form and tear the other man's throat out if he thought Niall meant any disrespect, but he knew the scarred warrior did not. "She does not see the scars."

"Nay." Niall seemed bemused by that fact.

Talorc did not answer. There was nothing to say. Niall frightened most women of their clan. Most of the men, too, when it came down to it.

"She sleeps in your arms as if she trusts you with her very life."

"Does she have a choice?" He was her husband. She had no better protection.

"No," Niall acknowledged, "but she is not afraid."

"She fears something." He'd noticed the trepidation right away and believed that meant she was weak. Now he wasn't so sure.

"Aye. But not you."

"She's nervous about the marriage bed."

"You claimed her last night. Every Chrechte warrior here could smell it. Hell, even a human soldier probably would have."

Just as he'd meant it to be. "Not completely."

"What are you waiting for?" Niall frowned. "You aren't going to try to annul the marriage?"

"You think she is a fitting mate for your laird?"

"Before we met her, I would have said no. She was English."

"Now?"

"She hasn't likened you to a goat yet."

"There is that."

"So, you *will* keep her?"

"She is mine."

"Yet you wait to claim her."

"I will not perform the Chrechte mating rite on any land but my own."

Understanding dawned in Niall's eyes. "So, that's why we're riding so damn fast. We didn't keep this pace on the way to the MacDonald holding."

"I want to get home," Talorc growled.

Abigail shifted in his arms and tilted her head back so she could see his face. "Did I sleep long?" she whispered.

"Aye."

She blushed but didn't say anything else.

"You can talk," he told her.

"We're off your rival's land?"

"Yes."

"My father's soldiers said nothing of having to pass through enemy territory when they were in Scotland escorting Emily."

"The whole time they were out of England they were in his enemy's domain."

"But our kings are allies."

Talorc shrugged.

She crossed her arms and glared. "You do that every time you don't feel like answering."

"What?"

"Shrug."

He did again. Just to see what she would do.

She laughed, a soft, muted music he wanted to kiss from her lips.

She screeched as he bent to do just that, but he swallowed that sound, too. She tasted like sleepy innocence.

When he lifted his head, she looked dazed.

Niall laughed, loud and long. "I believe your ways will take some getting used to."

The other Chrechte soldiers around them stared at Niall as if they had never seen him before. True, the man rarely laughed. Okay, until this trip, Talorc had not heard him do so in years, but that was no reason to gawk like a bunch of gossiping women.

He gave his warriors a look that told them so, and they went back to watching the terrain as they should do. Talorc never lost his awareness of their surroundings, even when his mouth molded to Abigail's.

"Will we be at the Sinclair holding soon?"

"We will be on Sinclair land late tomorrow."

He felt the tension fill her. She knew exactly what that meant. "You do not think it would be better to wait until we reached your keep?"

She did not say what would be better, but they were both fully aware.

"No."

"Oh."

His wolf would kill something if Talorc made the beast wait to claim his mate.

"Why did you take me off my horse earlier?" she asked.

"You were tired."

"You noticed?" She sounded chagrined by the possibility.

"Yes." He had, but he'd also noticed the way she'd been bonding with Niall, and rational or not, his wolf had insisted Talorc stake his claim.

"You are not as I expected."

"Why?"

"You hate the English and you would have killed my stepfather without blinking, but you have shown me consideration."

"You are my bride."

"Emily was to be your bride, but you were not so considerate of her."

"I had no intention of marrying Emily."

"So, why agree to marry me?"

He had lived almost three more years without a mate and realized he would probably never find one. "My king offered sufficient incentive."

"My dowry."

"Aye."

"At least you get something you want from this marriage." She spoke quietly, almost as if to herself.

"I want you, too."

"You don't want an English wife."

"You aren't English."

"What am I, then?"

"Mine."

Abigail was once again riding her own horse the next day when Talorc signed for his soldiers to stop. It was nowhere near nightfall and they had watered the horses recently. It had been another silent ride today, and Abigail had not minded a bit.

Trying to keep track of the conversations around her while on horseback was quite taxing.

She did not ask why they had stopped because she did not know if it was safe to speak.

Talorc swung down off his horse, said something to Niall and then crossed to Abigail's horse. He put his hands out. "Come."

She reached toward him, allowing her husband to lift her from the horse. He helped her to find her feet, holding on to her until her stiff muscles started working again.

"Why have we stopped?" Not that she was complaining.

"Would you like a bath?" he asked.

She looked around, unsure where such a feat might be performed. She saw no source of water, but she did not allow the apparent lack to dull her enthusiasm. If he offered, he had a way to make it happen.

"Yes!"

He laughed and then turned and walked away. She assumed she was supposed to follow, so she did. He led her to a cave opening. She hung back as he entered the cave.

He stopped inside the entrance and put his hand out. "Come."

She shook her head.

He nodded.

"What if there are wild animals in there?"

"You must trust me."

"It is not you I mistrust."

"Who then?"

"Wild animals." She swallowed, trying to wet her dry throat. "I do not easily make friends."

In truth, she had made none since discovering what the fever had taken from her. But her friendship with Jack, son of Jon the blacksmith, had predated her fever.

And he had not let her push him away afterward. He'd even ferreted out her secret—to this day she did not know how. But the young lad had told her it didn't matter and insisted on being kind to her.

"So?" Talorc asked.

"There was a boy I played with as a girl. My father's blacksmith's son. He was torn apart by a wolf. I saw his body." She shivered at the grisly memory, not faded one iota by the years that had come between. "It was horrible. Death comes too easily."

Talorc went curiously still. "You have nothing to fear from wolves."

"You think not?"

"I will protect you."

"What about bears?"

His lips quirked in a half smile, no impatience at her reticence in his face. "You have nothing to fear at all when you are with me."

She nodded and that seemed to please him.

"I had my soldier scout ahead."

"Oh."

She let him pull her into the cave and noticed immediately that rather than the dank, cold air she associated with caves, it was warm with a faint scent of sulfur. He led her down a long tunnel into a cavern lit by torches and ambient light from somewhere above. Their light reflected off the water of a large pool in the center. Beside the pool, the furs they had slept in the past two nights were piled invitingly beside the water.

Abigail stared around herself marveling at the warmth of the cavern. "A hot spring?" she asked in awe. She had heard of such a thing but never seen one.

"Yes. One of the reasons we fought for this section of land. The springs have healing properties."

"Really?"

"So it has been believed by my people."

"And these caves are yours now? Because of your king's gift?"

"Aye." Talorc smiled savagely. "Though it is my responsibility to keep them."

"Will you establish an outpost?" Her father had guard posts on the four corners of his lands.

Talorc shrugged.

"Do you simply not want to answer or do you not know?"

"I know you are delaying the inevitable with conversation."

Smart man. "I am nervous."

"I'm not."

She opened her mouth but honestly did not know what to reply to such arrogance, so she snapped it shut again.

He smiled, this time almost gently, and produced a soap cake. "You can have a proper bath."

"I . . ." This was the Talorc her sister had written of in her letters? Abigail could not believe it. "Thank you."

She had to blink back tears. No one but Emily had ever been so concerned for Abigail's comfort.

He looked around the cavern with satisfaction. "'Tis a suitable place for a Chrechte mating."

"Mating?" Oh, he meant joining their bodies. Heat crawled along her skin as images assaulted her mind from the discussion they had had back at the MacDonald holding.

For some reason, he looked chagrined by his own choice of words. "I simply meant the marriage claiming."

She nodded, having no desire to argue, even if she saw nothing simple about the physical consummation of their marriage. Though he looked as if he expected her to.

He indicated the pool. "You will bathe now."

"In front of you?" She'd learned already he had a much

different sense of modesty than she did—and Heaven help her, he seemed to expect her to adjust to his. But did he really expect her to bathe in front of him?

"Is that how it is done in your clan? Your men and women bathe together?" she asked, scandalized to her core.

"I did not offer to bathe with you, but if that is your preference, I will indulge you."

Before she could get the horrified *no* out of her tightly constricted throat, he had shed his plaid.

She stared in mute shock as he disrobed right there in front of her, as he had the past two nights in the privacy of their tent—*at night*.

"It's only midday. Surely you do not plan to accomplish the bedding right now?" Had she thought him considerate? He was worse than the goat her sister had called him . . . He was a *randy* goat with no sense of decorum or modesty. Or . . . or . . . or *anything* else.

"It is time."

"No . . . no . . . we should wait until to*night*. You said I could wash, with soap."

"I will wash you." He closed the distance between them before she realized he was moving. "Let me help you with this."

She pulled back, but it was too late. He had her belt undone that fast. The pleats of her plaid simply fell, leaving the Scottish garment hanging over her shoulder like a long blanket. He tugged and it was gone completely, falling to a pool of fabric around her feet.

She turned and leapt for the relative safety of the pool, grateful that unlike her older sister, Abigail had learned to swim. It was deeper than she expected, and warmer than any bath she had ever taken. Her head submerged before her feet hit the bottom of the pool. Water swirled around her from Talorc's entry into the pool as she kicked upward and away from where she had felt him come in.

His hands locked on her waist and she broke the surface right in front of him. He was looking at her quizzically. "Do the English bathe in their clothes, then?"

Chapter 7

"My blouse needed washing." Which was nothing less than the truth.

"It is not the time for laundry; it is time for you to become my wife."

"No . . . I . . ."

He leaned down and brushed a kiss over her wet lips. "Yes."

"But . . ."

"I have waited long enough."

"It has only been two nights."

"I will have you now."

She shook her head.

He nodded.

Just like outside the cave. Only this time, she did not have some puny ravenous wild beast to worry about; she had her new husband's amorous nature.

She leaned back, trying to put distance between them.

"Take off your blouse."

Taking comfort in the fact he had not mentioned her shift, she tugged the now-soaking blouse over her head and tossed it to the side. It really would need a washing tomorrow after that treatment.

He looked down at her and his eyes burned. "Perhaps we should develop a new tradition of washing your shifts on you."

She looked down and immediately tried to cover herself. The thin fabric was completely transparent in the water. "You should not look at me like that."

"I am the only man that should."

"Naturally, no one else should either."

He pulled her toward him in the heated water until their bodies brushed. "Get used to it. I like looking at you."

"It is not decent."

"It is."

"Talorc . . ."

"Come, let us wash your shift." He let go of her waist but immediately slipped one of his arms around her so that he held her just as securely to him. Only he now did so with one hand free.

Backing toward the edge of the pool, he reached behind him with his hand. "Aha." He held the soap up for her to see.

For a moment Abigail's need for cleanliness overshadowed her shyness and she reached for it.

But he shook his head. "I will play your handmaiden."

The idea was so ludicrous, she laughed. The sound might have been hysterical; she did not know. She could not hear the sound, and for once, she did not mind. Her nerves were too close to the surface of her control to care if her voice was working properly in this instance.

"You must be patient with me. 'Tis not my usual role."

She stared at him, unable to speak. He did not mean to wash her. He could not. And yet, he did not appear in the least like he was joking either. His mouth was set in a serious line while his eyes devoured her.

"I can wash myself."

"It will be my pleasure."

"But—"

No more words had a chance to make it past her lips before he began to wash her shift most thoroughly. Only every stroke of the soap cake over the fabric was a caress against the skin below it. He made sure the soap touched every inch of the shift before putting the bar on the rock ledge of the pool.

"I believe next I am to work the suds into the cloth, aye?"

Too choked to speak, she could merely nod warily.

Using his free hand, he did exactly that, being far gentler than the washerwoman and her helper in Abigail's father's keep. Indeed, every movement of his hand against the linen was more a caress than a scrubbing. And each touch left her more and more breathless.

"You have a strange way of washing clothing in the Highlands."

"You think so?"

A strangled laugh made it past her tight throat and she nodded.

"Then you will be relieved to learn 'tis not something I have ever seen done."

"Only lairds wash their wives' clothing thus?"

"Only this laird."

"Oh," she gasped as all pretense at cleansing her garment slipped away.

Knowing and clever fingers caressed her through the wet shift, causing it to rub sensually against her skin. She'd never known such sensation, not even when he had touched her in the tent. This was pure decadence, making her feel more naked wearing her shift than she had under the furs for the past two nights.

She did not know when he had released her to touch her with both hands, but they cupped and squeezed her buttocks through the fabric. She felt marked and possessed by that simple touch. Then one hand slid around to draw indecipherable patterns on her stomach. Bit by slow bit, his hand moved upward until he reached her breast.

Long, masculine fingers curled around her in an intimate hold that seared her to her soul. Using the wet fabric, he abraded her nipples until her thighs quivered with the tension of wanting more. Yet for all the pleasure she knew there was to be had in his arms, she could not make herself ask for it.

He continued to caress her bottom through the shirt and her legs parted of their own volition as she fought the urge to return the touch. More out of fear of doing it wrong than what it might lead to.

"I think my shift is clean," she said between panting breaths.

"Then I believe it is time to wash you." He removed the garment without another word.

She thought she had felt naked and vulnerable, but now she knew it had been as nothing compared to being in the water with the barrier of her undergarment gone.

She stared up at him. "Shall I wash you?"

His eyes widened, telling her she'd managed to give voice to the words, not merely mouth them. As the silence between them stretched, she wanted to duck her head, to hide from his probing expression. However, she could not afford to miss anything he might say, so she stood in a wealth of trepidation to see how he would respond to her boldness.

"Do you remember what I said in the MacDonald cottage?"

She nodded. Every word had been seared into her brain.

"You will touch me as I touch you."

"But I don't know how," Abigail admitted. No matter how much she wished she did.

She wanted to give him pleasure as he had given her.

"You believe I have a wealth of experience touching women?"

Possessive fury welled up in her, taking her breath for a second. "Don't you?" she asked, nevertheless.

"No."

Her shock must have shown on her face because he smiled. "Our clan believes that penetration is as good as speaking vows between two people."

"There is a long distance between touching and deflowering." Or so her sister had insisted.

Talorc shrugged.

She frowned. "What does that mean?"

"Perhaps I have touched a woman or two, but never with the intimacy of this moment."

"You'd better not have." She didn't know where the words or the ferocity came from, but she wouldn't take either back.

Talorc did not seem bothered. In fact, once again, he smiled.

She would have told him to wipe the smug look from his face, but he lifted her against his body and all her air left her.

"If you are going to wash me, do it now."

She did not know how he expected her to do so and said as much.

He rubbed his hardness against her once before releasing her on the other side of the pool, where she found she could stand without going under. "There."

She looked around for the soap but he grabbed her chin, making her look at him. "Just your hands."

She nodded, equal parts terror and desire fighting inside her. Then she reached through the warm water and brushed her hand down his arm. She'd seen her mother do that to her stepfather when he was tired or upset. It seemed such an intimate act.

Something a wife would do for her husband.

But from Talorc's expression, she knew he expected more. *She* wanted more. She took in a deep breath and then placed both hands flat against his chest. Skin hotter than the water covered hard muscles that felt like silk-covered granite under her fingers.

She used a washing motion but could not pretend that she was doing nothing more than a mundane chore. She trembled with the newness of touching another.

He made no move to direct her, allowing her to explore his torso in the guise of washing it. Neither spoke as she mapped his body with shaking hands.

She stopped with her hands resting against his stomach. "I want to touch you there."

He did not ask where "there" was; he merely nodded.

She did not move. "I'm afraid."

"Of what?"

It was her turn to respond with silence and a shrug. She could no more give voice to her fears than she could have stepped away from him in that moment.

"You have given me great pleasure these past two nights."

"You put your hand over mine," she reminded him. As if he could forget that tiny detail.

Without another word, his hands slid over hers and pressed downward. She let him guide her to the hard prick bobbing in the water. It jumped as her fingertips brushed along its length. He guided her fingers to curl around him and then moved his own hands to her hips, holding her in place.

The flesh in her hands was hot, hard and alive. So very alive.

She looked up into his heated gaze. "I feel like I'm holding the essence of your life."

Before she had a chance to feel stupid for saying something so ridiculous, he smiled a rogue's smile and nodded. "Many men would say that is exactly what you are doing."

"You said this would . . . it would . . ."

"Go inside you? Is that what has you worrying, wife?"

She swallowed and nodded.

"I'll fit as if you were made to hold me and no other."

"You're sure?"

"Aye."

"But . . . It's . . . You do realize there are small horses that would be pleased to be so endowed?" She had been raised in a keep after all; she'd seen more than one equestrian mating.

His head tilted back and she imagined his laughter boomed around the cavern. She could not hear it, but she could feel the vibrations through his body.

She was not sure why he thought her comment so amusing. She found it much more worrying.

He shook his head. "I willna hurt you, lass."

"You're so sure? You said you don't have much experience."

"I am sure." And that clearly was supposed to be that.

And truthfully? Right now, she was less concerned with what was to come than the fact he had given her permission, nay *instruction*, to "wash" him.

She moved her hands along the large prick and Talorc's eyes fell closed as a fierce expression took over his features. She let her hands learn him in a way she had not the previous nights in their tent. She explored the softness of the skin, pressing into the flesh to feel just how hard he was. It was like holding heated stone.

The massive warrior's body shuddered at her touch, and she could not help feeling as if she had accomplished something special.

Suddenly he lifted her from the water, breaking her hold on his manhood. "That is enough."

"You are clean?" she teased, shocking herself.

He gave her a heavy-lidded look that promised pleasure and something else . . . claiming. "It is time."

She could not respond. She would not deny her own desire. For that would be a lie, but she could not force agreement from her tight throat either.

For the longest time, he simply looked at her. His eyes seemed to glow yellow in the torchlight. "You are so beautiful."

"Not like you," she choked out.

He jerked as if surprised by her words. But how could he be? The Sinclair laird was a study in male perfection.

Long black hair gleamed darker than the night around handsomely chiseled features that bespoke relentless strength and fierce pride. His big, well-honed warrior's body was only the physical manifestation of that strength. Eyes that continued to astonish her with their bright blue depths revealed an inner power she had seen in no other man. They said Talorc could be nothing less than laird of his people; no other position would do for the man so clearly born to lead.

Right now those eyes glowed with striations of gold that sent pinpricks of sensation down her spine.

Strangely, she found that incredibly alluring rather than frightening. This man had authority over her life as only her parents had before him. He was so much stronger than either her mother or stepfather. His personality and form should intimidate, but she felt inexplicable safety. In this moment, Abigail did not worry Talorc would use either his mental or physical power to hurt her.

No, his intent to give her pleasure was undeniable. Baffled by the truth but unable to deny it, she craved the experience. Of all the scenarios she had entertained in her worried imaginings before leaving her stepfather's keep, none had included her being attracted to her Scottish husband. Even in her most closely held dreams, she had not let herself imagine desiring Talorc, wanting to be claimed by him—much less needing to claim him, too.

But he was everything desirable.

Each of his muscles was sculpted as if honed by the most talented of artists. And had they not been? Surely God had given her husband more than his share of masculine beauty as well as inner power only a select few in history would ever know.

"You are amazing to me," she admitted, not sure her voice was working.

He said something she could not understand.

Fear that she did not want in this place washed over her. "Please. I don't . . ."

Please don't talk. Please don't expose her secret before revealing the full mysteries of the marriage bed. Could she not have one time of normalcy in her life? One thing not marred or ruined entirely by her affliction?

"It is Chrechte."

Relief did not cancel out the fear that had become too much a part of her, but it was still welcome. "I do not understand Chrechte."

"You wouldn't."

"What did you say?"

"I called you an angel."

"An angel?"

"Aye. When Cait and I were children, my mother told us angels were beings with hair the color of spun gold and beauty to rival our own blessed Highlands."

"You see me that way?"

"'Tis the only way to see you."

"Oh."

"I also said you are mine. My angel."

"Oh." She would not . . . could not . . . deny that.

He lowered her until they were eye level. "Now you say it."

"I am yours." Though she would not call herself an angel.

He spoke again in the ancient tongue. Then in Gaelic, "I belong to you."

She didn't wait for him to instruct her to repeat the phrase. "You belong to me." At least until he knew her damning truth.

"I promised to protect you during our marriage ceremony and you promised to accept my protection. Now I promise to keep you as my mate for our lives forward."

Why did it seem he spoke the word *mate* with a finality

not even *wife* could embody? Could the lifetime promise be real? Or were even Chrechte vows subject to her defect? "I promise to protect you to the best of my abilities and to be your mate for as long as you want me."

He frowned at her addition, or was it her caveat? "Now it is time for the Chrechte blessing. I will speak it as both pack leader and your husband."

"That sounds nice." Better than the priest's hasty blessing as Talorc strode with her from the chapel.

He carried her from the pool and stood her on the furs. Then he dropped to his knees and tugged her down in front of him. Kneeling, they faced each other. His expression was so intent she could barely breathe. He tipped his head back slightly and said something, as if issuing a command. She did not understand, but he did not look at her expectantly, as if she should.

Then she thought she knew who he had spoken to as two warriors came into her sight. They took a stance behind Talorc as she realized they had not come into the cavern alone. All of his soldiers now stood in a circle around her and Talorc. None of them wore their plaid, or anything else.

She should be mortified—both by their nudity and hers, but she wasn't. It felt inexplicably fitting—as if she had been born to this obviously ancient Chrechte rite. It helped that none of the men were looking at her. They had their backs to her and Talorc, their heads tilted as if looking toward the heavens.

Each of the soldiers had a simplistic indigo marking of a wolf on his left shoulder blade. Talorc had that tattoo as well. Was that their Chrechte marking?

Her gaze slid from the big soldiers to her husband. He was looking at her with a patience she had not expected from a man who had declared it was time for them to consummate their marriage. He put his hands out and she laid hers in them.

He nodded and then began speaking.

The blessing went on for long moments in the language she had no hope of deciphering. Nevertheless, a sense of well-being grew inside her with each word he uttered. She did not know what the blessing entailed, but she could tell from the serious expression in Talorc's glowing eyes that it was important to him.

He stopped speaking, but neither of them moved. The air around them was completely still, indicating the soldiers had not moved either. They were all waiting for something. She could feel it. But she could not guess what it was.

He tilted his head back like his soldiers, drawing her attention entirely to him. His expression had turned feral, his eyes glowing once again with that strange light. Talorc opened his mouth and she thought he *howled*.

Unable to hear it, she could not be sure. Whatever it was, she felt a mystifying need to share the experience. Without conscious thought, she reached out with one hand and laid it on his chest so she could feel the vibration of sound through her fingertips. He *was* howling.

Truly. Just like a wolf.

And she thought the others were as well, their heads thrown back, their arms reaching high, palms out. The air shimmered with the sound she could not hear, making the hair on the back of her neck stand up and goose bumps rise on her exposed limbs.

Then, as suddenly as he had begun, he stopped. The other men lowered their arms, and she could feel that they had stopped howling as well. One by one, they came to her and Talorc. Each man dropped to one knee beside them, speaking some Chrechte pledge before bowing their heads and then leaving the cavern.

When she and Talorc were once again alone, he released her hand and cupped her face with both of his. "You are no longer English."

"I'm not?" She didn't know what she'd expected him to say, but it hadn't been that.

"You are my wife, mated to the Chrechte pack leader by ancient and true rite."

She didn't understand why he referred to his clan as a pack. No doubt it was one of the many new Highlander ways she would have to grow accustomed to. Regardless, if this rite had given her a place other than *unwanted English bride*, for however long, she was grateful.

"I will do my best to live up to the honor you have done me." She wasn't sure why she said that, only that she knew they were the right words to say.

His genuine, approving smile affirmed her choice.

Then he kissed her. At first the caress of his lips was like the brush of butterfly wings, the soft touch at odds with the power of her warrior husband. Her reaction was not gentle, however. The barely there caress of his lips lit the fire of passion that had banked during the Chrechte marriage ceremony.

It made her want the things he had promised. It made her crave the pleasure he had already shown her the past two nights in their tent.

This oddly gentle touch was like a benediction on the wanton woman clamoring inside her soul for release.

Placing both her hands on his chest, she felt the rigidity of his muscles beneath her fingers, his increased breathing and quickened but strong heartbeat. Each small detail evidence that he liked kissing her as much as she enjoyed him doing so.

The knowledge filled her with a fierce and unique pleasure.

Right here, right now, she could and *would* be a normal woman. A whole woman. His angel. Her lack of hearing did not matter when their lips were too busy connecting to speak.

She did not know how long they kissed, but little by little, his lips grew more demanding. Until there was no question that they required her total surrender. And she gave it, wanting nothing more than to know the reality of being a true wife to this powerful laird—at least for this one night.

Chapter 8

Her own breathing became shallow and she saw the pinprick of stars behind her closed eyelids.

Somehow he managed to maneuver her onto her back though his hands never moved from their tenderly possessive hold on her face.

His mouth moved over hers, deepening the kiss with his tongue as their bodies aligned in instinctive need. Growls vibrated in his chest as he claimed her mouth with wild strength, drawing her bottom lip between his teeth and carefully nipping it. He did not draw blood, but she knew instinctively not to pull back, not to attempt to assert independence in any form in this moment.

Her spirit rejoiced in the sensations. She had no desire to separate herself from him at all. She kissed him back just as fiercely, if not more so, nipping at his lips and dueling with his tongue to enhance the intensity of the kiss. For once, the cocoon of silence caused by her deafness only intensified sensations she more than craved.

The wildness she sensed in him called to a part of her she had not even known existed—animalistic desires and untamed cravings beyond her ability to comprehend.

Blanketing her, his big body pressed hers into the soft furs. Their skin touched intimately, and yet it was not enough. She hungered for *more*. More of his touch, more of the sensations swirling through her. She needed a deeper connection. She wanted what he had promised her on the morning of their wedding.

To join their bodies so perfectly that she would feel him inside her soul.

She did not know what to do to encourage him toward that pinnacle, but he had taught her one thing thus far. He enjoyed her touch with unabashed pleasure.

So, she touched him. Everywhere she could reach. Over bulging shoulders and biceps, along a back corded with muscles that felt like rock under his satin-smooth skin. Her hands glided down over his buttocks, cupping the hard, round globes. Yet rather than satisfying her, the movement of her hands over his body only increased her need.

She wanted to urge his hips forward with her hold on his backside, but when she tried, he did not move. His stubborn strength spoke a silent message of control that both frustrated and delighted her.

His possession of her mouth did not abate and his body moved over hers while she writhed under his weight.

But none of it was enough.

And yet, it was almost too much. She wanted more. She wanted to stop. Her mind warred with her body while her heart sang a song she tried to tune out. One thing they all agreed on: she craved deeper connection. And yet the connection she felt already scared her stupid.

She tried not to think as she moved her hands up his body and then traced the lines of his face with her fingertips. It was an intimacy as profound as the feel of his hardened male flesh pressing like a stone against her thigh.

At the first soft brush of her fingertips along his jaw, Talorc's body went rigid with the need to claim Abigail fully. He did not understand why that simple touch acted as such a siren's call to his feral nature when a similar caress along his flank had only fed the fire of his sexual need. It had not turned his desire into an inferno he was in danger of not controlling.

However, control it he must.

He would not hurt his sweet wife. Despite his wolf's nature, he was no beast to take what he wanted without thought or consideration. The Chrechte were not animals, but humans with the enhancement of animal natures. Nevertheless, it was easier to mate in kind. Humans were often too weak to face a Chrechte's full passion.

Abigail was more gentle than most, definitely too gentle for his wolf, but she responded to him blithely oblivious to her peril. She touched him with wanton carnality he would never have believed a gently bred Englishwoman capable of. While he could not read her thoughts, she broadcast her need with every move of her small, silky body.

And she kissed with the hunger of a Chrechte woman claiming her mate.

As soon as the thought formed, he banished it with an angry growl. For all that she looked like an angel right out of Heaven, she was human. She had been born and raised English. She was not his mate, but she was his wife.

This night their bodies would consummate that truth.

He grabbed both her wrists and placed them by her head. "Keep them there."

Her soft brown gaze was dark with desire, and she dared shake her head at him.

"Obey me."

This time it was her eyes that spoke denial, though her lips remained immobile.

"I mean it." He caressed her wrists with his thumbs. "Your hands are to remain in this exact position."

Her sensuous, bow-shaped lips twisted in mutiny. "I would touch."

"Your touch incites my lust, angel."

"Is that wrong?" She paused, looking at him with an unfathomable expression. "Between a husband and wife?"

"If it is the wife's first time to hold him within her body, it is dangerous. I would not hurt you."

"I know you will not." Again a pause as if she searched for words. "At least not more than necessary. Some pain is inevitable."

He wished he could deny it, but she spoke truth. Nevertheless, there was a difference between carefully breaking her maidenhead and rutting on her like a beast. Which he was in danger of doing if he did not maintain control. "Obey me," he repeated.

"What will you do if I do not?"

He could not believe his shy wife had the temerity to ask that question. He glared down at her, his passion making him more ferocious. "I will assure compliance."

She licked her lips, her eyes dilating with increased arousal, but she did not reply.

There was no need. Her reaction was as clear as his favorite loch. His angel liked the idea!

Without thought, he stretched her hands above her head and grasped both small wrists together with his left hand. His wolf howled in approval while Abigail gasped and then moaned, her eyelids dropping to half-mast.

He spent no time wondering why they should both enjoy him mastering her in this way so much. He was a warrior, not a philosopher. He knew only that the delicate bones of her wrists felt all too right in the grasp of his hand.

He lowered his head and kissed her again. Within seconds she was writhing as before, only with utter abandon. The movement of her pelvis would have thrown him off her body if he was not so strong. And yet he knew that was not her intention.

If the glazed expression on her beautiful heart-shaped face was any indication, she was not thinking at all. Certainly not enough to have conscious intentions.

Her instinctual responses were devastating enough. She spread her legs just enough to make the invitation clear, and yet, he was sure she was unaware of extending the offer. He rolled off her to lie on his side. Keeping grasp of her wrists, the position still left him the freedom he needed to touch her body and make her ready for the physical claiming.

She mewled at the loss of his weight and began to thrash her legs, undulating her body in beautiful, abandoned need. He had to throw one thigh over hers to keep her in place beside him.

Then he set about ensuring her arousal reached a fever pitch through which she would be only marginally aware of the pain that breaching her maidenhead would inevitably cause. He kneaded her breasts, teasing her nipples until she cried out in mindless desire.

He had touched every inch of her silken skin in the hot springs and he wanted to do so again, but both their need called out to him with too much urgency. He allowed his hand to slide down to the juncture of her thighs, sliding his middle finger between her swollen, wet labia.

He had not breached her vaginal opening beyond a fingertip during his nightly explorations of her body in their tent, but now he allowed himself to press deeper. He stopped only when he felt the supple barrier of her virginity.

She made a small, pained sound and he comforted her with small tender kisses on her face and neck. He whispered promises and compliments she did not respond to. The part of his brain that still functioned on a fully human level was grateful she was so lost to her desire she wasn't making sense of his words.

He would feel like an idiot later for saying them otherwise.

He did not pull his finger out, but massaged the thin barrier inside her body, that which proved she had not played love games as he heard many in the English Court indulged in. He had been told that the English Court actually revered love between parties married or promised to others as some sort of romantic ideal.

Both he and his wolf found the concept utterly distasteful.

And his beautiful, sensual bride was clearly not a practicing participant in such ludicrous games. She was wholly innocent and deserving of all his consideration for their first claiming.

With that thought in mind, he brushed his thumb over the nub of her pleasure. Her body jolted and he smiled to himself. He continued his ministrations, massaging her maidenhead in preparation to breaching it and her clitoris in preparation to her pleasure.

Only when his angel begged for more with both her body and broken little words barely whispered past her parted lips, did he move over her and fit his cock to her opening. He slid inside a mere inch, causing himself untold pleasure and her a level of shock.

"You are inside me." Awe laced each syllable.

He thrust gently with his hips, both he and his wolf working together to control the urge to take her quickly and without remorse. "I will be so deep inside you—"

"You will touch my soul," she completed and then tears spilled over her eyes.

Her body did not speak of pain; his wolf senses confirmed she was not in distress. The tears were some women's reaction to the claiming.

Even so, he asked, "You are well, angel?"

"In this moment, I am complete."

She wasn't, not yet, but he did not contradict her. Soon, she would understand. And then she would probably cry some more. Women. But so long as it was not from pain, he would tolerate her feminine emotionalism.

He pushed deeper and his head met the barrier of her innocence.

She stared up at him as if waiting for him to force himself through, but he had a better plan. He arched his hips so that he could get his free hand between their bodies. While he remained in stillness poised at her virgin's barrier, he caressed her clitoris with his thumb.

She whispered his name as her breathing grew even more ragged. He had not brought her to climax, but he had spent two nights teaching her body to crave the pinnacle of pleasure. It reached for it now, straining against him, and only as he felt the convulsion that signaled her orgasm did he surge forward to embed himself fully in her body.

His own cried out for movement, but he was a Chrechte warrior, not a callow youth to undo the careful preparation for this moment.

He allowed her to ride out both the pain and pleasure before he began to move. He could seek his own completion, and if he allowed himself, probably come with a couple of well-delivered strokes, but he wanted more.

He swiveled his hips on each downward thrust, and she gasped with obvious pleasure. He held himself with rigid control, building her pleasure again until he felt her body once again tightening around him. He allowed himself release as she screamed his name and came a second time.

Abigail woke with a residual soreness between her legs. No doubt it would be much worse if Talorc had not taken such care with her. He had made the consummation of their marriage incredibly special, but he had not stopped his ministrations there.

He had carried her to the bathing pool and washed her body with gentle hands while she dozed in his arms. She had been so exhausted. She did not know how long they soaked in the hot springs, but she could remember snuggling into his arms in sleep at some point.

She had woken alone though. Just as she had each morning of her marriage thus far. Her clothing was folded neatly on the edge of the furs. There was food to break her fast with there as well. She took her time eating, then combing her hair and finally doing her own pleats on her plaid when Talorc did not show up to help her.

When she came out of the cave it was to find Niall, not her husband, waiting for her.

She tamped down her disappointment and the embarrassment she hadn't been smart enough to feel the night before to ask, "Where is your laird?"

"He is your laird, too, lady."

"He is my husband."

Niall smiled, causing the only other soldier nearby to wince. Abigail ignored him and returned the big warrior's expression.

Niall crossed his arms, making the muscles of his biceps bulge. "Talorc hunts."

"I thought we would ride to the keep today?"

"He said we are to spend at least one more night here."

"But . . . why?"

"He is laird. He need not explain why." Which simply said Niall did not know.

She thought so anyway; maybe the warrior did know and didn't want to share. "And he's hunting right now?"

"Aye."

She looked over the clearing where four horses fed, her husband's dark stallion, the horse she had seen Niall ride, one she assumed the other soldier rode and the mare she had ridden for part of the journey—when she was not sharing a steed with her new husband. "He is hunting without his horse?"

"Aye."

"Is that common?"

Niall shrugged, but then surprised her by adding, "Sometimes Talorc prefers to hunt completely alone."

"What of the other clansmen? They are with him, aren't they?"

"They are hunting, but not with their laird."

"Oh." She didn't understand it but merely added the

instance to the growing list of things these strange Highlanders did and said that made little sense to her. "I see. Why aren't you hunting?"

"I am guarding you."

"Oh." She said again, when nothing more fitting came to her. Then she shrugged. She could not expect Talorc to dance attendance on her. And honestly, the less time she spent in his company, the less chance he would have to learn her secret. "Can you guard me on a walk? We have spent so much time riding, I crave the exercise of stretching my legs."

"If that is your wish."

"It is."

So, they walked and she asked Niall questions about what she should expect once they reached the clan.

He shrugged. "The Sinclairs have little love for the English. I fear your sister did not enjoy her short stay among us."

"She called Talorc a goat."

"Aye. It did not endear her to our people." Though Niall seemed more amused than offended by Emily's behavior.

"Will they judge me as harshly?"

"Some will, but most will accept you because you are their laird's wife."

"Wasn't Emily his fiancée?"

"He showed no desire or intention to follow through on the marriage. His followers acted accordingly."

"But he and I are married."

"Aye. He calls you his. It will make a difference for many."

But not all. The big warrior might as well have shouted the unspoken caveat.

Niall let out a deep sigh that surprised her, but his words shocked her even more. "I do not want your feelings to be hurt."

"Um . . . thank you."

He laughed. She couldn't hear the sound, but recognized the expression coupled with the movement in his Adam's apple. "You do not understand my concern for you."

She shook her head. She didn't. Her own mother had not cared if Abigail found acceptance in the Highlands, why should this battle-scarred warrior? She asked him as much.

"You are good for Talorc. You two are connected in ways neither of you are ready to acknowledge."

It was her turn to laugh. "I believe you are a romantic, big, fierce Niall."

He merely shrugged.

But she grinned, knowing she was right. "So, is there a maiden who awaits your return?"

"Many, but none who have claim to do so." A strange expression took his features, a mixture of sadness and yearning.

Abigail's heart twisted at the sight. "There is one you wished did."

Again, that annoying, enigmatic shrug. But she saw the truth in his eyes. She was right. He was pining. She wished she knew how to help him, but she did not imagine he would welcome the interference of a deaf Englishwoman into his love life.

"So, tell me about your family," she said.

"There is just me and my brother Barr now. Sean died in the battle that left me this." He indicated his scar. "And our father in the battle that took our previous laird."

"What of your mother?"

"She died birthing Barr and I. Two babies at once were too much for her human nature."

What an odd way to put it. "I'm sorry."

"Why?"

"Growing up without a mother must have been difficult."

"Easier than growing up with that harpy that gave you birth, I'd say."

"She was not always so cruel. I . . ." Abigail bit her lip and fought the urge to tell the truth. Despite her years of practice at hiding her affliction, lying did not sit well with her. "I disappointed her."

"Then she is a fool."

Abigail wanted to believe that was true. "Talorc's former second-in-command was your brother?" she asked by way of changing the subject. "Is it a family position or something?"

"Our families have been close for generations. Sean was the eldest, so he was the first to be chosen as beta, I mean second to our laird."

"And now your brother Barr holds his position."

"He's a fine warrior," Niall said with evident pride.

"I'm sure he is. For Talorc to choose him over you, he must be incredible."

Niall's face took on a ruddy hue, and Abigail had to bite back the urge to laugh again. She did not want to offend the man. After all, her praise had already obviously embarrassed him.

"I do not want the responsibility. Being second to our laird requires more than great skills as a warrior; it needs diplomacy." He said the last word with a distasteful grimace that left no doubt what he thought of that element to his brother's position. "I would rather knock heads together than help disgruntled clanspeople reach a *compromise*."

If he'd said "diplomacy" with a marked lack of enthusiasm, Niall made it clear that the word *compromise* left a foul taste in his mouth indeed.

This time she did laugh and was happy to see that Niall joined her.

Her laughter dried up as a huge gray wolf stepped into their path. Beside her, Niall jerked as if surprised. Who wouldn't be, to see a wild predator so close?

The wolf stepped closer and Abigail went rigid with fear.

The beast inhaled as if sniffing her and then raised his head and released a mournful howl. Then he barked. And if it wouldn't have meant she'd gone mad, she would have said he was trying to talk to her. A wolf.

"You need not fear, he will not hurt you," Niall spoke from beside her.

Funny, but she would have expected the big warrior to put his body between hers and the danger. Not that one of her father's soldiers would, but she had a different place in the Sinclair clan. Or at least, she thought she did. Perhaps they would be just as pleased to be rid of her by whatever means as her mother had been.

Abigail's eyes burned with tears, and no matter that she furiously blinked in an attempt to make them go away, one spilled over, burning a trail down her cheek.

The wolf whined and then barked at Niall, a clear growl of warning issuing from deep in the animal's chest.

"I am not the one causing her distress," Niall said, as if talking to a wolf was the most natural thing in the world.

Perhaps for the uncivilized Scottish warriors, it was.

The huge gray wolf barked once more and then turned and ran away, disappearing into the forest as if it had never been there.

Abigail wanted to turn away from Niall, to take time to collect herself. But as was so often the case, she had no choice but to look at him in case he spoke to her.

Eyes a shade lighter than the wolf's coat studied her. "Are you all right?"

"He didn't attack," she observed, rather than answer with a lie. "Why?"

"He had no desire to harm you. In fact, I think you hurt his feelings."

"Don't be ridiculous." She was in no mood for some strange soldier's jesting.

"I am not." Indeed, Niall looked all too serious. "Didn't you hear his sad howl and the way he whined?"

"I suppose he wanted me to pet him."

"Aye. Most likely."

"And get my hand bitten off?" Abigail shivered. "I don't think so."

"He would not have bitten you."

"How can you possibly sound so certain?"

"I know that wolf."

She shook her head but believed him regardless. "You're serious. That's why you did not get between me and the animal."

"If I had tried to touch you or stand between you, then things might have gotten ugly."

"That makes no sense."

"Yet it is true."

"Are you trying to convince me that Scottish wolves are so different from those found in the wilds of England?"

"Some. That wolf, yes."

"I will take your word for it."

"So, you do not wish to meet the gray wolf again?"

"No." But even as she denied the desire, she wasn't sure she spoke true. "Perhaps, if I could see him and know he would not hurt me. He was beautiful."

Niall nodded, as if satisfied by her answer, though she couldn't imagine why it should matter to him.

By the time the hunters who had ridden their horses returned in the early afternoon along with game for the roasting fire, she and Niall had established the beginnings of a true friendship.

Abigail insisted on helping to prepare the rabbits for the spit. Then she implored the soldiers to hunt again, this time for wild vegetables and berries to eat with the game at the evening meal.

Chapter 9

No matter how far into the woods Talorc ventured, the memory of Abigail's sweet, fresh scent drew him back to the clearing. He followed her and Niall on their walk, his wolf's paws silent on the forest floor. He masked his scent so that even Niall did not realize Talorc was nearby.

His wolf wanted to make himself known, to rub up against his angel and allow his full wolf senses the opportunity to take her presence in. He had revealed himself only to discover that Abigail was terrified of his beast. His presence had brought tears to her eyes, and not the good kind.

He'd forced his wolf to run away rather than risk frightening her further, or worse, making himself known to her. He could not afford to share the secrets of his people with Abigail.

Besides, he was supposed to be hunting. Not that they needed the meat; they could make his keep by nightfall. If they rode out, but they weren't riding today.

His gentle bride needed time to heal before getting back on a horse. She had soaked in the restorative waters of the hot springs last night. And he had left instructions with Niall to make sure she did the same today, but Talorc could not be sure that would be enough.

If the choice was between reaching home tonight but having a wife too sore to mate with and staying an extra day in the hot springs cave, he would choose the extra time away from his clan.

The only other time he had voluntarily spent time away from the people he was responsible to lead was when he had followed his sister and Emily to Balmoral Island. Caitriona's safety had taken precedence at that time. He had no such considerations now, but that hadn't stopped him from dictating a second night spent at the caves.

He refused to consider how aberrant that choice was for him to make. Nor did he have any interest in contemplating why he would make such a decision.

He only knew his wolf was in complete agreement and that was enough for him.

Thinking he should at least make some effort to hunt, he leaned forward and sniffed at a small pile of leaves. There was definitely something there, but it wasn't prey. Not of the animal variety anyway.

The smell was not that of his warriors and certainly not the enticing fragrance of his new wife. It was too fresh to be more than an hour old. Which meant someone who wasn't supposed to be here, had been.

He lifted his head, taking in the monochromatic image of his surroundings that he got in his wolf form. He was definitely still on his land, newly deeded to him by Scotland's king. A growl rumbled in his animal chest as he scented the ground around him again. Six distinct traces, two Chrechte and four human. All males.

A hunting party? A mistake? Or a challenge to Sinclair ownership of the territory dowered him by the king?

The Donegal laird was aging without a clear successor. He presided over one of the smaller clans and Chrechte pack within it, which was only a mere handful of shape-changers. Even without the king's intervention, the other laird would have ended up ceding the land to Talorc's much larger clan and Chrechte pack, and they both knew it.

Never a large group, the Donegal clan had lost too many to war. The laird's son had died at the hands of the same English bastards responsible for Talorc's father's death. The young warrior had been in the wrong place at the wrong time, patrolling his borders with a small band of soldiers when the English contingent bent on stealing the Sinclair Royal Treasure had crossed Donegal land.

That was the reason Talorc had not yet used might to press his claim to the disputed territory. His father had been responsible for bringing the betraying English bitch to the Highlands. Talorc did not dismiss the consequences of that act.

He had gone so far as to offer use of the springs to the Chrechte of the Donegal clan for their mating ceremonies and for use in clan healings, with the understanding that the Sinclair clanspeople's needs would take precedence. However, he would not tolerate the Donegal clan hunting on the newly claimed Sinclair land. Not in human or wolf form.

The Donegal laird had accepted both Talorc's generosity and his stipulation regarding the hunting.

So, what in the hell were six strangers doing on his land? Were they even from the Donegal clan? Neither of the Chrechte carried the scent of the laird. Talorc would have recognized it.

No matter where they were from, they didn't belong here and he meant for them to know it.

He followed their scent trail until it became clear the four humans and two Chrechte were headed in the direction of the hot springs. Toward his wife. Talorc's four-legged gait picked up speed until he was flying across the earthen landscape.

He lifted his head to howl a message of alarm to his warriors. Those that had gone hunting with him would head back toward the clearing, if they were not already there, and those he had left behind to guard his wife would be put on alert.

Acknowledging it wasn't merely his warriors who might have already made it to the clearing, Talorc pushed himself to go faster. His huge wolf's body picked up speed as the plants and trees he passed went by in a blur in shades of black and gray.

He burst into the clearing at a dead run, his keen wolf's senses telling him the interlopers were indeed ahead of him. He skidded to a stop behind six youthful warriors wearing the Donegal clan plaid, their stances that of challenge.

Niall and Airril had taken position in front of the entrance to the cave. They did not look unduly worried, but they were clearly ready to do battle if necessary.

Of the rest of his hunting party there was no sign.

Talorc willed his human form to emerge and seconds later the air shimmered around him as he became a man again. He let out a subsonic growl of warning that had two of the young men spinning to face him.

Damn it, neither could have had more than sixteen summers. The youth on the left showed more intelligence than his companion because the color drained from his face and he offered his neck in instant submission.

The four humans moved only after they realized their companions had done so. They didn't seem able to decide who posed the bigger threat, so they angled their bodies to the side. With more experienced warriors, such a maneuver might have been beneficial, but with these near children, all it did was make them more vulnerable.

Talorc glowered at them all with acute disapproval. The Donegal soldiers needed proper training. Badly.

The young Chrechte who did not have the sense to look frightened, frowned at his fellow clansmen before facing Talorc defiantly. "These waters belong to the Donegal clan. You can't have them."

"The king says otherwise."

The youth made a sound of disgust. "He carries the stench of the *Sassenach* and mimics their ways."

"You do not submit to your king?"

"I follow the way of the Chrechte. We fight for that which is ours."

"You challenge me for the right to this land?" Talorc asked.

"I do." The youth's voice shook, but his stance of defiance did not falter.

Talorc couldn't help respecting the boy's courage if not his wisdom.

"What is going on?" Abigail peeked from between the two Sinclair warriors blocking her way out of the cave. Her damp hair and glowing skin indicated she had been soaking as directed when the impetuous young Donegal soldiers arrived. He did not think that was the reason for the flush in her lovely face though.

She was staring at his naked body in a way that would have an effect on his manhood soon. "Do you always cavort around the forest in the altogether, Talorc?"

"I was hunting."

"So I was informed." She cleared her throat and closed her eyes for a second, only to open them again almost immediately. "I did not realize Scotsman hunted in the nude. You were wearing a plaid when you returned from the hunt the night before our wedding," she said almost accusingly.

"You have much to learn of our ways."

She sighed, making a production of it. "I suppose I do. I think I need to learn something of them now about why these children are here."

"We are men," the bolder Chrechte soldier insisted.

Abigail, to her credit, did not gainsay him but merely looked with expectation at Talorc. Obviously, his wife expected an explanation. He just did not know if she was going to like hearing it.

"These *warriors* do not cede the right to this land or the hot springs to the Sinclair clan." He gave them the respect of calling them warriors. More seasoned soldiers of their clan had not thought to challenge Talorc's claim.

If they had, Talorc was honest enough with himself to know he would not have been as lenient. More experienced men that had the gall to challenge him would already be dead.

"They are challenging you?" Abigail asked in confusion. "They don't respect the wishes of their king?"

"Aye."

"I see." She looked at the young Donegals, measuring each one with her soft brown gaze. Then she shook her head. "Brave, but foolish."

Her words so closely reflected his own thoughts that Talorc found his lips almost curving into a smile before he caught himself.

Showing his first bit of wisdom so far, the Chrechte boy remained silent in the face of Abigail's observation. His compatriots looked like they were already questioning the intelligence of their actions, but none of them appeared ready to back down.

Again, he could respect that.

"Are you going to accept the challenge?" his wife asked after a moment of silence.

"Yes."

Five of the six young soldiers flinched, but the bold Chrechte youth merely looked more determined.

Abigail crossed her arms and nodded. "Good."

"You approve?" he asked in shock.

He would have thought his gentle wife too compassionate to commend behavior so far from her civilized world.

"It is obvious these young men's honor demands you win the land."

He nodded, still bemused by his wife's easy acceptance, not to mention her insight into the ways of their people.

"Besides, you will not kill him." She did not make it a question.

"I won't?"

She just looked at him.

It bothered him that she seemed able to read his intentions so clearly, but she was right. He would not make the cost of bravery for these young soldiers be their lives.

Before he could say anything else, the hunting party returned. Though he did not know where they had been. The fragrance of roasting meat told him they had been back to the clearing at least once already.

"Were you able to find anything?" Abigail asked them.

They both looked at him for instruction, having responded to his warning howl.

"My wife sent you on an errand?"

"Aye, she did," Niall answered for them. "She wanted vegetables and berries for the evening meal."

"And did you find any?"

The two men nodded.

"Enough?" he asked.

Both men looked unsure, eyeing his wife with something between respect and apprehension.

Niall chuckled, the sound rusty from disuse. "It appears your wife likes her vegetables."

Talorc nodded. "Then go find more, Earc. Fionn, you will stay to face the challenge these young warriors have made on behalf of their clan for rights to this land."

He would not have the youths face Niall. None but the boldest Chrechte would be able to do so without pissing himself, and Talorc intended to face that challenger personally.

Both men did as he said without another word.

He faced the six Donegal youths again. "All who have come in challenge will fight, except him," he said, indicating the Chrechte who had offered his neck already.

The boy who had already offered his submission bowed his head as if in shame. Talorc growled and the youth's head snapped up. "You are omega, there is no shame in submitting to the more powerful alpha."

An omega's place in the pack had not always been a respected one, but when the Chrechte realized their warring ways were on the verge of decimating their people, that changed. Initially, it had been an omega who first suggested the Chrechte should insinuate themselves into the surrounding clans, rather than warring with them. Once the wisdom of the recommendation was acknowledged, respect for the thinking of the omegas grew.

Since then, omegas were given a place of honor on the pack councils. They were considered both wise and level-headed, which in most cases was exactly right. They were also considered strong in ways brawn could not defeat, because omegas had managed to eke out lives among their more powerful Chrechte brethren despite being the physically weakest. Generation after generation. It was not something easily dismissed by thinking men.

In addition, each omega now stood as a living reminder to their pack that no matter how strong the Chrechte might be, they could not escape the weakness among them—that of mortality. They had to respect life in order to continue thriving. They were still influenced by their wolf natures, but not controlled by them. Those that were often died young, and that, too, stood as a prominent reminder for those that came after.

"Talorc, don't you think you could refer to these young men in more humane terms? Or are there more meaning to the Gaelic words you are using I do not understand?"

"I am not being offensive," he assured his wife and then wondered at his doing so. Did it matter that his English wife thought him rude?

He wasn't civilized, damn it, and had no desire to be.

Giving vent to his irritation, he crossed his arms and glared at the other Donegal Chrechte. "Why did you bring an omega to a challenge?"

"He is my younger brother. I cannot leave him unprotected, but he refused to stay in the forest while I challenged you."

"I will share my brother's fate," the omega wolf said quietly.

Talorc's respect for these young soldiers grew. He had no doubt they would lead the Donegal clan and pack one day. He nodded his acceptance of the explanation. "You," he said looking at the omega, "stand with Niall and my lady during the challenge."

The omega dipped his head in acknowledgment of the order.

Niall led Abigail away from the cave and the men squaring off to challenge. The omega followed, taking a position on the other side of Niall. Away from Abigail, as was proper. He showed no fear in the huge warrior's presence, patently trusting Talorc's Chrechte honor as the superior alpha. One day he would learn not all of the wolf nature were worthy of that faith, but not today.

Talorc instructed Airril and Fionn to face the four humans.

Then he nodded toward the leader Chrechte. "Come face your challenge, boy."

"I am no boy."

"You are no alpha either, not yet."

He could tell his final two words had given the young soldier pleasure by the expression that flitted across his face before seriousness settled back over his features. "My name is Circin."

"And I am Talorc, laird of the Sinclairs and pack leader to my Chrechte brethren."

Then he waited, letting Circin make the first move. Talorc countered it, glad when it took some effort on his part. He would be sorely disappointed in the Donegal laird if the man hadn't seen to any training in the young

Chrechte warrior under his care. Talorc made his own move, explaining why it was a good counter, but how it could be better.

Circin's eyes widened at the instruction, yet he did not allow the flow of words to splinter his focus. Even so, it was obvious he was listening to everything Talorc said. And in doing so he earned another measure of Talorc's esteem.

He allowed the sparring to continue long after the human boys had been defeated and submitted to Airril and Fionn. He could have taken Circin down to forced submission at any time. However, he wanted to teach the young wolf moves usually reserved for the Chrechte because they required greater speed, strength and stamina than most human warriors possessed.

Circin showed his appreciation in voluntarily baring his throat when Talorc pulled him into a nearly unbreakable hold. The younger soldier could have held on to his pride until Talorc forced an acknowledgment of his superior force. The laird was glad to see the boy understood how to take dignity in defeat.

It was a lack in that respect that had led to their people nearly wiping themselves out in the past.

Talorc had allowed Circin to fight long enough that there should be no shame in his loss of the challenge. Yet the young man's honor should be fulfilled as well, since he had fought for right to the land and lost.

Nevertheless, it was good to check. Talorc did not need an enemy cropping up from a source he was close to naming friend. "You are satisfied?"

Circin nodded, sadness tingeing his gaze. "I am."

Even knowing the outcome before the first blow was struck, there could be no joy in defeat.

"Good." He placed his right fist over his heart.

Circin copied the action and bowed his head.

"Tell your laird the Sinclair laird would consider it an honor to train Chrechte warriors from his clan should he desire it."

Circin's eyes lit with excitement. "You mean it?"

"The first thing you need to learn, boy, is that an alpha never says something he does not mean or cannot back up," Niall chided from his position between Abigail and the omega.

"Even Muin?" Circin asked.

"Muin is your brother?" Talorc asked, rather than reply.

Circin wiped blood from the corner of his lip with the back of his hand. "Yes."

"An omega is always welcome among his Chrechte brethren, regardless of what colors they wear."

"You adhere strictly to the Chrechte laws."

"Aye." Even if the Balmoral had believed for a time he did not.

"I will pass your invitation on to my laird."

And would not take no for answer, if Talorc's guess was accurate.

He was not surprised when Abigail invited the Donegal warriors to share in their evening meal. He was only surprised by the fact her presumption in doing so did not bother him. He supposed that she was his wife after all.

"I could not help but notice you did not take your horse hunting," Abigail said, breaking the silence she had maintained since inviting the other soldiers to eat with them.

His wife was a curious mixture of timidity and boldness. She had not hesitated to confront him before he faced Circin's challenge, but she had spent the hours since then watching everyone else and saying very little. 'Twas odd. In his experience, women tended to talk more than men, often filling a peaceful silence with unnecessary verbal noise. Abigail was the first woman he had met who might actually speak less than his warriors.

"I did not need a horse."

"Perhaps you should reconsider that notion." She paused, giving him a look from between her lashes. "Considering the fact that your soldiers returned with game and you did not."

Everyone around the fire went silent at his wife's innocent observation, waiting for his response.

He wasn't about to admit that his wolf had spent the morning preoccupied with a woman who had responded with naught but fear at his presence. He frowned at her, letting her know he had no intention of justifying his failure to return with game.

"Perhaps it was forgetting your plaid that caused your lack of success. You scared the prey away." The edges of her lips curled upward, though her expression remained demure.

She was teasing him. His shy little human wife dared to tease the Sinclair. The look of astonishment on Earc's face and subtle mirth on Niall's said they realized it as well. The other men wore a mixture of trepidation and concern, clearly mistaking his wife's words as criticism.

"Highlanders have been hunting without covering for as long as they have claimed these lands."

"Hmm . . . ," she replied noncommittally.

"Are you worried about my ability to provide for you?" he asked, keeping his expression hard and unreadable.

Crossing her arms she gave him an arch look that about had him falling backward. "Maybe I am." She wasn't buying his pretend annoyance, not even with worthless English gold coin.

A gasp from one of his warriors said they had though.

"You needn't concern yourself, lady. Our clan provides for the laird as he provides for us," Niall said, adding his own bit to bait Talorc.

"It would seem that is a good thing," she replied and took a delicate bite of the roasted rabbit.

When Talorc did naught but give Niall a halfhearted glare and a shake of his head, Circin frowned much more fiercely. "You accept such an insult from your warrior?"

"Niall did not insult me, nor did my wife." He looked at Abigail, who was definitely smirking now. "Did you?"

"Nay, my laird. I would never do so."

Circin looked wholly unconvinced. "But—"

"In fact, I have full confidence that my wife will readily promise to eat only that which I proved for the next week."

"Certainly," Abigail said promptly.

Only then did the Donegal youth catch on. "You were teasing your laird."

An almost silent giggle issued from her throat. "Yes."

"No one teases the Donegal laird."

"Not even his wife?" Abigail asked.

"Our lady died ten years ago."

"That explains it. He's probably still grieving," Abigail said, clearly tongue in cheek.

The young soldier nodded quite seriously. "Aye. That he

is. The biggest part of his heart died with her. They were true mates."

"It is good for a husband and wife to be friends," Abigail observed, clearly mistaking the meaning of the word *mates*.

Circin gave Abigail a confused look that went right past her as she studied Talorc's face. He stared back.

"Do you agree?" she asked, a wistful expression on her pretty oval features.

"'Twould be enough to wish not to be enemies," was all he was willing to concede.

How could he be friends with a woman born and raised *Sassenach*? He would never have a true mate now that he had accepted her into his bed. He would not be able to father children, for a Chrechte could not have offspring with a human unless a true mate bond existed. He, who believed strongly in preserving the Chrechte, would not be able to pass his own wolf nature on to the next generation.

The thought had him surging to his feet. "I will take the first patrol."

Abigail paced, her attention drifting to the cavern entrance every few steps. It remained as empty as it had been since she said her good-nights to the warriors and found her way to her and Talorc's temporary sleeping chamber.

Her husband had disappeared at the end of dinner and not returned since. At first, she had been relieved by his absence. His cruel comment regarding not being enemies with his wife being enough to wish for had put her on the verge of tears. Coupled with the way he had ignored her all day to hunt, on foot yet, left her in no doubt about how he saw her.

As an unwelcome interloper.

Just like her parents.

For just a little while, when he had taken such tender care of her after consummating their marriage the night before, she had let herself begin to believe it might be different.

Only, no matter what he had said during the Chrechte marriage ritual about her no longer being English, regardless of how deeply emotional their physical joining had felt to her, he did not care for her. She had been a fool to think one day he might. An absolute fool. The intense physical intimacy that had been so transforming for her had meant less than nothing to him.

She was his enemy. That she was his wife could not cancel out that salient fact.

She could not credit her own stupidity in allowing even a tendril of hope to grow that there might be a place for her among his clan, even once they learned the truth of her deafness. Talorc would be only too happy to use the deception as an excuse to get rid of his unwanted English wife. Just as she had first believed.

She swiped at the moisture trying to pool in her eyes. She would not cry. She would not.

Nor would she have Talorc return to find her pacing with impatience for his arrival.

With that thought in mind, she stripped to her shift and climbed between the furs to force or feign sleep. Either would work, so long as Talorc did not realize how hurt she was to learn her idiotic hopes had been just that.

Chapter 10

Only one torch burned in the cavern when Talorc entered sometime after midnight. The water of the pool looked like obsidian in the muted amber light. He contemplated soaking in it before joining Abigail, but he recognized it for the stalling tactic it was and turned from the pool to look at his wife.

She slept fitfully, having kicked off the fur that should be covering her beautiful body. She was wearing her shift, though she had not done so since attempting to the night of their wedding. If preserving her modesty was her goal, she had failed miserably. The undergarment had ridden up her thighs until the pretty blond curls that covered her mound were revealed.

Her shapely legs glowed in the soft light, beckoning him to touch. Everything about his wife's body appealed to his senses and his wolf's nature. Instead of pouting like a little boy deprived of his lifemate, Talorc should be grateful he at least found Abigail desirable.

He hadn't her sister.

He did not know why he had avoided the lovely blonde gracing his furs tonight. Their situation was less her fault than his. He, at least, could have chosen to disregard his king's desires. Again. Abigail's stepfather might have offered to refuse the marriage, but the reality was Abigail's mother would have made her life even more a misery if the baron had been fool enough to do it.

And Talorc would have been forced to kill him. After all, he had decided to accept the marriage knowing the cost of doing so from the moment he sent his demands to his king.

Besides, he wanted his wife. One of the few compensations from this ill-conceived marriage was the fact he was free to have sex with her as frequently as they both desired. And yet he had stupidly avoided her for a good part of the night.

It might be past midnight, but he had finally wised up.

Stripping off his plaid, he joined her on the furs, his cock already standing at attention and his wolf clamoring for touch. Talorc reached out and traced the curve of her soft, feminine belly with one fingertip.

Her forehead wrinkling like she was frustrated, Abigail shifted toward him in her sleep. He moved as well, readily allowing their bodies to settle against each other. She seemed to like that as she stopped moving and the lines of her face smoothed to peacefulness.

If he did not know better, he would think she was part Chrechte, the way she reacted with almost animal-like instincts.

Leaning down, he took a deep breath, inhaling her addictive fragrance. Emily had not smelled this good; no woman ever had. But his lovely wife's natural perfume was like wildflowers on the floor of Heaven to his wolf's senses. Unable to help himself, Talorc nuzzled into the smooth skin of her neck.

She tilted her head back in an unconscious gesture of submission that went straight to his sex and his wolf's spirit.

He continued to nuzzle her until the urge to scent her in the way of his people grew irrepressible. He rubbed his cheek against hers on one side of her face and then the other. His wolf cried out for Talorc to change and to scent his mate properly, but he resisted. Abigail would no doubt have heart failure were she to wake to a giant gray wolf rubbing his muzzle against her cheeks and neck.

She'd been terrified enough meeting him in the woods. She had an unhealthy fear of wild animals he would have to help her get past. 'Twas a good thing he had no intention of ever revealing his wolf nature to his wife. Even if he could trust her with his secrets, her terror would remain a barrier between them.

So, scenting her as a man would have to do. It would be enough to mark her as his for the other Chrechte. Now that they had access to water for washing, his fastidious wife would not leave the scent of their lovemaking rubbed into her skin.

Unfortunately.

Abigail's breath hitched and then changed to reflect a waking state. Her smell changed subtly as she experienced some kind of agitation. Tension crept into her limbs even though she had not moved. He lifted his head to meet her eyes.

She blinked sleepily at him, something unreadable in the brown depth of her gaze. "You're here."

He did not ask where else he should be, considering he had spent most of the night away from their temporary bed. He simply nodded and then covered her lips with his before she could say anything else, or ask any questions he did not want to answer.

She went rigid against him, all implications of unconscious surrender disappearing as she jerked her face away from his and broke the kiss.

He reared up to lean on his arms above her. "What is wrong, angel?" Then a thought struck him. "Are you still sore?"

She did not reply, keeping her face averted so he could not read her expression.

That bothered him more than he cared to admit and he carefully grasped her chin to turn her head so their eyes met. "Answer me."

She stared at him, her soft brown gaze shimmering with what looked like resignation.

"You are sore. It is all right. We will wait until you have healed." He was no monster.

"I am not sore."

"Then why did you turn away?" he demanded with exasperation.

"How can you share your body with your enemy?"

"I would not." Disgust at the idea laced his voice.

Her brows drew together in confusion. "You said I was your enemy when we were eating the evening meal."

"I did not."

"You did. I do not always understand . . ." She hesitated and blew out a clearly frustrated breath. "Gaelic. I do not always understand Gaelic perfectly. It is not my first language, but I know the word for enemy."

He mentally reviewed each word he said to her over the evening meal and comprehension finally dawned. "I said it was enough that you and I are not enemies, I do not expect us to be friends."

Her eyes glowed with pleasure, but dimmed almost as quickly as he finished speaking.

"You do not think we can be friends?"

She was formerly English. She was a woman. She was not Chrechte and could never know of that important part of himself. There was only one answer to her question, but he could not force the negative out. So, he shrugged and watched with amusement as her eyes narrowed in what could be only described as an adorable glare.

"That is not an answer."

"Aye, my angel, it is."

Her lips parted, but before she could argue, he covered them again with his mouth. This time, he took advantage of the opening and thrust his tongue forward to claim her sweetness.

Unlike a moment ago, her response was instant and blatant. She had really been bothered by the idea that he saw her as an enemy. Women were strange creatures with minds unfathomable.

He would never bed his enemy, but he would not be overly worried if *she* considered him less than trustworthy. He would still bury himself in her softness. Not that she would distrust him. He was the Sinclair, and by her words and actions, she had shown she knew what that meant—at least to the extent that she trusted her safety in his hands.

For her to refuse intimacy because she thought he viewed her in a negative light when she so clearly enjoyed making love was overly refined thinking. 'Twas most likely the result of her more *civilized* English manners.

Now that she had decided she could allow herself a natural response, she burned him with the fire of her need. He reveled in the carnality of their kiss, rubbing his naked body against hers. Her small hands grabbed onto his shoulders, her nails digging in and sparking satisfaction in his wolf's spirit at her flagrant possessiveness. He lowered himself, covering her body completely with his in a move demanded by his Chrechte blood.

He rubbed his body against hers, scenting every bit of skin that he could reach. His bones shuddered with the need to change, but he controlled it.

Barely.

His wolf howled for release. He willed the beast to submerge itself in pleasure.

Lifting her arms above her head, he nuzzled one of her armpits. An aphrodisiac like no other, the scent of her pheromones made him crazy. He nipped the tender skin right where arm and shoulder joined. Her body jerked, her hips pressing up into him. She wasn't trying to buck him off though, not with the way her smaller calves wrapped around his, holding him to her with unmistakable intent.

He approved and let her know how much by rubbing his hard cock against the apex of her thighs. She made a choked noise, her hips bucking again and again. It was amazing how perfectly their bodies were attuned, considering she was not part wolf.

He threw his head back and howled out his pleasure and his need.

Then his head dipped forward of its own volition and his lips sought out the join of her shoulder and neck. He opened his mouth over the sensitive spot, his teeth brushing the skin there, making them both moan in a feral recognition as old as time. He bit down, gently but firmly, worrying the mark he had made the night before.

A keening sound broke from her throat and his body went rigid with pleasure at the recognition of his claiming. His wolf howled so loud inside him that his head reverberated with it. Her entire body bowed, lifting his much-larger form several inches before she collapsed back into the furs.

He shifted his hips until his granite-hard erection pressed into the slick opening to her soft body.

"Do it." Her hands grabbed at him, pulling him down. "Do it. Do it. Do it. *Claim me.*"

He could not have stopped himself if he had wanted to. He claimed her with his bite and with his manhood.

As he surged inside, two things happened. The first was an overwhelming sense of coming home, even stronger than he had the night before. So strong, he could not begin to deny it. So strong that it paralyzed him into temporary immobility.

And the second was that he heard her cry out his name. *In his head.*

He recognized the soft cadence of her voice, but there was a timbre to it he had not heard from her before, a richness that her spoken words did not have.

No. It was not possible. She was human. She was his king's choice, not Talorc's. *She was not Chrechte.* She must have said it out loud and he just thought he had heard it in his mind.

That had to be it.

All inner arguments fled as the pleasure built with unprecedented speed between them. She moved under him with wanton sensuality. His hips thrust of their own accord, moving his hardness in and out of her with a speed and strength he would not have thought she could handle, much less rejoice in so clearly.

He slid his forearms under her knees and pulled her legs up so he could thrust more deeply.

"Yes. Yes. Yes . . ." Each affirmative barely whispered past her lips, but the intensity of the demand was more obvious than if she had screamed the words.

He spiraled toward climax. The strange sensation that he could feel her doing the same only increased his pleasure. Building it and building it. Until they reached an orgasm together that was so intense his shy wife screamed out so loud it would have shattered his inner ear.

If the cry had not sounded inside his head.

He put his head back and howled in indescribable pleasure as he planted his seed deep in his wife's body and cried out her name in his mind.

" *Abigail.*"

Her breath seized in her chest and Abigail's body convulsed with another wave of wondrous bliss as she heard her name shouted in her husband's pleasure-drenched voice.

Heard it.

Heavens above and all the saints besides. Could it be true? Had she truly heard Talorc yell her name as he reached his own pinnacle of gratification? Yet, how could it be anything but real? She who had heard nothing, not even a ringing in her ears, for too many silent years, had heard her own name called out.

She gasped at the sheer miracle of it, tears of joy burning with welcome sting in her eyes.

Grabbing his face with both hands, she demanded, "Say it again. Say my name again."

But as she spoke, cold dread lapped at the edges of her joy. She had not heard her own voice.

He stared at her with satiated pleasure and obligingly complied with her frenzied request. "Abigail."

She watched his lips form the syllables she knew made her name, but no sound penetrated the cocoon of silence she lived in. Desolation choked her even as she begged, "Again. Please?"

Talorc's brows drew together and he asked her a question with his amazing blue eyes.

She could not answer it though, only beg again, "Please." Though each word she uttered eroded the hope that had blossomed at what she had thought was a miracle.

Because she could not hear her own words and now questioned whether she had indeed heard her name. But if not, then what? It had been so long since anything but silence had assailed her, she could not remember sound. She fought the forgetting of normalcy, but each year drew her further into a world that felt as if it had never had sound at all.

Still, how could she have imagined something she never even experienced in her dreams anymore?

"Are you not well?" he asked.

And she read the meaning on his lips, in the concern now masking his features, but she did not hear.

How could she answer?

They had just shared a pleasure beyond belief and she was allowing the imaginings of her mind to ruin it. She was not well, but it was no one's fault but her own.

She forced a smile and pulled his face toward her, intent on hiding behind a kiss. "How could I be anything else?"

How indeed?

And he cooperated in helping her hide, kissing her with a tenderness and leftover passion that assuaged the pain of her self-delusion.

He did not take her to soak in the hot spring this night, but led her on another sensual journey that did not end with any inexplicable experiences. Then he kissed her after—right into slumber.

Talorc woke with his arms wrapped protectively around his mate. Not just his angel in a flight of fancy, but his *true and sacred mate*. If he could believe the evidence of his mind and senses. How was it possible?

The arguments against the probability of finding a sacred mate the way he had were just as valid as the day before, but none of them mattered in the face of one inescapable fact: *He had heard her voice inside his head.* They were capable of mindspeak. Not all true mates were, but it was an indisputable sign that the mating was blessed.

It also meant that until Abigail or he died, they would be physically capable of mating with only each other. Not that he would have considered doing otherwise. The Sinclairs, particularly the Chrechte among them, placed high importance the physical act of sex. Most members of the clan, warriors and women alike, considered it a sacred bond, not to be broken.

Even more important, the sacred mating bond meant that not only could Abigail have Talorc's children, but most likely she *would* have them. What had seemed an impossibility the night before now had a strong chance of happening. Talorc would send his wolf nature into the next generation if he was blessed with Chrechte offspring rather than human.

It was enough to make him howl in delight. However, his joy was tinged with melancholy.

He could not tell Abigail of his full nature and risk her revealing the secrets of his people to outsiders. Thus he could not share some of the benefits of the true mate bond with her, like mindspeaking. Since he had accepted a while ago that he would most likely not find his true mate, that should not bother him. But it did.

Knowing the mental intimacy they were capable of made him long to participate in the ancient Chrechte act. Yet part of him was relieved he had a reason to avoid it. The true bond was disconcerting enough; the deep intimacy of mindspeak was not something he was comfortable sharing with a woman he had met only a few days before. Particularly a human who had been born and raised in England.

He must be careful not to speak into her mind as he had done when shouting her name during his first climax the night before. He could not risk revealing the true state of their mating before he was ready. If that time ever came.

Abigail's first view of the Sinclair holding was more than a little imposing. Her sister's letters had described a keep similar to their father's, with timber fence surrounding the motte and bailey. Not so now. In the almost three years since her sister had first gone north, that timber had been replaced with stone, and the Sinclair keep looked more like a castle. A solid, impenetrable fortress, to be precise.

A wide moat surrounded the high stone wall. The water was dark, indicating a depth that would prevent easy crossing.

Horse hooves clattered as their party went over the single access point, a narrow bridge that led to the only opening she could see in the wall. Clanspeople had come out of their cottages to welcome their laird home and followed the horses across the bridge. They were joined by more men and women in the bailey.

Some called out, many cheered and children ran in games of tag around the men mounted on their huge steeds. It was a much different picture than the one Emily had painted of her first view of the Sinclair holding. Both warrior and warhorses showed their superior training because the children were never in danger of being trampled.

Talorc maintained their forward movement, however, crossing the bailey to guide his horse onto a path up the motte. Stone walls rose high on both sides, casting a shadow over them all, those riding and on foot alike.

Abigail could not tell if the steep hill was man-made like her father's motte or a happenstance of nature. The path beneath her horse's feet was composed of dirt and moss-covered stones. It felt solid, indicating the hill had been created many years ago, whether by God or man. No rainstorm would wash away its foundation as tragically happened back in England on occasion.

Sybil had worried and lamented about such a thing happening since she had taken her daughters to live in the Hamilton keep.

The gate at the top of the path was open and Talorc rode through, his bearing proud and imposing. A contingent of warriors, every bit as ferocious looking as the ones that had accompanied them north, waited in the courtyard. They stood in front of a single circular stone tower centered on the flattened top of the hill. The tower soared well over thirty feet into the air, competing with the fierce soldiers for Abigail's curious attention.

Talorc dismounted and greeted the warrior that looked

to be Niall's twin with a fist to his heart. The other man copied his laird's movement, adding a nod toward Talorc that was almost a bow but not quite.

Abigail smiled at Niall. "That is your brother, Barr, is it not?"

"Aye."

"He's almost as handsome as you, but he lacks the mark of strength you carry on your face."

Tipping his head back, Niall laughed out loud, making Abigail grin. She liked to see joy on her new friend's face.

The warriors around them stopped greeting their laird and stared. So did the clanspeople, looking at Niall as if he'd sprouted Medusa snakes on his head.

Niall's mirth transformed to a fierce glare, causing all but a red-haired man standing near Talorc to affect immediate interest in something else. The red-haired man was smiling and staring at Niall with what could only be described as a love-struck expression. Not that Niall seemed to notice, he was too busy trying to intimidate his friends.

Abigail shook her head, giving up on trying to keep track of the conversations around her. She could only see a few people's lips, and she didn't have enough experience watching them speak yet to accurately read more than every other word. She could not see her husband's mouth at all. However, when everyone, including the clanspeople that had followed them from the lower bailey fixed their attention on Abigail, she surmised he'd said something in regard to her.

Panicked, she looked at Niall. "What did he say? I was not paying attention."

Niall gave her a strange look but didn't hesitate to reply. "Our laird introduced you as his wife. The soldiers and clan are now at liberty to speak to you."

"You mean they weren't before?"

"You dinna notice none of the soldiers spoke to you on our trip north?"

"I thought they might be shy." Or that they hadn't liked her because she was English. "You spoke to me."

"I had my laird's leave to do so."

"Wow, Sybil would throw a fit worthy of a yowling, scalded cat if my father presumed to dictate who could and could not speak to her."

"Does that mean you intend to throw such a fit?" Talorc asked, having approached without her noticing.

She shook her head with a smile. "Not at all." If he but knew it, he had just made her life all the easier. The fewer people that spoke directly to her, the less chance her secret would be revealed.

"Good." He put his arms up, indicating he would help her from the horse. "Come."

She didn't hesitate, sliding from the white mare's back right into her husband's strong arms. He set her from him immediately but put one hand on her shoulder. "I have already introduced my wife, I now tell you that Abigail of the Sinclair is *your* new lady."

Surprise rippled through the crowd, but it was no stronger than her own sense of astonishment. Even Abigail recognized a seal of approval when she "heard" it. Talorc was telling his people he expected them to accept her.

Amazing.

She knew he had not done the same for Emily. Her sister had felt hated by the Sinclairs.

An old man approached, a scowl on his wrinkled features. "You ask us to pledge our loyalty to this *Sassenach*?"

"Nay."

Abigail felt her heart plummet. Had she misunderstood?

"I do not ask. I demand it. As is their right, any who

wish to challenge me may do so. Be assured, however, that I will consider the least slight to my mate a challenge for my position as laird."

The old man stepped back, clearly reeling from his leader's words.

Abigail felt a bit faint herself. Talorc had just announced to all who cared to listen that he considered her his friend. Warmth suffused her along with guilt she had kept buried deep inside since she began hiding her deafness from those around her.

She did not want to deceive her husband, but terror at his reaction to the truth prevented her from admitting it. Even now. Her plan had been to reveal her affliction upon reaching the Highlands so that Talorc would send her to live with her sister, Emily, among the Balmorals. With that goal in mind, telling the truth of her lack of hearing would have been easy.

Or so she supposed, but now it felt impossible. Once again hope was blooming inside that there might be a place for her among the Sinclairs. A true place. A position of belonging. And she did not want to give that up.

Chapter 11

The redheaded soldier Abigail had noticed earlier stepped forward. "I will show our lady to your quarters so she can rest from her journey, my laird."

Talorc nodded. He turned to Abigail. "Wife, this is Guaire, seneschal to the Sinclair holding."

"Seneschal? I don't know this word."

"It is similar to a steward," Guaire replied in English, earning himself a glare from the other warriors around him.

Except for a slight tightening of his shoulders, he ignored the reaction, showing he was used to such from the others. For some reason that bothered Abigail. She knew she was going to like this soldier. He had been happy when Niall laughed and that pleased Abigail.

Niall was one of the few people in the world she counted as friend.

As they walked away, Talorc must have said something because Guaire stopped and looked back at his laird. Abigail swiveled her head so she could read her husband's lips as well.

"You will give her your arm on the stairs and assure her safety."

"Aye, my laird."

"I'm no bumbler, Talorc." She was deaf, not lacking in grace. "I'm not about to go tumbling down the stairs."

"Nevertheless you will allow a soldier to aid you whenever you use them."

She gave him one of his famous shrugs, refusing to agree to such a ridiculous instruction and unwilling to lie either.

As she and Guaire left, Abigail was actually grateful for her inability to hear the many whispers and comments that had to be going on behind them.

They stepped into the hall and Abigail sucked in a breath.

The interior was every bit as imposing as the exterior and far more austere. No colorful silks adorned the stone walls to give the hall a more cheerful aspect. No chairs surrounded the huge fireplace, conspicuously unlit despite the late-afternoon chill in the cavernous room. The sun might shine outside, but it had not penetrated the thick stone walls of Talorc's tower home. The only furnishings in the great hall were two long tables with backless benches down each side.

"How many of the soldiers dine in the hall?" she asked Guaire, rather than commenting on the cheerless aspect of the huge room.

"Ten of the elite soldiers live here in the hall as well as Talorc's advisor, Osgard, and myself. Another ten to fifteen of the unmarried soldiers will join us for the midday or evening meal."

"The married soldiers never share a meal with their laird?" That surprised her. Talorc struck her as a leader who would prefer to stay connected to all his people.

"It would be considered rude to leave their wives and families for such. Is it not the same in England?"

"Well, I know that all Sir Hamilton's soldiers were on rotation to eat in the great hall once a month. It was considered an honor."

"As it should be."

"Of course, their families were welcome to join them. Some did and some preferred not to. My mother liked to lord her position over the other women living in my step-father's barony."

"Interesting." Guaire did not appear as if the comment was merely a polite one. He looked intrigued. "I do not think we have had a child at the laird's table since Talorc and Caitriona themselves were children."

"Perhaps it is time to change that."

Guaire smiled at her, his expression saying he was amused but approved. "Perhaps it is."

"How long have you lived in the laird's tower?" she asked as Guaire guided her up the stairs.

The stone steps curved in a gentle spiral along the wall up to the first story, which was a good fifteen feet above the great hall. She understood Talorc's insistence on her having an escort a little better. The stairs were not wide enough for two people to walk abreast and they had nothing between them and a sheer drop to the main floor.

Guaire led her one step ahead, while her hand was held firmly in the crook of his arm. "Since the laird's sister left to live with the Balmoral clan. I had been seneschal for two years already then, but not afforded the privilege of living within my laird's home."

"Well, I'm glad you do now. The stairs are very narrow," she observed.

Guaire led her across the small landing at the top of the stairs and through a doorway there. "It is a tactical advantage."

"Talorc seems very concerned with the safety of his fortress."

"Not the safety of the fortress." Guaire stopped and gave her a look that conveyed his desire for her to understand. "Our laird cares greatly for the security of the people that live within it."

"Because of what happened to his father?"

"More like because of what his father's actions allowed to happen to the rest of the clan. Our former laird was only one of many that died when his bitch of a wife betrayed the clan to her English friends."

"I can't imagine an English force coming this far north to wage war on a Scottish clan. What could they possibly hope to gain?"

Guaire shrugged and she was sure it did not mean that he did not have an answer, but that it was one he didn't wished to share. "Does it matter? They came and they killed."

"Yes." At the behest of a woman who should have been loyal to the old laird and his people. And Abigail's husband *still* called her his mate. It was a miracle to her way of thinking. "I must be grateful Talorc accepted me so readily."

"He did not have a choice. You are his mate, a true one if he willingly acknowledged so to the Chrechte warriors."

"I didn't even realize he saw me as his friend. It is an honor I plan to live up to."

Guaire gave her a puzzled look. "Friend?"

"His mate."

The redhead's leaf green eyes widened. "He did not tell you what it meant to be his mate?"

"We discussed it last night." Sort of. In a roundabout way. "We both feel it is a blessing for a husband and wife to be true friends."

Guaire seemed to be choking on something, but he just shook his head and led her down the hallway that bisected the first story. He pushed open the first door on the right. "This is Talorc's chamber, now yours as well."

Considering the sparsity of furnishings and decor on the main floor, she should not have been surprised by this room. However, it would make a monastic cell appear decadent by comparison. A pile of furs much like the ones she and her husband had slept in on the trip north occupied a spot against the far wall. There was a chest under the window but no chairs or chest of drawers.

The only decor, if you could call it that, was a huge well-oiled sword and a selection of knives hanging above the fireplace mantel. She turned in a circle and noted torch holders on either side of the door. That was something at least. A small indication that her husband acknowledged they were no longer cave dwellers.

"It's, um . . . is he having a bed made?"

Guaire's look was definitely tinged with humor this time, and maybe a little pity. "I do not believe so."

"You would know, I'm guessing."

"Aye."

She sighed. The furs had been comfortable enough the past few nights, she supposed. "He is a man of few indulgences."

"I think 'few' may be overstating the case."

That was what she was afraid of.

* * *

"She is your true mate?" Barr asked Talorc with nothing less than shock.

He and a small group of Chrechte warriors had come into the great hall after Talorc had dismissed the clansmen.

Talorc looked toward the floor above as if he could see his beautiful blond wife through the timbers. He sighed at his own foolishness. She wasn't even up there. Guaire had taken her on a tour of the fortress. "Aye."

"But . . ." Clearly his second-in-command did not know what to say because he did not finish his thought.

Osgard's feelings were easily read. He was furious, his craggy, aged features tightened in fierce lines. "Impossible."

"You doubt my ability to read the signs?"

"Your father insisted Tamara was his true mate as well, but we all know how that turned out." Osgard snorted. "The man was infatuated and that was that."

"I am not infatuated with my wife." He was protective of her, possessive in a way he never would have anticipated, but that was all because of the wolf. She was not just his wife. She was his sacred mate. "I have no intention of sharing the secrets of our clan or our people with her."

"Your father did not intend to tell your mother about the Royal Treasure either, but he did it all the same."

"I am not my father," Talorc growled.

Osgard was still hurt from his former laird's betrayal, but no one knew the pain of looking up to that man as sire and having all feelings of respect and admiration wiped out in a single night. No one but Talorc.

"Our lady does not know she is your mate?" Niall asked, scowling.

"She thinks it means we are true friends." And Talorc refused to feel bad about that. Abigail was human. She would not understand anyway.

The fact that her sister seemed to in her bond with Lachlan of the Balmoral was not something Talorc wanted to examine closely.

Talorc's words startled a laugh from Osgard. "The English are fools."

"What is foolish about a woman mistaking a word that has more than one meaning?" Niall demanded. "There is no honor in making a gull of your sacred mate."

"That is not my intention. She is not one of us; she does not need to know she is anything more than my wife. 'Tis all she expects as a human."

Niall looked far from convinced.

Osgard frowned at the scarred warrior. "Has she ensnared you, then?"

"Our lady does not seek to snare. She is innocent and kind." Niall crossed his arms in a stance that said he would not be moved. "I count her friend."

Barr gasped.

"She does not fear me. She thinks I am romantic and kind." Niall rolled his eyes. "She sees the best in people. 'Tis a strangely appealing trait. You'll see."

Osgard puffed up with anger as only an old Scotsman could. "I see the lass has you and our laird bamboozled."

"She's nothing like Tamara," Talorc insisted, and he realized how deeply he believed the words as he spoke them. "She would never deceive me as that woman did my father."

"Your feebleminded father believed the same."

"Enough!" Talorc accepted much from Osgard, but this was going too far. He surged to his feet and loomed over the old man. "My father was your laird. He made a mistake in trusting the wrong woman and paid with his life. I learned from that mistake and will not repeat it. You should need no more than my word to accept that fact. Insulting his memory as you have just done is an affront to the title he wore."

"Better cause offense than to watch this clan taken down by another scheming Englishwoman. I'll not do it."

"There is no falseness in my mate!" Talorc felt his eyes change and the world went black-and-white.

Osgard flinched back as all the color leached from his wrinkled skin. "My only concern is for the clan," he said with much less vigor than before.

Talorc could respect the older man's motivations, if not his opinions. "I'll see to the protection of my people, as I have from the beginning of my leadership. But know this. My wolf demands protection of my *sacred* mate just as surely."

Osgard grudgingly nodded, and then sighed. "I did not intend to speak insolence against ye, for all that I see you as the son I lost in that bloody, fiery battle, you are my laird, and I respect both your decisions and your commitment to your clan."

The words were a major concession from the old warrior, and Talorc treated them with the respect they deserved, pounding his right fist over his heart with a nod.

Though it was late afternoon when they arrived at the Sinclair holding, Abigail declined Guaire's suggestion she take a nap before the evening meal. "I would rather get acquainted with the motte and lower bailey if you don't mind escorting me."

"I would be delighted."

Abigail smiled. "You are very kind. You do know I'm English, don't you?"

"You used to be English. Now you are married to our laird. That makes you a Sinclair."

"That is similar to something Talorc said on the journey here."

Guaire nodded. "'Tis truth we're speaking."

"I hope the other clanspeople are of the same mind." Though she took leave to doubt it.

However, she was pleasantly surprised to discover that most of the Sinclairs were actually quite amicable when Guaire introduced her. She'd met a group of women who spun the wool harvested from the sheep the clan tended. They dyed and made it into the Sinclair plaid as well as other plaids of similar colors for trade with clans at the twice-yearly gatherings.

The only building larger than the spinning cottage in the lower bailey was the smithy. Abigail was delighted to learn that Magnus, the blacksmith, was married to a woman originally from the clan Abigail's sister had married into. She was even happier when Magnus called his wife from their cottage behind the smithy to meet the new laird's wife.

A lovely woman, with a sweet smile, Susannah welcomed Abigail to the clan. "I'm sure you'll find many friends among our clan just as I did when I came."

"Thank you."

They got to talking about their family members on Balmoral Island and Abigail said, "I brought gifts for Emily, but I do not know when I will be able to take them to her. Are there messengers that go between the two clans very often?"

"No more often than necessary," Magnus replied laconically.

"The lairds have approved our visit to the island after the next full moon so I can visit my family," Susannah said with a smile. "My mother is eager to see our children."

Abigail smiled. "That's wonderful."

"Your family is now the Sinclair clan," her husband admonished with exaggerated patience.

"And I'm not going to pretend my mother, my brother and his wife no longer exist just because I've married one of the reclusive Sinclair clan."

"We are recluses? The Balmoral live on an island with no other clans."

"And it's not an island you mind visiting. You like the hunting there."

Magnus didn't reply, but Abigail wasn't disturbed by the couple's banter. She was more adept than most at reading the language of the body, and it was clear the blacksmith and his wife held no real animosity over their discussion.

Susannah rolled her eyes and spoke to Abigail. "My point, before my husband interrupted with an old argument, was that we could take your gifts and deliver them to your sister if you like."

"That would not be too great a burden?" Abigail asked, truly moved at the offer and blinking back moisture. "I should love to let my sister know I am well and living in the Highlands now." She could not trust Sybil to send word of Abigail's new circumstances to Emily.

"I will pass on any messages you like," Susannah generously offered.

"Thank you so much. If you do not mind, I will include a letter with her gifts."

"You can write?" the blacksmith asked curiously.

"Yes. Emily taught me."

"She is independent, that one. Our laird can read as well," Magnus announced proudly. "As can our Guaire. 'Tis why he was chosen seneschal."

"That and the fact he is the only clan member who can read that does not shake the pleats from his plaid when the elite warriors gather together in one place." Susannah smiled with approval at Guaire.

He shrugged, but his expression said the clanswoman had a point.

"Your parents must be proud of you for being chosen for such an important role in the clan," Abigail observed as she and Guaire walked away from the smithy.

"No doubt they would have been pleased, but my father died during the war with the English baron's forces."

"And your mother?"

"She caught a fever the next year and never recovered."

"I'm sorry."

"Thank you. Sadly, the fever was not one we had experienced before the battle with the English. Our healers did not know what to do."

"Often there is nothing you can do," Abigail replied, remembering her own fever that left her life without sound.

Abigail's further meetings with the men and women of the Sinclair clan continued to go surprisingly well. That was until they returned up to the motte and reached a small cottage located behind the kitchens. Guaire introduced Abigail to Una, the housekeeper and head cook for the residences of the tower.

The widow, who was only a few years older than Abigail and quite beautiful with her dark red hair and doe-like eyes, gave her new lady a once-over that left no doubt she found her laird's new wife lacking. "You're his forced English bride, then?"

"Una!" Guaire admonished. "The laird expects the clan to welcome her."

"She's English," Una spit out, her lovely features twisted in ugly disapproval.

A small boy who clung to his mother's skirts, peeked from behind her and scowled at Abigail. "We hates the English."

Guaire gave Una a look that would have had Abigail taking a few steps back and served to make the other woman avert her eyes at least.

Ignoring her for the moment, he dropped to one knee and looked right into the young boy's eyes. "We do no hate our laird's wife. Where she comes from is of no matter. She is a Sinclair now."

"Tamara was a Sinclair, too, but she had her English baron lover bring his forces to our land and wage a coward's war, attacking with fire while our clan slept," Una replied with venom. "Too many of us lost loved ones to an Englishwoman's treachery to forget it."

It was this attitude that had caused Emily so much distress and fed Abigail's earlier concerns about meeting the clan. However, Abigail had spent the past several years being reviled by her own mother. She had developed a core of solid stone. She would not be cowed by irrational hatred.

"MacAlpin betrayed his own people. We don't distrust the Chrechte because of what one man did," Guaire stood and replied before Abigail had a chance to defend herself.

"It's not the same."

"No, it isn't," Abigail agreed. "MacAlpin wanted power and Tamara had her own reasons for betraying your clan, but I have nothing to gain by making enemies here. I have nothing to return to in England."

"Why should I believe you?" Una asked belligerently.

"Because I'm telling the truth, but maybe you will need time to accept that."

"Time is not something she has," Guaire said, his face set. "I will make sure the laird is made aware of your stand on the matter, Una."

Una blanched, proving she might be prejudiced, but she wasn't stupid.

Abigail shook her head though. "No."

His brows drawn together in a frown, Guaire said, "The laird's instructions in the matter were clear."

"My mind is made up." Abigail crossed her arms over her chest and gave Guaire her best no-nonsense frown. "I will spend the next month getting to know Una and she will come to know her lady, not the English hobgoblin she imagines that has her so frightened."

"I am not afraid," Una denied with disdain.

"What will happen in a month's time?" Guaire asked, ignoring the other woman's continued posturing.

"If she cannot learn to respect, if not actually like me, then she will be relieved of her position as housekeeper and head cook for her laird."

Una's mouth opened and then snapped shut without forming any words.

Guaire shook his head at her. "It is more than you should expect. Talorc made it clear he would consider disrespect shown to our lady as a direct challenge to his leadership."

Una sighed. "I know. I was there."

Abigail tensed. "That changes things." She wished it didn't, but the fact that Una had witnessed Talorc's words meant Abigail could not choose her own course in the matter.

For the first time, Una looked at Abigail with something approaching respect. "In what way?"

"I cannot allow such a challenge to my husband's authority stand. As much as I find it distasteful to do so, I must inform him of our discussion. However, I will attempt to convince him to allow you the month's grace. In fact, I will ask him to give the entire clan a month to get to know me before he takes seriously any disparaging comments about or toward my person."

Una and Guaire stared at her in varying degrees of shock.

"You would—"

"Talorc is not known for his patience," Guaire said, interrupting Una.

"That is quite all right. I am convinced I have enough for both of us."

Chapter 12

Abigail had reason to regret her certainty not an hour later as she argued with Talorc in their chamber. "Una needs time to come to know me before she will trust me."

"I am her laird. She knows me well enough."

Abigail opened her mouth but could not think what to say for a moment. That was an undeniable point. "I do not believe she intended to show you disrespect."

"I do not agree."

"Talorc, please! Do you not think this transition is hard enough for me? Must you put me in a place of enmity with your people without giving me a chance to prove myself?"

He looked astonished at her accusation. "That is not what I am doing."

"But it is. I imagine Una is well liked among the clan. She is beautiful and takes care of not only the laird, but his most trusted soldiers. If you banish her for being a little cranky, I wouldn't blame the other clan members for finding the fault in me. They'll have a real reason to hate me, not an irrational prejudice."

"Our hatred of the English is not irrational."

She threw her hands in the air. "That is exactly what I mean. If even you, who considers me a friend, can say something so hurtful, how can you expect every member of your clan to be more circumspect?"

"I meant no insult, I did not say that I hate *you*."

Cocking her elbows, she fisted her hands on her hips and just looked at the maddening man her king had dictated she marry.

Their gazes locked, but she refused to look away. And something told her he never would.

"You dare to challenge me?"

"Is that what I'm doing? I thought I was disagreeing with you." She could tell right now this would be an ongoing argument in their marriage.

"I will not allow my people to mistreat you."

"I'm not asking you to. I'm not an idiot. I just want you to give everyone a chance to get to know me and realize I'm not like Tamara."

Talorc picked Abigail up by the waist and drew her to him. "You are nothing like that evil bitch."

"I'm not, Talorc. I'm really not." She needed him to believe her.

He didn't reply, but he did kiss her, long and deeply. Kissing led to touching and touching led to disrobing. Soon, they were writhing together in the furs. By the time she could string two thoughts together again, she was naked and snuggled atop her husband's chest.

Sound vibrated through his chest and she knew he had spoken. She lifted her head, affecting a sleepy yawn. "What?"

"I said you will be the death of me."

"I do not think so. You kissed me, if you will recall."

"You challenged me."

"Considering the consequences, I believe I will have to challenge you more often."

He growled in mock outrage and rolled her under him to begin kissing her yet again. She loved his taste and could have kept at their current occupation in perfect bliss for the next hour, but Talorc lifted his head and looked toward the door.

Someone must have knocked. Chills chased down her spine as Abigail acknowledged yet another source of revelation for her secret. What if someone knocked and she did not hear them? She would have to keep the door open when she was in the chamber. There was no help for it. Unlike in her room in her father's keep, she could not feel the vibrations of the floor when someone approached the door.

Or perhaps she had merely been preoccupied? She lost all sense of her surroundings when her husband started touching her.

He brushed a lock of hair back from her face. "We must go down for the evening meal, angel."

"I am not overly hungry, are you?" she asked, placing her hand on his neck and caressing the sensitive spot she had discovered earlier.

He needed more time to calm down in regard to Una. Abigail still hoped to convince Talorc of her plan to give the clan a month to get used to her.

"I might be convinced to forego the evening meal if I thought other, more pressing appetites were going to be fed."

She made no comment about how they had just been fed, but leaned up to press her lips to his throat. Many aspects of her new life were precarious, but not this.

The marriage bed was everything he had promised it would be and more. So much more.

Here, she felt like a complete woman, like her deafness did not matter. She did not need to hear to make him shudder above her like he was doing now while her lips moved along the strong column of his throat.

In this one place, where touch ruled, the silence of her world meant nothing.

The next morning, Abigail was both chagrined and relieved to wake alone. Again.

She had not managed to extract a promise from Talorc to allow his clan time to accustom themselves to their new lady, one who had been born and raised in England. A country and its inhabitants even he expressed nothing but disdain toward. She worried that even now, he was banishing Una. Abigail would feel terrible if that happened.

She knew too well what it was like not to have a secure place to call home, one in which she belonged without question.

However, as much as that possibility distressed her, Abigail could not regret having the privacy to face a more personally terrifying prospect—the risk she was going mad. Perhaps the Church was right in teaching her deafness meant she had an affliction of the mind, that her fever had robbed her of her reason as well as her ability to hear.

Though why such an infirmity should take so many years to show itself, she could not begin to comprehend.

Abigail refused to believe she was possessed by a demon, as the priest taught such impediments indicated, but she could not deny *something* was amiss.

The night before, Abigail had once again been certain

that she heard Talorc's voice. It was a wonderful, masculine voice, one that made her giddy with warmth and filled with joy. Even the memory of it caused her to lament her perpetual silence more intensely than she had for many years. Only the voice could not be real, for just as in the hot springs cave, she heard *nothing else.*

The voice had to be completely conjured by her imagination, which was a disquieting enough thought. She refused to entertain the other possibility that the voice was that of some demon that supposedly caused her deafness. The fever had stolen her ability to hear and that was that.

According to Emily's friend the abbess, priests were too quick to point to a demon when faced with the inexplicable. The learned woman had said so in one of her first letters to Abigail. They had continued a correspondence with each other that Emily's move north had forced Emily to drop.

Now, Abigail had no more notion of how to maintain the friendship than her sister had done. It was the single relationship she truly regretted leaving behind. The abbess had known of Abigail's deafness and never thought less of her for it. Other than Emily, the abbess was the only person who had ever been so accepting.

However, for the first time since losing her hearing, Abigail felt a niggling worry that the priests might actually be right. Because in addition to imagining she heard Talorc once again shouting her name during climax, Abigail had also heard the howling of a wolf.

Her stomach cramped at the implication of her mind playing such tricks on her.

She covered her face, wishing she really could hide so easily from what ailed her. She couldn't and pretending never made reality any easier to bear in the long term. Fighting back the tears, she made herself face her fears.

She had not gotten this far by giving in at the first sign of adversity.

The voices in her head were simply one more thing she had to hide from those around her. It was not as if imagining she heard her husband's voice, or even that of a wolf, could cause her or the Sinclair clan any harm. In some ways, it was no different than being deaf.

It did not make her a demon instead of the angel Talorc claimed her to be. It didn't! But how she wished she had her sister here to talk this over with, or some way to correspond with the abbess.

Loneliness swamped Abigail, but she refused to acknowledge the low feeling. Forcing herself to face the day before her, she crawled from the furs and stood to survey the bedchamber. She was gratified to discover a pitcher of what must be water beside a large wooden bowl already half-filled with it. Both sat under the window on a small table that had not been there the day before.

Who had thought to provide her with such a kindness?

It didn't really matter if it had been Talorc or Guaire who had thought to provide this most welcome nod to civility; Abigail was just thankful someone had.

She wasn't surprised she had not woken when the table was brought into the room. She had discovered that her tendency to wake at the least sense of someone nearby had flown the first night she slept in Talorc's arms. Her husband made her feel safe. She did not even feel any anxiety at the thought that someone had been in the room while she slept. They would not dare to be there without her husband's sanction.

If only he could protect her from her own weaknesses.

What would she do if the voices in her mind persisted?

What if they got worse? Could she risk having children, knowing that her mind was so unstable?

Abigail tried to banish the unanswerable questions, but the implications of this new affliction plagued her through her ablutions. Her worries grew until her hands shook so badly it took three tries to get her pleats to stay tucked into her belt, much less straight.

This would not do. She had to get ahold of herself. She could not change her circumstances; she could only pray she did not hear the voices again. With that thought firmly in mind, she left the room.

Abigail was halfway down the steps when she sensed she was being watched.

She looked away from the steps in front of her toward the great hall. At first she thought it was empty, everything was so still. Then she noticed the old man who had vocalized his displeasure at Talorc's marriage the day before. He was glaring at her from his place at the far end of the nearest banquet table. And if looks could catch fire, she would be singed for sure.

She tried a tentative smile, but his glower did not waver. Already upset by her earlier thoughts, Abigail came close to stumbling on the stone steps but caught herself in time.

Suddenly, Niall was there. He said something to the old man Abigail could not catch. The gray-haired warrior frowned at her and shook his head.

Niall looked up at her, his own disapproval evident. "Talorc said you were to be accompanied coming down the stairs."

"I'm perfectly capable of walking down a set of stairs," she said, but she could tell by his look that she had not projected her voice enough to be heard.

Wonderful. She put her hand against her throat and tried again, glad the vibrations grew stronger, which meant her voice was louder.

Sure enough, Niall's confusion cleared, but he did not look appeased by her words. He crossed the room and was taking the stairs two at a time before she'd come down two more steps. His features set in implacable lines, he put his arm out to her.

She rolled her eyes but accepted his assistance and allowed him to guide her down the stairs. When they reached the bottom, she saw that Guaire and Una had arrived. She smiled at her new friend and tried not to frown at the woman who had been less than pleasant the day before.

Regardless of Una's attitudes, Abigail was relieved to see that she was still acting as housekeeper to the tower. At least, that was what Abigail assumed the other woman's presence with Guaire indicated.

Guaire smiled and nodded at Abigail. "Good morning."

"It would not have been a good morning if our lady had slipped on the stairs," Niall replied, his displeasure now firmly fixed on the seneschal. "The laird gave instructions for his lady to be accompanied at all times."

"I am aware of that," Guaire answered, looking just a bit harried. He stepped away from Niall's approaching form in what was probably supposed to look like a subtle maneuver.

But the stiffening of Niall's posture said he'd noticed all right. And taken offense. "So, why was she coming down to the great hall alone?"

"Because I am no child and did not feel like waiting to descend the stairs until someone came along to hold my hand," Abigail said with asperity. Honestly, how could they all not see what a ludicrous directive it was that she needed a babysitter to descend the stairs?

"Una and I were on our way to see if our lady had woken when we arrived to find her coming down with you," Guaire said. The look he gave Niall was filled with resigned longing.

From the way the big warrior crossed his arms and frowned, Abigail surmised he was entirely blind to the other man's feelings. Which was probably for the best. If Niall did not return Guaire's regard, he would most likely only hurt the seneschal's feelings were he to discover them.

Those with afflictions such as blindness and deafness were not the only ones the Church taught their followers to revile as tainted.

Still, she wished there was something she could do to help.

"Was the water in the pitcher still warm when you woke?" Una asked, interrupting Abigail's thoughts.

"Yes, it was fine. Very welcome, in fact."

"I am glad."

"It was your idea," Abigail said as the thought came to her and then wished she'd kept her mouth shut.

But Una did not look offended. "Aye, the laird would have happily left you smelling of him to let all in the keep know who you belong to."

"As if there could be any question."

They shared a moment of female understanding, until Abigail realized Niall and Guaire were still arguing over her being left to come down the stairs alone. Normally, she would have paid attention to their conversation, but she'd been so shocked by Una's consideration, she had forgotten to watch the men's lips.

"Will you two please stop apportioning blame? If you must assign responsibility, then place it where it belongs. With me. I am no child to hide behind another's plaid. I walked down the stairs alone. There you have it, my heinous confession. And you may as well get used to it, because I'm not going to wait around for someone to escort me when I want to go somewhere."

"You would defy your laird?" Niall demanded.

"Of course she would. I spent only a few hours with her yesterday and already I know our lady well enough to recognize a stubborn nature that rivals that of our laird. You spent days traveling in her company, how could you not notice the same thing?"

"I noticed that our lady respects our laird too much to dismiss his instructions out of hand," Niall gritted out.

Abigail, who had had quite enough of being discussed in the third person, glared at them both. "Of course I respect my husband, but I am his lady, not his slave or his child." And this was far too dangerous a subject to continue pursuing, because when pushed, she would have to admit that refusing to obey her husband wasn't really all that acceptable. "I had hoped to get something to break my fast. Would that be possible?"

Niall nodded. "Guaire will see to it."

"I am the housekeeper now? I may not be an oversized Chrechte, but I'm no woman. In case you had forgotten, I am seneschal here, not handmaiden."

Niall looked like he wanted to explode, but he clamped his jaw and turned on his heel instead, leaving without another word. Guaire's green gaze filled with pain as the other soldier stomped away.

The older soldier surged to his feet. "I suppose you are

happy, sewing discord already," he said to Abigail before making his own less-than-happy exit.

"That one has a temper," Una observed.

Abigail asked, "The older warrior?"

"Oh, Osgard can be unpleasant right enough. My dam says he's never been the same since losing both his wife and son to the English attack." Una sighed and shook her head. "But I was speaking of Niall. He always holds back with you, Guaire. You are lucky he sees you as such a friend."

"What do you mean?" Abigail asked, thinking Una had to be exaggerating Niall's angry nature. Her new friend was sweet.

"If any other soldier had said something like that to Niall, he would have been knocked flat and had a knife drawn on him for good measure."

"Never say so."

Guaire sighed. "It's true, but he did not hold back with me because we are great friends." He looked terribly dejected in that moment. "Far from it, in fact."

"Why then?" Abigail asked out of curiosity.

"He thinks I am too weak to bother with."

"Nonsense. You may not be as big as some of our Chrechte warriors, but you are no weakling, Guaire. You might use your brain to serve our laird, but you have never neglected your soldier's training. I would trust my life with you . . ." Una gave the redheaded man a wink. "That is, if I wasn't laying some heads open with my own bread board."

Abigail smiled as the other two laughed, though Guaire's humor seemed forced.

That morning heralded a new direction for her interaction with the English-hating widow. Una shared with Abigail that her laird had forgiven her initial insult to his lady, after dressing her down but good. However, he had stressed his expectation that she help Abigail find her place in the clan. Una had not acted in the least surprised by this.

But Abigail had been thrilled to discover her husband had listened to her and given the other woman another chance. She hoped that meant he would not be too hard on the rest of the clan as they got to know her as well.

Una appeared to take the laird's directive to heart this time and spent time each day familiarizing Abigail with the domestic working of the fortress. Abigail's suggestions for meals and changes to the great hall were accepted without rancor, though she soon realized doing things as they had been done in her father's keep was not always possible or desirable.

One thing she stood firm on, and that was a rotating invitation to each of the clanspeople and their families to dine with their laird. Talorc noticed immediately that different clan members now joined him at the long banquet table for evening meals. Rather than get angry, he had thanked Abigail for thinking of it and made sure he spent time speaking with each evening's special guests.

While her husband trained his forces and oversaw improvements to what Abigail already considered an impenetrable fortress, Guaire helped her to become acquainted with the clan's many industries. Not only did the Sinclairs keep several herds of sheep and harvest the wool for their own use, but they produced goods for trade with other clans as well.

Their blacksmith and his two apprentices provided services for the surrounding clans, and Guaire boasted that other Gaels came from as far as Ireland to trade for the weapons Magnus forged. Despite the fact that its own laird did not sleep in a proper bed, the Sinclair holding even boasted a carpenter and his apprentice son.

Abigail was more than a little impressed by their hard-working creativity and told Guaire so. He nodded, "Aye, we've a good, strong clan, but we can thank the sound leadership of our laird for a lot of it."

A burst of pride warmed Abigail's insides to be married to such a fine man. She did not know what her sister Emily had found so lacking in Talorc of the Sinclairs, but Abigail thought him to be a king among men. Her feelings for him grew steadily with each passing day and her plan to rejoin her sister became a secondary consideration to the hope of staying with the man she was coming to love permanently.

All was not blooming roses and sunshine among the Sinclairs for her, however. Hiding her affliction became increasingly difficult the more people she came to know and the greater the clan's acceptance of her grew. Every night she went to bed thanking God for another day that her secret had not been revealed.

And while Una's attitude had markedly improved, Osgard's had not. Oh, he was careful enough in her husband's presence, but when they were alone, he often made hurtful comments to Abigail. Una told her to ignore the old man's words as he wasn't really pleasant to anyone.

Sometimes that was a harder task to undertake than others. Like one morning when he "kept her company" while she mended one of Talorc's shirts in the great hall.

"I suppose you've noticed you're never left alone."

It was difficult to sew and watch the older man's lips, but Abigail had spent years learning to do this sort of thing. Thank goodness. The last person she wanted learning of her deafness was the crotchety old man.

"Yes, I had noted it." How could she not? She'd assumed her husband was watching out for her safety and felt good because of it.

"Ye know 'tis because your laird and your clan dinna trust you."

She stared at him, at a loss how to respond. She could not be sure he was lying, but she hated to think his words could be true.

He nodded, warming to his theme. "Ye cannot be left without supervision lest ye betray us in some fashion."

Tears burned the back of her eyes, but she absolutely refused to show weakness in front of the cranky old man. She focused her attention completely on the small stitches she made with her needle, unwilling to dignify the barb with an answer.

It was easy to ignore him since she didn't even know if he was speaking unless she looked at him, and that she refused to do. He'd pricked her with enough poison for one day.

Over the next few days, she wondered which was the truth: that her constant escort was the result of her husband's concern for her safety or her trustworthiness? She was too disheartened by the prospect of the latter to ask one of her new friends for their opinion.

Even with Osgard's animosity and the stress of hiding her inability to hear, Abigail found her life among the Sinclairs the happiest it had been since her sister Emily had come north.

The only thing missing was Emily herself. Even though Abigail no longer wanted to go live with the Balmoral, she desperately wished she could see her sister. To be so close and yet still unable to speak to her beloved sibling was hard indeed, but Talorc would not consider a trip to Balmoral

Island right now. He said he had spent too much time away from the clan already.

Abigail suggested going by herself with an escort. However, he was even more intransigent on the subject of her traveling there without him. She would not complain, though. Magnus and Susannah had taken Abigail's gifts and letter to Emily and returned with gifts and a long missive from her sister.

And Talorc had promised to extend an invitation to Emily to come for a visit.

Circin and his brother Muin arrived with two other Donegal warriors, both of whom were not even shaving yet. Guaire arranged for the four to sleep with the unmarried warriors in the barracks built into the thick wall surround the motte and tower. Talorc spent even longer days training with his soldiers after that, and often came to their bed exhausted.

Never too exhausted to make love, however. And no matter how long her own day had been, Abigail's body always responded to her husband's passion-filled touch.

Chapter 13

A week after the Donegal soldiers had arrived for training, Talorc found Abigail working what had been an overgrown herb garden, tucked away in the courtyard behind the tower.

She'd discovered it soon after her arrival at the Sinclair holding. Abigail had begun clearing the weeds immediately, thrilled to find something she could make her own. Next to reading, gardening was her favorite pastime. She'd learned much about plant and bed preparation watching the gardeners in her father's keep and working with them when they allowed it.

She also knew a great deal about healing with herbs, having researched everything she could about the art in hopes of healing her own ailment. Though she'd never discovered a cure for her deaf ears, she had learned to treat a wide variety of illnesses and injuries.

She was digging in the dirt around a fragrant stand of lavender when she noticed her husband's approach. She looked up with a smile. Though she hated doing so, she avoided him as much as possible during the day on the supposition that the less time they spent in each other's company, the less likely it would be for him to discover her secret.

Her heart always filled with gladness when she saw him, however. And she was sure it showed on her face. "Good day, Talorc."

Her current escort bowed to his laird in greeting. Talorc returned the greeting and then dismissed the young soldier to other duties.

"You plan to rescue my mother's garden?" he asked Abigail.

Shocked, she rocked back onto her heels. "This was your mother's garden?"

"Aye."

"She was an herbalist?"

He gave Abigail that look that said she was still a mystery to him and he blamed it on her English roots. "She studied the art of healing both body and spirit with herbs, if that is what you mean."

Abigail nodded. "I wish I could have known her."

For a woman who had gone so long speaking so very little, Abigail too often found her foot in her mouth now.

Thankfully, Talorc did not look offended by her unthinking observation. "I too wish you had that opportunity."

"Thank you." She bit her lip. "Does it bother you I am working in her garden?" Perhaps it had become so overgrown because Talorc had not wanted anyone else to touch his mother's plants.

"No. It is fitting."

"Because I am now lady of the Sinclairs as she was?"

"Because you are my wife and a sweet angel. She would have liked you."

Abigail's heart was about burst from the praise. "Thank you for saying so."

"It is never a hardship to speak the truth."

If only he knew. Some truths caused nothing but pain.

"She kept a diary of her recipes. Perhaps you would like it?" he asked.

Warmth suffused Abigail. "I cannot think of anything I should like better."

"Nothing, my angel?" he asked with a wicked glint in his blue eyes.

She felt a blush crawl up her neck and could not speak in reply to save her life. She loved this playful side to her husband and saw it all too rarely.

"Thank you," she said, meaning both his generosity and for sharing this side of himself with her.

"You need not thank me, but if you insist, you can do so by waiting for your escort before coming down the stairs of a morning." His frown was marred by the twinkle in his gaze.

She grinned. "I'll consider it." But they both knew she wouldn't.

It was shaping up to be one of those arguments like the one between the blacksmith and his wife regarding the disparity between the Sinclair and Balmoral clans. Neither held any true rancor over the subject, but neither would they change their view in regard to it. It felt good to have something like that between her and Talorc, something so normal and domestic.

"I now understand why you argued so fiercely for me to give my clan a month to get used to you. You were hoping that by showing leniency, I would learn to tolerate your flaunting of my authority."

She widened her eyes in mock innocence, though she would be devastated if she truly believed he thought her guilty of such. "I do no such thing."

"You think not?"

"It's a ridiculous instruction."

"You are a stubborn woman."

"I thought I was your angel."

"A willful one."

"It runs in the family."

"It is a more charming trait in you than your sister."

"How can you say so?" she asked even as her heart swelled with the implied compliment. "Emily is everything that is wonderful in a sister."

Talorc grimaced. "And the Balmoral would say she is everything that is wonderful in a wife."

"But you do not say so?"

"She called me a goat." He gave Abigail one of his rare smiles. "She is not you."

Her hand flew to her mouth and she shook her head. She would not cry like a ninny, but no one had ever said anything so lovely to her. Not even Emily. That it was her usually taciturn husband made it all the more special. "Thank you."

He shrugged and she grinned, knowing he had done so on purpose to tease her with what she still considered a non-answer.

Then his eyes grew serious as they usually did only at night in their bedchamber. "You are mine."

Abigail could not hold it in any longer. She jumped to her feet and leapt into her husband's arms. "Is it any wonder I am in love with you?" And without a thought to propriety, she kissed him exuberantly, first on his lips and then all over his face.

She could feel his laughter rumbling in his chest. Leaning back, she looked him in the eye, her expression as earnest as she could make it. "You are the best husband any woman could ever wish for."

She rejoiced daily that he and Emily had not found each other as pleasing.

Talorc looked down at her with mock severity. "Such a display is most unseemly, my angel. Clearly this is behavior you learned in England."

"Yes, because Sybil was always so open with her affection." Abigail could not hold back the laughter bubbling up and made no effort to do so.

The idea of her mother kissing her father, much less anyone else, in the courtyard of their keep was so ludicrous it was impossible to even imagine.

Talorc did not laugh, but his half smile might as well have been a belly rolling mirth as far as Abigail was concerned. "I see I will have to teach you the proper way to treat your laird in a public setting."

"By all means, teach me," she offered saucily and without the least worry. After all, her feet were no longer on the ground because his hold on her was so secure.

"You should not kiss your husband thus," he said quite severely.

She cocked her head to one side. "I shouldn't?"

"Nay." His blue eyes darkened with heat. "You should do it like this." He took her mouth with possessive passion, his lips moving against hers in ways guaranteed to scramble her mind.

Forgetting where they were, she returned his kiss with enthusiasm, burying her hands in the hair at his nape.

When he pulled his lips away, she was breathing heavily. So was he.

She brushed at his neck. "I seem to have gotten dirt from your mother's garden on you."

"'Tis your garden now."

"I will share it with her, and keep her memory alive there for our children."

Just like that, the emotion grew thick between them.

Talorc traced the line of Abigail's lips with the hand not clasping her to him. "Thank you."

Unused to being the recipient of such gratitude, she rubbed at the soil clinging to the sweat on Talorc's neck. "What shall we do about this dirt?"

"Lucky for me, I was planning a swim in the loch."

"You were?"

"I thought you would like to join me. I remember how much pleasure you found in the water at the hot springs."

A blush of equal parts embarrassment and pleasure heated her cheeks. "I should like that very much."

"Good." Rather than release her as she had expected, he put his free arm under her knees and swept her up against his chest.

"I can walk." But she didn't say it with any heat. After all, she enjoyed being held this way.

"I like carrying you."

She giggled in pure joy.

He nodded at someone else and only then did Abigail realize they had an audience. Men and women of the clan were smiling at them and calling out teasing comments. For once, Abigail did not allow the fact she had been unaware of them bother her. Nothing could diminish the pleasure she felt in this moment.

She loved her husband and had had the courage to tell

him so. While he might never repeat the words back to her, he clearly cared about and liked her. That was miracle enough for Abigail.

She rode to the lake on Talorc's horse with him, feeling a sense of belonging unlike anything she had ever known. They played in the water, not even pretending their primary purpose was bathing. Afterward, they made love in the sweet green grass, surrounded by the scent of heather.

As she climaxed she heard his voice saying something in what she recognized as Chrechte. She pretended it was "I love you."

If she was going to hear a voice that existed only in her imagination, it might as well say something she would never see spoken on her husband's lips.

Later Talorc sat on a rock and smiled at Abigail's efforts to do her own pleats. Determined to prove that she could dress her pleats every bit as efficiently as her laird husband, she was concentrating on getting each fold precisely the same when she heard Talorc's voice inside her head for the first time outside of making love.

"Abigail, run!" The urgency was so strong, she obeyed without thought, only to trip on her unpleated plaid and go crashing to the ground.

Air rushed over her and she looked up in time to see a huge gray wolf. Her mouth opened in a silent scream, but the wolf did not attack. He sailed right over her.

She scrambled to her feet, yanking her plaid off as she went. She looked for Talorc, but he was nowhere to be seen. She turned her head and saw a wild boar and the wolf in a fight. Abigail ran to Talorc's horse, screaming her husband's name.

She scrambled onto the big black stallion's back and kneed him into movement. She had to find her husband. Something must have happened to him.

Terrified but unwilling to leave the man she loved behind, she turned the horse toward the forest from which the wild boar had come.

"Abigail! Go back to the keep," Talorc's voice demanded in her head.

"I won't leave you," she said in her own head, feeling more than a little crazy for replying to the imaginary voice.

"Obey me." The voice had never sounded so harsh.

But it wasn't real and no matter how insistent it sounded, she did not have to listen. She wasn't leaving Talorc behind. She skirted the fighting wild animals, but kept her attention on them in case they lost interest in each other and came after her.

With a spray of blood, the wolf tore out the boar's throat. The big gray beast put his head back and howled. Heavens above, she really was going mad. She felt an insane and almost irresistible urge to stop the horse and approach the wolf, to commend it for fighting so bravely and effectively.

The beast turned his head to look at her. Showing she truly had lost all sense, she halted the horse and stared back at the blood-covered wolf. If she didn't know it was impossible, she would have thought the look the wild animal gave her was one of possession. That made no sense.

Without warning, the wolf spun and ran into the forest. Filled with trepidation and undeniable curiosity, she kneed the stallion to follow.

They had only gone a couple of yards when Talorc came striding out of the forest. He was covered in blood, explaining where her husband had been. He must have been fighting another boar. Guaire had told her the wild pigs with deadly tusks sometimes traveled in groups.

Talorc had been protecting her, and just like the massive wolf, he had clearly won his fight. He gave her an indecipherable look before turning to dive into the lake.

He did not come out until all the blood was gone.

Abigail had managed to get her plaid on while her husband bathed. He said nothing as he donned his own clothing.

"You are not hurt?" she asked. She had not seen any marks, but she could not be sure.

His jaw set, he shook his head.

"Did you see the wolf? I believe the beast saved my life." She bit her lip. "Not that you did not protect me, too. Clearly you were in your own battle in the forest, but a second boar came into the clearing."

"A second boar?"

She nodded and pointed to the bloody carcass. "Over there."

Talorc stared at her for several tense seconds but said nothing.

She had spent years in silence, but this one felt more than a little uncomfortable. "I must rethink my view on wolves. Niall told me the gray wolf I met at the hot springs would never hurt me. You will probably think me mad, but I believe it was that wolf that helped you save me today."

"It was."

"You know this wolf, too? Is he a mascot for the clan then?"

"A mascot? No."

"But he is a friend to the clan."

"That is one way to put it."

Wishing her husband did not look so very stern, she nodded. "What caused the boar to charge, do you think?"

"It is their mating season. Our presence may well have been the only cause."

"Oh."

He turned and headed for his horse. She followed, not sure what was going on between them. They had been so happy before the wild boars attacked. It had been upsetting to be sure, but Talorc acted angry. Though not overtly. It was like fury simmered under the surface and she did not understand why.

Was it because he believed he had not protected her enough? If the gray wolf had not shown up, the boar might well have gotten her. Talorc was the sort of man that would find reliance on another, even a wild beast, a trial. He often acted as if he believed he and he alone was responsible for the safety and well-being of his people.

He pushed himself and his warriors harder than any English baron she had ever seen or heard of.

Their ride back to the fortress was a silent one. Despite riding pressed one to the other, Talorc held himself apart from her behind an invisible but undeniable wall of hostility. Abigail made no attempt to speak, not knowing what to say. She only wished she understood what had upset Talorc.

When they returned to the keep, he led her directly to the great hall. She was surprised to find a handful of his elite warriors seated at one of the banquet tables. The evening meal was still a couple of hours off and the warriors did not usually come inside to congregate this early in the day. But Niall, Barr, Earc, Fionn and Airril were all there, along with Osgard's glowering presence.

Una served water and mead to the seated warriors before scurrying from the hall with a single, baffled, backward glance at Abigail.

Guaire was there as well, standing on the other side of the room from the warriors, though he looked as puzzled by the presence of the other men as Abigail.

Talorc stopped in the middle of the hall with her. "Turn your back to the soldiers," he instructed.

"What? Why?" She worriedly bit at her bottom lip. Turning her back on others was a recipe for disaster in Abigail's silent world.

Anger simmered in his blue gaze. "Just do it."

She did not understand his request and liked it even less, but she did not think now was the time to argue.

Hoping against hope that he would not speak while her back was to him, she turned. Talorc moved so that he had a view of both her face and the soldiers behind her. Because of his position away from the other soldiers, Guaire was the only other person whose face she coud see.

With a sick feeling, she suddenly began to realize what might be happening. Her stomach lurched while her hands grew clammy and her head buzzed with dizzy terror. She could not force herself to ask again what was happening because she feared she already knew.

She was being tested, and if what she suspected was true, the covering she had worked so hard to hide her secret behind was being ripped away with ruthless efficiency. She could pretend to "hear" whatever Talorc had instructed his men to do behind her. She could keep lying through her actions, if not her words, but there was no strength left in her for the subterfuge.

And it probably wouldn't work anyway.

As he stared at her, a look of horrified understanding dawned in Guaire's usually warm green eyes. The horror turned to unmistakable pity as she felt the color drain from her face.

Talorc knew. They all knew. Her affliction had been laid bare.

Somehow Talorc had realized the truth of Abigail's infirmity at the lake and he had brought her back here to test his new knowledge in front of his warriors. Darkness played at the edges of Abigail's vision, but she refused to give in to the weakness. She would not faint.

But it took several deep breaths before her body was in agreement with the conviction of her mind.

Pain lancing through her, she faced her husband in silent entreaty.

But there was no mercy to be found in him. His countenance was so dark with anger she flinched away from him.

A look of disgust crossed his features. "Have you kept so much of yourself hidden *you* do not know *me* any better than that? I will never hit you."

The words were harsh, but his expression was harsher.

It was just as she had feared. He knew she was deaf and now he hated her. She was flawed and he did not want her anymore. Like many in the Church, he believed her infirmity deserved punishment rather than compassion.

"You are deaf," he said with clear antipathy, confirming her fear.

Everything inside her stilled as hope drained away to

leave her hollow. The time for acknowledging the truth had come. "I—"

"Dinna lie to me," he said, interrupting her confession. "Though that is all you have done since the moment of our meeting."

She shook her head. That was not true. She had hidden her affliction, but she had not lied about anything else. Not ever.

His glare turned sulfuric. "You cannot deny it. I shouted a warning when I heard the swine coming through the forest, but you did not react in any way. Then, just now, I had my soldiers yell a war cry and you did not so much as twitch though such a noise would have sent even a seasoned warrior running."

"I was concentrating on my pleats." And she had not been looking at him to read his lips. She did not care about what had just happened. He had only been testing the new knowledge, not discovering it.

"There were many signs, I cannot believe it took me so long to realize the truth."

"I had many years' experience learning to hide my affliction." And she had had a compelling reason to keep it hidden, one that grew more important each day—her love for and desire to stay with the man who now hated her.

"How is it that you speak?" he demanded.

"I did not lose my hearing to a fever until my tenth year."

"And you have lied about the truth of your condition since then?"

"Yes."

"How?"

"Emily."

"I should have known."

"Don't you denigrate her. She was the only one who cared enough to try to save me. She worked with me, hours every day, so I would continue to speak normally. I learned to read lips with her help and constant guidance. No one in our keep knew of my affliction except my mother and stepfather. And eventually, my sister Jolenta." She hated sharing the pain of her past but owed her husband as much truth as she could give him.

He did not ask if her deafness was why her mother hated her so. He must realize it was.

"I told Osgard there was no deception in you. I was a fool." She could have stood it if only anger showed in his eyes, but hurt lurked there as well.

Abigail's heart broke. "No."

"Yes! Perhaps your bitch of a mother convinced you to lie to me initially, but you have had ample opportunity since then to admit the truth."

"I was afraid."

"Just like the rest of your countrymen, liars and cowards, every one of them."

"No, it's not like that."

He looked at Guaire. "Take her to our chamber."

"Talorc, please." She grabbed his arm, but he shook her off.

"You have already made a fool of me, will you add to my humiliation by disobeying me in front of my warriors?"

"Why not? You revealed my secret in front of them."

"You deceived them as well; they deserved to witness the truth, too."

"I wanted a chance to fit in." She didn't expect him to understand or care. The only one who ever had was Emily, but she told him the truth anyway.

"There is no place in our clan for deceivers and cowards."

She felt the words like blows and went to her knees from the pain.

A gentle touch landed on her shoulder. She looked up through eyes swimming in tears to find Guaire's face covered in compassion.

He put his arm out. "Come, my lady."

Before she had a chance to take it, she was being lifted with jerky movements into Talorc's arms. He carried her toward the stairs, his entire body radiating fury and repudiation.

Unwilling to hide from anything any longer and needing to face the full ramifications of her situation, she looked toward the table of Sinclair soldiers. They were glaring at her. The expression on Osgard's face was one of smug satisfaction, but that did not hurt nearly as much as the revilement she read in Niall's eyes.

He had been her first friend among the Sinclairs. Now he was her enemy.

Chapter 14

Talorc dropped her onto the pile of furs in their bed-chamber. "If you value your safety, you will stay here."

She could think of nothing to say to such a threat being issued from the lips of the man she had come to equate with her safety.

He turned and only then did she realize Guaire had followed them up the stairs. "Stay with her. Allow no one in this room until I return."

Guaire nodded without a word.

Then Talorc left. Guaire locked the door.

"Am I prisoner?" she asked, making no effort to modulate her voice.

But Guaire heard. He frowned. "Nay. Talorc does not want you hurt. The clan will need time to adjust to the knowledge that you have been hiding the truth about yourself. If you want my opinion, most of the Sinclairs will understand, even the Chrechte. Only those who saw how much you hurt our laird with your deception will hold it against you."

"I did not mean to hurt him."

Guaire sighed and leaned against the door. "I believe you."

"He won't."

"I have never seen him so happy." Guaire looked away from her, though she could still read his lips. "I did not believe he would ever grow to trust an Englishwoman. Not even if she was his wife."

"I destroyed that trust." Desolation blanketed her. Would he ever call her his angel again?

"Aye."

"I did not want to be sent away."

"He would not send you away, no matter what. You are his true mate."

"I do not think Talorc considers me his friend any longer."

"Unfortunately, I think you are right."

Talorc's fury was only a thin mask for pain so deep it would buckle his knees if he let it. His wife, the paragon of virtue he claimed as his sacred mate, the woman he had come so close to admitting love to, was a liar. A coward.

Osgard made a sound of disgust echoed among the other warriors at the table. "I guess you canna expect anything better from an Englishwoman."

"I expected better," Talorc gritted out.

Just as his father had with Tamara. Talorc had spent years proving himself to his clan, protecting them and being so careful not to share in his father's act of criminal stupidity.

To discover he had been deceived just as neatly by a woman he had grown to trust hurt more than Talorc would ever admit out loud.

Without a word, Niall pressed a cup of mead in front of Talorc and without another word, Talorc drank it.

Osgard left the table and returned several minutes later with a small cask filled with drink much stronger than mead. Talorc proceeded to imbibe in more than his share over the following hours and through dinner. At some point he called for one of his soldiers to take a message to Scotland's king, telling him of Sir Hamilton's treachery and demanding redress.

He was deep in his cups when Barr said, "You've got to admire her ingenuity."

Talorc turned on his second-in-command with a glare.

Barr merely shrugged, not appearing nearly as drunk as his laird. "She didn't just fool you, she fooled everyone at her father's keep and within our holding as well. Tamara hoodwinked only your father, and that was only because he was thinking with his little head, not the big one. Our lady is a clever one, not just a woman used to manipulating men with her pretty face."

"She's a sight more than pretty," Earc said, slurring his words. "Our lady is beautiful."

Osgard probably would have argued, but he was slumped over the table, snoring. He'd never been able to hold his whiskey as well as Talorc's dad.

"Aye, beautiful and smart," Fionn intoned drunkenly. "Just like an angel."

Talorc frowned at his soldiers, Fionn's words stinging in a way he would never admit. "She lied to us all."

"She hid a frailty. Like a good soldier," Barr said. "We do not reveal our weaknesses to others."

"She is no soldier," Talorc roared, though perhaps not as impressively as he would have before that last cup of rotgut. "She is my mate."

"Aye, she is that."

Airril looked at Talorc blearily. "Did you ask her why she hid her affliction?"

"'Tis not an affliction. She is deaf, not diseased," Talorc responded angrily.

"He didn't ask. We were all right here when he tested her." Earc was looking distinctly green.

If he was smart, and all Talorc's Chrechte elite were intelligent, Earc would not drink any more tonight.

"Nay, I did not ask. What could it matter her why's of lying to me?"

Barr guided Earc to the floor as the man lurched alarmingly. "You won't know until you learn what they are."

"She said she was afraid," Fionn slurred.

"There. She's a coward." Though the words felt hollow as he said them.

"She's your mate. 'Tis your responsibility to find out what had her so feared." Barr's tone left no room for argument.

And that was one of the reasons Talorc valued him so as his second: the other warrior was not afraid to speak his mind when it was needed. Not that he always agreed.

Right now, he wasn't sure what he thought. Except that the table looked damn comfortable as he slumped forward to rest against it.

After a sleepless night in which Talorc did not return to their bedchamber and Guaire did not leave it, Abigail returned to the great hall just after sunrise. She'd left

Guaire sleeping on the pallet she'd insisted making with some of the furs from her and Talorc's bed.

She had a feeling her husband wasn't going to like that, but then he could have come back and told Guaire the man could go to his own chamber for the night. As it was, no matter how many times Abigail assured the seneschal she would be all right on her own, he refused to leave her.

His presence had stopped her from collapsing in sobs. As much as she might have wanted to do so, she was grateful to him for inadvertently helping her keep her strength up. Then again, considering how astute the man was, his help might have been entirely deliberate.

At least she still had one true friend among the Sinclairs.

The stench of stale whiskey assaulted her nose when she was halfway down the stairs, so she was not wholly unprepared for the sight that met her eyes as she looked up after reaching the bottom. The soldiers from the night before, every one of them members of the elite Chrechte, were passed out in various poses of drunken disarray.

Talorc slept slumped over the table, but at least he was not passed out on the floor like Osgard. And Niall.

The big, scarred warrior's eyes opened as Abigail stood staring, contemplating her next move.

She opened her mouth to speak, but he turned away with clear intent to ignore her presence. He rolled to his feet and left the hall without once looking back or speaking to her. So, that was it then. His attitude had not softened with the passage of a night, or drinking a great deal of whiskey apparently.

His twin brother, Barr, woke next. His eyes looked clearer than Niall's had, his expression more open as well. "Good morning."

"Good morning," she whispered, not sure she wanted to wake the others.

"I do not see Guaire."

"I left him sleeping."

Barr nodded. "Talorc is going to have kittens when he realizes you descended the steps without escort again."

"I believe that is the least of my worries this morning."

"You deceived him and he feels stupid because of it."

"He's not stupid."

"Aye, I ken. And he knows it, too, but what he knows and what he feels are not always the same. 'Tis the same for all of us, don't you think?"

"I suppose." She wrapped her arms around herself and surveyed the sleeping warriors. "It looks to me as if they are all feeling drunk at the moment."

"Or not feeling anything at all."

"Sometimes I wish I could achieve that," she admitted, barely giving sound to her voice.

But Barr heard. These Chrechte had the hearing of a predator. "Dinna try it with rotgut. The headache the next morning is not worth it."

"Perhaps it would be best to speak to Talorc later, then."

Her husband's head came up from the table then, his blue gaze bloodshot but still piercing. "What is there to talk about?"

She could not believe he had asked such a foolish question. "The revelations of yesterday."

"You mean my discovery that you have been lying to me since the moment we met?"

"I never told you I could hear."

"You never told me you couldn't."

"No, I didn't."

"Why?"

"I would prefer to discuss this in private." Once again, she let her eyes skim the passed-out warriors around them. "Enough of this drama has been played out in the great hall for your soldiers to enjoy."

"I see no need to discuss this at all."

She crossed her arms. "I have a right to know what my future holds." She'd spent most of last night thinking and had come to several conclusions. The most important being, if she could convince Talorc to let her stay, she wanted to remain a Sinclair.

She knew it would not be easy, but nothing in her life had been since the fever that had nearly killed her as a child.

She had also decided she would not hide from the truth, whatever it might be. So, her husband would talk to her. And that was that.

Talorc did not reply, but he got up from the table, said something to Barr she could not see and headed up the stairs. Abigail followed, unaccountably disheartened by the fact that he had not insisted on her taking his arm for the ascent.

She'd taken two steps when he stopped and spun around, stomping back to her and grabbing her hand. "I'm probably less steady than you." But he did not let her hand go.

"I do not know where you get this idea that I am clumsy," she said to his back.

If he replied, Talorc did not bother to turn his head so she could see it.

When they reached their bedchamber, Guaire had left. Relief was quickly replaced by disappointment as Talorc released her hand and stepped away. His body jerked when he spied the pallet the soldier had slept on. Talorc glared at Abigail.

"Don't look at me like that is my fault." She waved her

hand at the makeshift bed. "You are the one that ordered him to stay with me. When you did not come to our chamber last night, he was forced to sleep here. I tried to convince him to leave, but he refused to do so."

"As he should have done." But Talorc gave the smaller pile of furs a less-than-pleasant look.

Hoping out of sight would result in out of mind, Abigail gathered the furs and made to put them back on her and Talorc's bed.

Talorc grabbed her arm. "Don't."

"Why not?"

"I will not sleep in a bed with another man's scent."

Oh, brother. "Are you trying to tell me you think you can smell Guaire on our blankets?" Superior warrior or not, that was just plain crazy.

"I can. I will provide more furs for our bed. Until then, we will do without."

"Why not? It is not as if we make do without a real bed to begin with. What is a little more discomfort?" she grumbled under her breath as she squatted to roll the furs in a neatened bundle on the floor.

When she straightened, Talorc was frowning even more fiercely at her. "You do not find our bed adequate?"

"It's not a bed. It's a pile of furs," she insisted stubbornly, and then realized how irrational she was being. Right now was not the time to discuss their sleeping accommodations. "Never mind. As long as we share them, the furs are more than adequate."

A flash of something like regret showed in his eyes. "I did not intend to sleep in the great hall last night."

That was good to know anyway, though she was not sure what it meant in light of what he had said the night before.

Focusing on the mundane rather than issues with the power to shred her newfound happiness, she lifted the bedroll. "What do you want me to do with these?"

"I do not care."

She set it in the corner. "Fine." She would give the furs to Guaire later. No doubt he could make use of the soft, luxurious pelts.

"Why did you deceive me?" The smell of whiskey still clinging to him and his plaid showing evidence that he had slept in it, Talorc leaned back against the door.

For all that, he was still the most handsome man she had ever seen. It was a wonder she ever had any breath in her the way it escaped at the very sight of him. But now was not the time to dwell on how attractive she found her laird husband.

She opened her mouth but did not speak. She had to tell him the whole truth. She would never again lie to him, through word or deed. Only she was pretty sure the truth would not help her case.

"You are the one who said you wanted to talk." Back to belligerence, he glared accusingly at her.

And she was sure it was only going to get worse.

"In the beginning, I knew that if I told you of my affliction, you would refuse to marry me."

"You knew this how?"

"No man wants a flawed bride."

"Everyone has flaws."

"Are you trying to imply you would have married me regardless of my infirmity?"

He shrugged. "To perpetuate your deception, you had to want to marry me. Why?"

Funny how he did not simply assume it was because every woman was supposed to aspire to the married state.

The abbess would approve of Talorc's intelligence, Abigail thought. "Marriage to you would bring me to the Highlands. I hoped that once you discovered my secret, you would send me to live with Emily, rather than back to England."

"You married me to be reunited with your sister."

He was smart. She'd always known that.

"Yes."

"Why not simply go to live with her? Your mother did not seem enamored of your presence."

That was putting it mildly. "Sybil wanted a more permanent solution to my presence in her home."

"Bitch."

Abigail flinched, not sure if he meant Sybil or her.

"I told you I would not apologize for saying such. Your mother has stone for a heart."

"Only when it comes to me."

"Why?"

"Why do you think?"

"If I knew I would not ask."

"Because I am damaged. There is no place for me in her life." Just as Talorc had said there was no place for Abigail among his clan now.

Even now, hours later, those words sliced through her like a dagger.

He said a word she did not know. She didn't ask him to translate because she was fairly certain she didn't want to know it either.

"If your plan was to get me to bring you to the Highlands and then reject you for your weakness so I would send you to live with your sister—which was a hopelessly flawed plan, by the by—why did you not tell me the truth once we reached my fortress?"

This discussion had gone better than she could have

hoped and the fact that he was still asking questions gave Abigail a sliver of hope. Just enough to prick at her though, not enough to truly lift her spirits. "By the time we had reached the Sinclair holding, I knew I did not want to leave you."

"You continued to deceive me with the hopes of staying with me?" he asked as if to clarify. "You were so certain that revealing your secret would result in my rejection of you?"

"Yes." To both.

He did not react to that admission in any way.

When the silence between them had stretched the point of pain, she asked, "What will you do with me now?"

"Are you still hoping to be sent to live among the Balmoral?"

"No." Hadn't she just confirmed she wanted to stay with him?

He looked at her with bad-tempered demand.

If he wanted it spelled out, then spell it out she would. "I want to stay here, as your wife, if you will have me."

"Why?"

"I love you. I told you that yesterday."

"You could have been lying."

Her broken heart shattered a little more. "I wasn't."

"Have you lied to me about anything else?"

"No, but I have hidden something from you."

"What?"

"I began hearing a voice in my head. I like to think it is you, but it can't be anything except my imagination. I do not hear anything else. Well, besides the one night I heard the howl of a wolf."

"Is that all?"

"Yes."

He nodded and then turned to go, as if all had been settled between them.

"Doesn't that worry you?" she asked desperately. "The voices in my head?"

"No."

Was that because he intended to get rid of her? "Are you going to send me away?"

"You are my wife."

She had no reply for that, and before she could conjure one up, he had gone.

Talorc ran through the forest in his wolf form. He had swum in the loch to clear his whiskey-addled head, but it had done nothing to dispel his confusion in light of his wife's revelations.

She had deceived him just as Tamara had deceived his father. Only his father had realized his wife's true nature too late. Talorc was now all too aware of Abigail's clever manipulations, but he had no desire to banish her.

The problem was that, like his soldiers, he admired his wife's ability to hide her weakness. He could not help feeling proud that she was so talented at reading lips and speaking, no one had guessed at the fact she could not hear. The admiration he felt was at odds with the sense of betrayal choking his insides, and yet he could not rid himself of it.

No more than he could rid himself of the desire, no— *the need*—to keep his wife. Not that he had much of a choice. Were he to banish Abigail from the Sinclair holding, he banished any hope of children to carry his Chrechte lineage along with her. As a true-mated Chrechte, he was not physically capable of engaging in the mating act with anyone but Abigail. At least, until that mating was severed through death, or a betrayal so great, even his wolf spirit would reject her.

Apparently, his wolf was not bothered by Abigail's perfidy. He felt as possessive and protective toward her as ever. He still craved her approval and the opportunity to scent her in his wolf form. It was a craving that grew stronger each day, becoming acute when the least incident indicated another man's encroachment on what he considered his territory.

The wolf had howled in displeasure at the sight of the furs Guaire had slept on in Talorc and Abigail's bedchamber. Talorc had wanted to throw the damn things out the window. He hadn't, showing remarkable restraint in his opinion. Particularly when his mate had rolled them up so carefully, her scent mixing with Guaire's on the fur.

His angel had much to learn about the Chrechte nature. And him.

She claimed to love Talorc, but in the same breath, Abigail had indicated she thought him capable of throwing away his wife for something so insignificant as an inability to hear. Surely that was a grief she had to bear, not him. Her deafness did not impact *him* except that he had to be more diligent in his protection, knowing she was less aware of her surroundings than he had believed.

It also explained the times he thought she ignored him when in fact she simply had not realized he'd been speaking.

How could that be a bad thing?

Yet she had hidden the truth with a diligence that both worried and impressed him. No Chrechte had ever hidden their nature with more talent and ingenuity than his wife hid her deafness. When the time came for him to trust her with the secrets of his people, he could not doubt her ability to maintain his confidences.

But he could not help his concern at the knowledge she had deceived him so well and so easily. She had assured him she had not lied about anything else, but could he believe her?

She had married him with the intention of using him to gain access to her sister. *She had spoken her marriage vows and the ancient Chrechte pledge of troth without meaning the words at all.* That truth twisted something deep inside him, hurting in a way he had not done since losing each of his parents. His sacred mate had spoken her Chrechte promises like a child with her fingers crossed.

That, at least, caused his wolf to grieve.

Despite the fact that she was English and human, he had given his oath in good faith, both before the Lowlander priest and in the cave before his Chrechte brethren. From the very beginning, he had made no plans to find a way out of the unwanted covenant. The fact that his angel had approached their marriage with such spurious intentions acted like a spear right through his gut.

He hated discovering she had the power to hurt him thus. It made him angry to have his emotions at anyone's mercy, even his mate's, but particularly a mate whom he could not trust. It was a state he had convinced himself he would never experience. Talorc had been so sure he would never make the mistakes of his father.

Yet here he found himself vulnerable to an English human woman. 'Twas an anathema to be sure.

She claimed to have changed her mind about using him, as if he should now believe she wanted to be with him. As if that should make her actions acceptable.

It did not. It only showed she was capable of betrayal for the sake of her own agenda, just as Tamara had been. Even if Abigail had come to love him as she claimed, she had started out with the intention of using him, of throwing away their marriage and their Chrechte mating.

Just how much like his dead stepmother was Abigail?

It was that question that kept him in wolf form running through the woods rather than returning to the fortress, to his wife.

Chapter 15

Talorc did not send Abigail away. At least not that day.

Of course, he wasn't around to order her banishment. He'd disappeared after their discussion early that morning and had not returned to the fortress since.

He wasn't training the soldiers. Barr was doing that today. Without the help of his twin, Abigail noted when she walked by the training ground in the lower bailey on her way to the smithy. She wanted to ask Magnus if he could make her a three-pronged, handheld digging tool for her herb garden.

She approached the blacksmith with some trepidation, unsure what her reception would be. However, not only was he as respectful and helpful as always, but he even smiled when she described what she wanted.

"Aye, I can make that right enough. It's a clever idea, it is."

"Thank you." He must not have heard of her deception.

But his next words dispelled that thought. "Is it true, then, that you canna hear?"

"Yes."

"You're a sly one, you are."

She opened her mouth to defend herself, but the look of approval on his face forestalled her.

He nodded. "You're a fitting mate to our laird."

"Um . . . thank you."

"A Chrechte has to be stealthy and good at keeping a secret."

"But I'm not a Chrechte."

"Nay, you are not, but you've got the heart and the smarts of one." From the way his chest puffed out and his eyes gleamed, it seemed that was highest praise coming from the blacksmith.

And that was only the first of several such strange conversations Abigail had that day with members of her clan. Far from making them hate her, learning of her affliction and how well she had hidden the weakness increased her stature in their eyes.

She only wished the same was true of her husband, but then no one else knew she had planned to use him to get to her sister.

As incomprehensible as she found it, the fact was her husband seemed far more offended by her deception than her deafness. The clan admired her deception and appeared to have no qualms about her deafness. Indeed, they showed awe at her ability to discern their presence since she could not hear their approach.

That was, everyone but Niall. He ignored her completely.

She watched in awe herself from the other side of the bailey when Guaire took him to task for it. Perhaps she should not have eavesdropped, but old habits were hard to break. Besides, she found the exchange fascinating.

Guaire glared up at Niall with green fire in his eyes. "What is the matter with you?"

"Aren't you standing a little close, Guaire?" Niall asked, rather than answer the seneschal's question.

Guaire's fists clenched at his sides. "Does my nearness offend you?"

"You are the one that runs in the other direction whenever I get within breathing distance."

"That isn't true."

"It is."

"I'm not running right now."

"I noticed. It looks like you will face even the scarred demon of your nightmares if it is for your laird's wife."

"Don't call yourself that!" The tendons in Guaire's neck stood out, making it clear he shouted.

Niall didn't look in the least repentant, just grumpy. Really, really grumpy.

Guaire took a deep breath, obviously pulling himself under control. "You are treating her cruelly."

"How I act toward Abigail is none of your business, seneschal."

"She's my friend."

Abigail found herself smiling at the claim, despite the seriousness of the argument between two of her favorite Sinclairs.

"Is she?"

"What is that supposed to mean?"

Yes, what did that mean? Abigail would like to know, too.

"You spent the night in her bedchamber."

"You dare to imply—"

"I'm not implying anything." Niall rubbed his hand over his face. "Just leave it, Guaire."

"I won't leave it. Our lady deserves better than you are giving her."

"I would protect her with my life."

Abigail believed him; there was nothing but sincerity and an inexplicable sadness in his eyes.

"She is more than a responsibility to you." Guaire was not giving any quarter. "She is your friend. Or at least I thought so."

"I believed so as well."

"What? So you don't believe it any longer?"

"She deceived my laird. She hurt him. She deceived me."

"She had her reasons."

"They don't matter."

Abigail feared her husband shared his warrior's belief.

"They do."

"She doesn't need my friendship, she has yours."

Abigail could not stand it any longer. She headed toward the two arguing men. So intent was she on reaching them she did not immediately take note of the vibrations of the ground. When she did, she instinctively moved to the side, turning to see what was making the earth shake.

Talorc's giant black stallion was almost upon her. She'd moved away from his path, but not enough. Realizing it, she dived to the ground, rolling farther away from the deadly path of the beast.

She felt the rush of air as he charged behind her. Now that was what she called close. Shaking a little from the near mishap, she stood and dusted off her plaid. Only then did she notice the soldiers running toward her.

Niall got there first. "Are you harmed?"

"No." She tried a tentative smile that was not returned. "Just a little shaken."

"Several of the clan yelled a warning, but you did not hear." He didn't appear to be making an accusation so much as an observation.

Nevertheless, a blush of humiliation crawled up her body. "No, I do not hear anything."

"How did you know to move away, then?" he asked, curiosity and concern both there for her to see in the way he watched her.

"I felt the earth pound beneath my feet."

"Aye, that is our lady," one of the soldiers said.

The sting of humiliation faded a little.

Guaire reached out and squeezed her shoulder. "Well done." He glared up at Niall. "Even if some are too damn stubborn and mean to admit it."

She grabbed Guaire's hand. "Don't."

"I'll not tolerate him treating you so coldly."

"Guaire . . ." She sighed and said what needed saying. "My deception hurt him."

"I do not need you defending me to my . . . to Guaire," Niall said, a sulfuric glare encompassing them both. Then he stormed away, toward the training ground, knocking two soldiers right on their bums on the way.

"What is the matter with him?" Earc asked.

Abigail and Guaire both shrugged helplessly. Barr came walking up, leading the still-agitated beast between two of the more seasoned Chrechte soldiers.

"Is he all right?"

"Is who all right, lady?" Earc asked.

"Talorc's horse," she said, replying to Earc but fixing her gaze on Barr.

"He is under control."

"You must find whoever is responsible for upsetting him so. I dare say you'll find the culprit among the youth. A prank they had no idea could have such serious consequences, but that cannot be repeated." She bit her lip, looking at the poor lathered horse. "I wish Talorc were here, he could calm the beast more quickly."

"If our laird were back from hunting, I do not believe his first concern would be for his horse," Barr said with an amused look.

Abigail grimaced. "If you say so." But she wasn't convinced of Barr's point of view. Not at all.

"What's got Niall in a more foul mood than usual?" Earc asked. "Even with a hangover, he isn't usually such a bastard."

Barr glared at the warrior.

"That is, I mean . . ." Earc stumbled over his words most uncharacteristically.

Barr looked at Abigail's hand still resting on Guaire's. "I believe you will find the reason for my brother's anger in something other than the tail end of a whiskey cask."

Abigail dropped her hand, still not really understanding what had Niall so upset. She thought it was discovering her secret, but now Barr implied Niall was jealous maybe? Of what? Her friendship with Guaire? That made no sense.

He was not so petty.

Without further elucidation, Barr led the horse toward the stables.

Guaire watched the other man's progress for several seconds before shaking his head and sighing. He turned to Abigail. "Are you ready to return to the keep?"

"I don't think you can call that stone castle a keep,"

she said, renewing an argument they'd had when she first
arrived.

"But castles are taxed, my lady."

"Then by all means, lead me to the *keep*."

They made it there eventually. After several clan members had expressed both their gladness that Abigail had not
been hurt and their appreciation of her cleverness in moving out of the horse's way despite her inability to hear the
shouted warnings.

Talorc returned to the fortress just before the
evening meal. His hunt had been successful and he delivered the boar to Una in the kitchens.

She praised his hunting skills and then gave him a look
of commiseration. "I am sorry, laird."

"What are you sorry for?" he asked, with little interest.
His thoughts were elsewhere, as they had been all day.

"That you were tricked into marrying a woman both
flawed and so full of deceptive wiles." She made a *tsk*
sound and shook her head. "I don't know why the rest of
the clan is behaving as if she managed some great feat in
deceiving us all."

He didn't either, but he was grateful if that were true. He
wasn't looking forward to having to protect Abigail from
her own clan.

Not really wanting to get into a discussion with the
widow, he simply shrugged. And then could not help
thinking the action would have had his angel glaring at
him rather than looking overly sympathetic as Una did.

Feeling uncomfortable from the brief conversation for
no reason he could fathom, Talorc went to the great hall to
join his soldiers and his wife.

She was already seated in her customary place at the banquet table. Her hair shone golden, her curls smooth as if she had just brushed them. She'd donned one of her embroidered blouses with her plaid and it struck him she had made her best efforts to look lovely for him.

At least it had better be for him.

He looked down at his plaid with small blood spatters caused by carrying the pig and gave a mental shrug. He was no woman to worry about his appearance, but perhaps he could have washed off the sweat from his walk back to the fortress before joining her in the hall.

There was nothing to be done about it now. He walked toward the table, his attention fixed on his wife.

She was blushing and looking mildly distressed. He frowned and listened to what was being said around him. The hall was abuzz with something to do with his horse and his wife. Had she tried to ride him? He thought the stallion had shown a great deal of tolerance for her thus far.

She looked up with shock on her porcelain features when he touched her shoulder to let her know he was there. "You have returned."

"As you see."

"Was your hunt successful?"

"Yes. We will have boar tomorrow." They would have had it today, but the one he'd killed the day before had been scavenged by other predators. It was only to be expected when he had left it there for them to find.

He took his seat beside his wife and turned to Barr. "What has happened with my horse and my wife in my absence?"

"Someone tormented the stallion into a lather and then released him from the stable on a rampage."

Talorc had barely taken Barr's words in when Earc said with relish, "Your wife was directly in the horse's path."

A subsonic growl of fury rumbled in his throat, making the other Chrechte around the table send back immediate growls of submission. Only the fact that she was sitting there looking unharmed in any way kept him from roaring out his anger.

He turned abruptly to face his wife. "You are well?"

"Right as rain." She even smiled.

"Someone saved her. Who?" he asked Barr.

"She saved herself. She didn't hear the shouts of warning, but she noticed the earth trembling beneath her feet," he said with clear admiration.

Hell, Talorc was more than a little impressed himself. "Where was her escort?"

From the look on Barr's face, that was the first time the question had occurred to him. "I do not know, Talorc. Who did you assign to escort her today?"

Talorc's memory flew back to that morning and his leave-taking from the fortress. He had not assigned anyone the specific duty of watching his wife. He rotated the duty amongst his soldiers daily, so none missed too much training time. Despite the fact that he had not assigned a soldier to the task, his wife knew better than to leave the tower without an escort.

"You know you are supposed to be escorted when you leave our room," he censured her.

A wisp of something like anger passed through her beautiful brown eyes before she blinked and it was gone. "I was never alone."

"If you had an escort, you never would have been in danger."

"I avoided the danger on my own. I've been doing so for years."

"She's a liability to the clan. Anyone can see it," Osgard said angrily from his place down the table.

Talorc looked at his wife to see her reaction to the old man's words, but she appeared not to have noted them. It struck him then that she rarely looked in Osgard's direction. Considering the fact that she could not "hear" him if she did not see him, her behavior effectively eliminated the crotchety warrior from her notice.

It was an effective way to deal with his advisor's annoying inability to accept his new lady. Talorc had to admire the simplicity and ingenuity of it as well.

He turned so she could not see his lips either and glowered at his advisor. "She is my wife."

"To hell with the clan, then?"

"Watch yourself, Osgard. You will go too far with your prejudice and find yourself living with your great-niece in an already crowded cottage."

"It wasn't the clan in danger today, but our lady," Guaire said from his customary place on the other side of Abigail.

"I wasn't actually in any more danger than anyone else," Abigail asserted, obviously having read Guaire's lips.

Osgard snorted, but several soldiers nodded in agreement, their respect for their lady clear.

"What did the stable master have to say?" Talorc asked Barr.

"He did not see anyone."

"No one at all?"

Barr shook his head. "He was training one of the young mares in the paddock, so was nowhere near the stable at the time your horse got out."

"And the stallion?"

"Shows signs of being whipped on his left flank."

Talorc let out a growl that had several warriors' heads snapping up. "Did you check for scent?"

"There was naught but the stable master and his helper, and nothing in the whip marks themselves at all."

Talorc frowned at that. Whoever had played the prank clearly knew enough to avoid detection by masking their scent. In addition, they had been careful to use an implement that they had not touched at the end used to whip the horse. "You think one of the boys?"

"It could be." Barr was a cautious man and would not accuse without some indication of guilt.

Not even youths known for their pranks.

Despite being unsure what her husband was feeling toward her, Abigail found the evening meal surprisingly pleasant. It was more relaxing than any meal she had eaten in the presence of others since coming downstairs for the first time after her fever when she was ten. She did not have to worry about revealing her secret anymore.

The release of pressure was most amazing. No one got impatient with her when she missed something they said. Everyone acted like her ability to understand them was some great talent, that *she* was something special.

Not someone cursed.

"Did you hide your deafness among your English family?" Earc, ever the curious one, asked.

"Of course. Only my mother, stepfather and eventually my younger sister Jolenta knew."

"Why 'of course'?"

"At best my affliction was considered a great misfortune."

"And at worst?" Earc prompted.

"Many priests teach that to be so infirm indicates possession by a demon."

"Are English priests so gullible, then?" Fionn asked. "Or are you expecting us to be by believing you?"

"I assure you, it is the truth." She only wished it was not. "The abbess says they cry demon when they cannot explain why a fever leaves one person deaf or blind but another untouched by any such difficulty."

"Your abbess sounds like a wise woman," Guaire said.

"I never met her. We only corresponded through letters, but I counted her friend. She was the only person besides my sister Emily who found value in me after discovering my affliction."

Talorc took hold of her face and turned her head so their eyes met. "Stop calling your deafness an affliction."

The rest of the room ceased to exist for her. "It is—"

"An infirmity, though not much of one in your case. You have learned to compensate for it in amazing ways."

"I have no choice. I did not want to live the rest of my days in a nunnery's locked cell." She shivered at the thought that still plagued her dreams some nights.

"You had a choice, but you did not give up." He shook his head, looking puzzled, but she did not know what by. "The only true misfortune is the idiocy your parents showed upon learning of your changed circumstances."

"Emily protected me from my mother's wrath." As much as she had been able to anyway.

"There should have been no wrath. You did not make yourself deaf."

"She always blamed me. I was supposed to make a good match and forward her social ambition."

"Marriage to a laird should please any mother."

"Sybil was just glad to get rid of me, but my younger sister Jolenta was jealous."

"It matters not. You are now mine to protect."

Abigail stared at him, not sure how to take that. Just yesterday, he had said there was no place for her in the clan. Now he acted as if he had no intention of banishing her. She wanted to know his plans but was not about to ask about them in front of his soldiers.

Someone must have said something because Talorc frowned and looked over his shoulder. He spoke, his face averted so she could not read his lips. Osgard got up and stormed from the great hall.

"He does that a lot," she said quietly.

Talorc returned his attention to her. "What?"

"Osgard is of an age to be revered, but he acts the child, storming off." She bit her lip, hoping she had not gone too far in criticizing the old man.

"He paid a great price when my father's second wife betrayed our clan to her English lover."

She gently pulled her face from his hold and turned to Guaire, refusing to hear again how she was held responsible for the heinous actions of a dead woman. "When is the next trade gathering?" she asked the seneschal in what she hoped was not an obvious bid to change the subject.

"In the early fall."

"Will we attend?"

"The Sinclair always sends a delegation."

"He does not go?" Abigail asked, disappointed. "I would have liked to go."

Guaire looked past her to Talorc and then had to bite back a smile. "I believe your husband would like your attention."

She turned to Talorc, determined not to answer if he

made another comment about the infamous Tamara or the betrayal of the English. From the fierceness of the frown on his face, that was exactly what he was thinking about.

She stifled a sigh. "Yes?"

"Would you like to attend the gathering?" he asked, each word bitten off.

Shock had her eyes widening, but she was no fool, no matter what Sybil said. "Very much so."

"Then we will attend."

"Will I see Emily there?" Excitement coursed through her.

Talorc's countenance, which had just begun to lighten, went dark again. "I do not know."

"She is my sister and I love her."

"I know how much."

"Please, Talorc . . ." She pleaded to him with her eyes not to get into her sins in front of his soldiers.

"I will make sure the Balmoral is made aware of our intention to attend."

Pleased at her husband's kindness, tears of frustration still clogged her throat as she forced out a simple "Thank you."

"No need to thank me. It is my duty to provide for your happiness."

Rather than feeling defeat at his reasoning behind his kindness, Abigail was glad. "Few husbands would see it so. You are a good man, Talorc."

"Chrechte know their responsibilities to their mates."

"Is a friend more important than a wife?"

He didn't answer, choosing instead to ask Barr a question about the soldiers' training that day.

She leaned toward Guaire and whispered, "He can be very abrupt."

"He is laird. He does not waste words."

"Is an answer a waste of words?"

When Guaire shrugged, the knowing expression in his eyes told her he remembered her complaint about that particular gesture so favored by the Highland warriors.

She giggled and soon his chuckle followed.

When her gaze traveled around to the other eaters in the hall, she found Niall glaring daggers at her and her giggles faded to nothing. She could not forget that along with her husband's trust, the revelation of her secret had lost her a friend.

Later, tired, Abigail excused herself to retire.

"I will escort you to your chamber, my lady," Guaire offered.

But Talorc stood abruptly. "I will go up with my wife."

Abigail took her husband's hand with some trepidation. She was not sure she wanted to be alone with him where he would feel free to continue berating her for her deception.

He noticed her hesitation and frowned at it, his hand closing firmly over hers. She looked back at the table and saw Niall give Guaire a look that made little sense.

The huge warrior looked hurt in some way, but Guaire had done nothing to hurt him.

Chapter 16

Talorc locked their door after leading Abigail inside the bedchamber and then leaned against it, facing her. "You and Guaire have grown very close."

"He reminds me of Emily."

Her husband's shoulders jerked in surprise. "My soldier reminds you of your sister?"

She giggled at the implication. "Not because he is feminine. He may not be as fierce as you, but he is a strong soldier. I would trust my safety in his hands," she said, repeating something similar to what Una had said once.

"So, how does he remind you of Emily?"

"He saw value in me before he learned my secret and that did not change after."

Talorc's brows drew together. "According to what I saw at dinner tonight, many members of the clan feel the same."

"Yes, it is amazing. Only Guaire was already a good

friend, and then he showed himself to be a true friend both standing by and standing up for me. Even with Niall, who intimidates most clan members."

"Like Emily did when you first lost your hearing," Talorc said, clearly able to draw a logical conclusion.

"Emily saved my life twice." Abigail wanted to make her husband understand why her sister was such an important part of her life. "When I had the fever, no one wanted to risk exposure to nurse me."

"Not even your mother?"

"Especially not my mother."

"So, Emily nursed you?"

"Yes."

"You said she saved your life twice."

"Fear of the inexplicable is strong in my father's keep."

"Yes?"

Abigail nodded. "If the rest of the keep had been made aware of my loss, they might well have insisted on ridding the keep of me."

"Your father would have submitted to the demands of his people?"

"I know only that my mother would not have been disappointed to see me gone."

He said that word again, the one she did not understand.

Unable to meet his gaze directly and say what she wanted, she peered up at him through her lashes. "I did not believe I would ever have a person in my life who was more important to me than my sister."

"You want me to believe I am that person?" The tension in his body was easy to read.

Emotion clogged her throat. "Yes." More than anything.

Several long seconds passed in silence while he watched her and she watched him from beneath her lashes.

"I want proof."

Her head snapped up. "What?"

"Prove to me how much you want to be with me." He put his arms out. "Come here."

This she could do.

Without hesitation, she walked right into those arms that always made her feel so protected and safe. His spicy, masculine scent washed over her, filling her with longing. She looked up at him, letting her love shine for him to see if he wanted to. "Please, don't send me away, Talorc."

He did not reply, but his mouth claimed hers with raw passion. He tasted like the mead from dinner and that feral flavor she associated with him alone. It was a heady combination and she didn't know how long the kiss lasted. The pure bliss went on and on and yet felt like it was over in a moment. She was so dazed by it, he had to touch her eyelids to let her know he had something to say when he lifted his mouth from hers.

She allowed her eyes to flutter open.

His expression was all fierce possession and wild desire. "Mine."

"Yours." If only she could know as surely that he was hers.

"Show me."

She nodded, finally understanding what he wanted her to do to prove his place in her heart. He wanted her to offer the one thing that was not and had never been part of her deception, something far removed from her sister and anyone else.

The untamed passion she felt for him.

With that in mind, she undid his belt, letting it fall to the floor, her hands already busy tugging at his plaid. She needed to get to bare skin, not just because he wanted her to prove something to him, but because she craved the intimacy he gave only to her.

The blue, green and black tartan came away from his magnificent body with ease. He had not worn a shirt, so the loss of his plaid left him totally, gloriously naked. His body glowed with vitality, his muscles rippling with tension under his golden skin.

His manhood was half-filled and getting thicker by the second, his testes hanging low and heavy with seed. Knowing he would be planting that seed deep in her body soon, she quivered in her core, the thought of having his child unbearably sweet.

The smell of dried sweat and musk filled the air between them, calling to her senses like an earthy elixir. She did not understand it, but he brought out an unrefined element in her character that had her responding on the most basic of levels with and to him. Like an animal with its mate, she found not only the sight of him pleasing, but his smell and taste as well.

"You like to look, don't you, my angel?"

Her heart leapt at the endearment and she nodded, still reveling in the saturation of her senses.

But the way he felt under her fingers was the most wondrous thing of all. To have the freedom to touch him anywhere, any way she liked, and to have that freedom extended even now was beyond believing. In the best possible way.

Unable to resist taking advantage of that freedom, she reached out and caressed him, sliding her hand down his neck, across his chest and down his stomach until it hovered just above the nest of hair that crowned his manhood. Her entire being shuddered in pleasure at the jerk of his body and his rapidly burgeoning erection that showed the instant effect she had on him.

Curling her hand around him, she hissed at the heat emanating off his hard flesh. "So hot, so strong," she whispered, watching his face for more signs of his pleasure.

They were there, in the way his eyes closed beneath his furrowed brow, and his lips parted to suck in and release his panting breath.

He thrust toward her with his hips, his hardened staff sliding against her fingers. "So good."

She dropped to her knees and kissed the spongy tip. His knees bent and then he straightened them, and she could tell he remained standing by will alone. She nuzzled into the black curls of his pubic hair, inhaling the unique scent of his sex. His now-rigid penis rubbed against her cheek as she searched out more of the enticing fragrance.

He grabbed her head between his big warrior's hands and guided her so her mouth slid along his stretched, taut foreskin. She blinked at the dark red head, pearls of liquid weeping from the slit. Then she lifted her gaze to his.

He raised one brow as if asking what she would do now.

She knew what she wanted. To taste. She leaned forward the scant distance between her mouth and his manhood and lapped at those delicious-looking pearls, loving the salty sweetness.

He used his hold on her to guide her mouth farther onto his hardened shaft. "Please . . ."

She didn't want to miss his words, but the pleasure in her mouth was irresistible. Her eyes slid shut as her head tipped forward to take him in as deeply as she could. He hit the back of her throat and she concentrated on relaxing her throat and enjoying the sensation. She sucked as she pulled backward, swirling her tongue over his head. Delectable.

His knees tried to buckle again and she repeated the move, increasing the suction of her mouth until her cheeks hollowed out. Continuing the loving with her mouth, she began stripping her own clothing off. He liked looking at her and she wanted to give him *everything* to show him that she was his.

She had to slide her lips off the silk-wrapped stone column of his flesh in order to remove her blouse and shift though.

He took the opportunity to move to the furs, where he lay back, propped up on his elbows, his strong, muscular legs spread wide. He beckoned her with one hand. "Come here."

The expression of need on his face filled some of the cracks in her heart.

She did not bother to stand, but crawled across the floor, her breasts swaying and her gaze fixed on his.

His gorgeous blue eyes widened and then narrowed to slits as his body shuddered in pleasure.

Power surged through her with the knowledge that by simple acts such as this, she could make the mighty Chrechte laird come undone.

She stopped on her hands and knees between his legs. "I love you."

Something flared in his face, but he remained silent. Waiting.

She licked her lips and watched as his Adam's apple moved to indicate he had groaned. Placing one hand on each of his thighs, she leaned forward until her mouth once again closed over his member. Feasting on the pearls of moisture that continued to leak from it, she concentrated on pleasuring just the bulbous tip.

She used one hand to slide his foreskin back to give her better access and lightly dragged her teeth across his slit before dipping inside with the very tip of her tongue. His hips bucked and he took hold of her head again, his fingers buried in her blond curls. She sucked and licked and gently slid her teeth along his hardness, barely letting them touch. He began to thrust on his own, but never so hard he choked her.

It was wild, wanton and utterly decadent.

And then he was coming, his essence filling her mouth and bursting across her senses. She swallowed, taking him into her with joy that marked her soul as his lips and teeth often marked her neck.

"Abigail. My angel. My true mate."

This time she didn't blink at the voice. She did not try to hear it, or anything else, again. She just enjoyed it. She did not care if it was her imagination or not. That voice spoke in a tone of awe, affection, maybe even love. She let the emotions wash over her. It did not matter in that moment that they were fantasy; they fed her hope and the kernel of happiness that she always felt in his presence.

He lifted her from her place between his legs with gentle hands, his expression almost reverent. "Sweet wife. My angel."

Tears pricked her eyes and she did nothing to force them back. The feelings were too big to hold inside.

He pulled her up to lie on the furs with him, his hands caressing her as she settled against the ultrasoft pelts. "Now, I make love to you."

"You already did."

His eyes closed and then opened, the blue surrounded by a golden glow that sent shivers through her. "You are perfect for me."

"Even flawed?"

"We are all flawed in one way or another."

Her mother did not ascribe to that theory, but Abigail could thank God that her husband did. "You are perfect for me."

"As it should be."

Then he went about proving to her just how perfect for her that he was. Big calloused hands skimmed over her body with touches both gentle and demanding, drawing forth an uninhibited response. He caressed her neck, her belly, her thighs and finally her breasts, nipples and that spot of ultimate pleasure between her legs. She cried out in sheer delight when he entered her, responding eagerly to the long, drawn-out pace he set.

Her climax took her by surprise, sending her body rigid as she felt his seed, hot and wonderful, inside her.

They curled together in the furs that she loved better than any wood-and-rope bed because she and Talorc shared them.

Chapter 17

Abigail could not believe the difference it made in her days having her clan know of her inability to hear.

She no longer had to constantly maneuver herself so she could see people's faces. Knowing she needed to read their lips, the clan members made sure they faced her when they spoke to her. No one got impatient when they had to repeat themselves, and that made her more willing to ask them to do so. People made sure she "heard" important news personally, not relying on her overhearing it.

She was aware of what went on around her on a level she had never achieved before. And it was magnificent. She felt like she truly belonged.

Each day in this new, open environment, she relaxed more. She tried new things, ventured farther afield in the holding, meeting clan members that did not often visit the fortress. Guaire was often her companion, but she missed Niall's friendship. That was not to say she did not see him. Along with the intensely curious Earc, he frequently accompanied her and Guaire on their forays to visit herdsmen and other far lying clan members.

But Niall acted as the silent escort, rarely speaking to Guaire or Abigail, and turning a fierce frown on them any time they touched in friendship.

Una had gone back to treating her laird's wife less than warmly as well. Abigail tried to talk to other women about her chilly demeanor, but the housekeeper denied any negative feelings. Nevertheless, in ways both subtle and overt, Una made it clear she would prefer Abigail leave the domestic duties to her.

However, Abigail refused to give up her place of domestic leadership in the tower. She was Talorc's wife and would not allow another woman to make her feel inadequate in the role. Whatever grudge Una held against her, Abigail was still lady of the keep. Full stop. Period.

While she had no desire to lord her position over others as her mother did, she was not about to be walked over either. Thus, she moved delicately into a more solidly supervisory capacity each day. She made it a point to give personal direction to the women who helped Una do the cooking and cleaning for Talorc and his elite warriors.

And continuing in her campaign to make the great hall and the rest of the tower more of a home than a fortress, Abigail instructed Una in further additions and changes she wanted made.

Chairs now flanked the great fireplace and fresh flowers graced the banquet tables. A long plaid, about four feet wide, hung down the wall behind the table at which Talorc, Abigail and her husband's highest-ranking soldiers sat. She was embroidering the Sinclair coat of arms in black thread on a piece of blue silk she had brought with her from England, which she planned to sew onto the banner's center.

Una resisted the changes, complaining to others about the fresh flowers and additional furniture to dust in the great hall. When she thought she could get away with it, she also countermanded Abigail's orders to the other women.

Abigail was contemplating what to do about that while she worked in the now-thriving herb garden. Despite the widow's negative attitude, Abigail did not want to remove Una from her position. She kept hoping Una would settle to Abigail as her lady and start acting accordingly.

In that way, she was very different from her mother, she knew. Sybil would have had the woman thrown out of the keep and off her husband's lands for such behavior. No question.

Abigail wondered sometimes if she gave Una so much tolerance because she could not stand to be like her mother. Was her compassion good for the clan, setting a positive example of tolerance? Or did her unwillingness to take direct action weaken her position as lady and therefore the sense of stability in the clan?

She could not decide the answer to these questions and was wishing her sister were there to advise her when a commotion caught her attention out of the corner of her eye. She turned to see what was going on and stopped still to stare in shock.

Talorc and Barr were walking with a big, black-haired warrior wearing a dark blue, green and pale yellow plaid. He had his arm firmly around a much smaller woman holding a baby.

Abigail rubbed her eyes to make sure they were not

deceiving her, but the same glorious vision showed upon opening them again. Her brain might trick her into thinking she'd heard her husband's voice, but this had to be real. She wanted it to be so badly, she ached with it.

Abigail gave a glad cry when she allowed herself to accept the recognition of gold and brown curls surrounding a beloved face.

Emily!

Abigail popped to her feet and rushed to her sister, dropping her little trowel, her skirts flying. Emily was running, too, her expression mirroring Abigail's sheer elation. Abigail threw her arms around the other woman, little one and all.

Kisses on her cheek and a one-armed hug that was hard enough to take Abigail's breath told her it was true. Her sister was really here. Tears tracked down both their faces as they grinned at each other.

"I worried I would never see you again," Abigail choked out.

"I knew God would not be so cruel, but I will admit I never considered he would use Talorc of the Sinclairs to restore you to me."

Abigail's gaze flicked nervously to her husband to see how he took her sister's words. While they had reached a rapprochement of sorts and their lovemaking was more intense than ever, he had never openly acknowledged her words of love, though she told him each night, and often at least one time during the day. It went without saying that he never said the words back.

They had never discussed her plan to use him to get to her sister again, but the knowledge of it was a barrier between them. Invisible, but felt all the same.

However, right now, there was nothing but indulgent pleasure on his face.

Grateful for that much understanding, she smiled at him, her joy making her simple. "My sister is here."

"I noticed." His lips quirked at one side drolly.

Emily touched Abigail's cheek in a long-familiar gesture to get her attention. "He invited us to come."

"Oh . . ." She looked back at Talorc, her eyes filming with happy tears. "You are too good to me."

Talorc leaned forward and kissed her softly. Right there in front of her sister and brother-in-law. And not on her cheek, but on her lips. "I would not withhold your family from you."

Dazed by the kiss, Abigail turned to what was no doubt a goofy smile on her sister. "Is he not wonderful?"

"I am willing to concede he is not a goat," Emily teased with an eye roll.

Her husband threw his head back, obviously laughing.

Talorc frowned at Emily in censure, but the amusement in his blue eyes belied any true anger. "It is about time you acknowledged the truth."

Abigail shook her head, so happy she could explode with it.

Talorc brushed the shell of her ear with his forefinger, his indication he wanted to say something to her. With a brilliant smile, she gave him her full attention. "Yes?"

"Wife, this near-decrepit warrior is the man your sister chose to marry over me." He waved his hand at the other man. "Lachlan, Laird of the Balmoral."

"It is a true pleasure to meet you," Abigail said, her hand to her throat to make sure she had enough volume to be heard. "I am selfishly grateful that my sister married you rather than the man your king intended for her. Talorc accepts me as I am."

Even if Lachlan did not understand how important and extraordinary that was, Abigail knew Emily would.

"I too am happy with events as they turned out," the big warrior replied, a twinkle in his dark brown eyes. "Who knew a simple kidnapping could have such far-reaching consequences?"

"Emily kidnapped you?" Abigail asked in mock astonishment.

Though her sister had never shared the full circumstances surrounding her marriage to the wrong laird, Abigail had never believed it was something so uncomplicated as Emily and Lachlan meeting and falling in love, with Talorc stepping conveniently aside as Emily had implied in her letters.

Lachlan laughed again and he smiled at his wife. If Abigail did not know better, she would insist they were communicating somehow. Their body language implied it, but neither of their lips moved.

Emily smiled softly at Abigail. "We have both found our happiest paths by God's grace." She winked. "And I did not kidnap my husband, though I did do a good job of getting myself invited along for Caitriona's kidnapping."

"That is a story I would like to learn."

"I'll tell you later," Emily promised. She looked at her husband with mischief. "Every last detail."

Lachlan made a big production of groaning.

Abigail shook her head with a laugh. "I can see he is a good match for your humor and wit."

"Yes." Emily smiled in blissful contentment. Then she indicated the baby girl in her arm. "This is Abigail Caitriona, our daughter."

The precious little one with her mother's violet eyes and father's dark hair reached for Abigail.

Still reeling from learning her sister had named her first child after her, Abigail's hands shook as she extended them to take the baby. Emily relinquished her daughter with a smile.

Abigail tucked the baby close. "She is beautiful." She smiled down at the infant. "Hello, sweeting. I am your aunt."

The baby reached up to pat her aunt's face.

"We call her Gail," Emily said.

"Oh, that's lovely."

"Her doting papa started it. He said Abigail Caitriona was too big a mouthful for such a small body."

Abigail choked on a watery laugh. "I should think so."

She looked at Talorc, letting her desire to have their own child shine in her eyes. He looked back with a tender heat that caught at her heart.

Emily stared at both of them with nothing less than shock. "I would never have guessed Talorc had it in him."

"What?" Abigail asked.

"Love."

Then Emily's eyes widened and she shot a chagrined glance at her husband.

She sighed and looked at Talorc. "I am sorry, that was unkind. It's just that, while my sister's letter said she was happy with your clan, I never imagined she could be this at ease. My own experience was so different, but there is no denying Abigail's contentment. She is glowing with it."

"They all know my secret, and for the most part, no one cares." Abigail ignored her sibling's allusions to Talorc being in love with her. She knew it was not true, but if she said so to Emily, her big sister would no doubt get defensive on her behalf. Abigail wanted nothing to mar this visit with Emily, particularly not the troubles that nipped at the edges of that contentment she so clearly rejoiced in.

"We are proud of her cleverness," Earc said. He had been watching over her as she gardened and had held back from his usual peppering of curious questions quite manfully thus far.

"Aye, the entire clan is proud," Talorc affirmed, evidently willing to overlook Emily's allusion to love as well.

Emily's lovely violet eyes grew misty again. "It is a miracle."

Abigail knew exactly what she meant: the clan's acceptance and appreciation of her. "Yes."

She spent the rest of the day reacquainting her sister with the Sinclair holding and relearning her sister's words, movements and heart as well. Emily told Abigail about her life among the Balmorals, in much richer detail than she had ever been able to go into in a letter she knew would be read by both her father and Sybil as well as Abigail.

"I am so glad you found another woman to call sister. I missed you so much, but at least I still had Jolenta. I prayed for you to find someone to take my place," Abigail admitted.

"No one could take your place in my heart, but Cait is another sister of the soul. I know you will find the same when you come to Balmoral Island to visit."

"Isn't she Talorc's sister as well?"

"Yes."

"Won't she come here to visit?"

Emily bit her lip, a clear marker that she was hesitant to speak freely.

"Just say it," Abigail demanded.

"Talorc promised not to take Cait's little son, but she

worries that if she brings him to visit, Talorc will decide he belongs with the Sinclairs rather than the Balmorals."

"Why would he?"

"Because the babe's father was Sean, Talorc's second-in-command before Barr."

"Niall and Barr's older brother?" Abigail asked in shock. "I knew they had been married, but I did not realize she was pregnant when he died."

"Yes. And she was big with child when Drustan decided to keep her."

"This is part of the story you need to tell me, is it not?"

"Yes, but it's too long a story to get into before we have to return to the great hall to eat."

The evening meal was a full celebration that ended with both lairds insisting on carrying their wives up the stairs to the sleeping quarters. Abigail couldn't help noticing and being amused by the fact that Lachlan seemed every bit as concerned about Emily's safety on the narrow stairway as Talorc was about her.

"It's a tactical advantage, I'll give you that," Lachlan said to Talorc. "But it is not practical for a laird with a family to consider."

Talorc looked at the stairs, then at the sleeping baby in Emily's arms and finally at Abigail, where his gaze lingered for long seconds. "I see your meaning," he said with a look she could not decipher.

She had no trouble deciphering the angry frown Guaire sent toward the other end of the table. No doubt Osgard had said something rude again. Ignoring him was getting more and more difficult, but she wasn't about to whine to Talorc like a spoiled child. She had enjoyed more acceptance from her clan than she ever would have hoped for.

One man's intransigent insistence on unpleasantness

was not significant. Not even if he found his twin in the tower's housekeeper's attitude.

Niall at least was never mean with his words, nor did he ever attempt to undermine her with others. Whatever was going on with her estranged friend, she had hope of one day renewing their camaraderie.

The next week was one of the most convivial of Abigail's life. She and her sister worked in her herb garden together while Gail napped in the shade. When the baby was awake, they played with her and spent more time visiting amidst Abigail's clan.

Emily exclaimed over and over again about the friendly attitude the clan treated her with now that she was wed to someone besides their laird. "I can only think my absolute lack of desire to marry their laird showed in my every action."

"He learned from the way he treated you and established my role with the clanspeople immediately."

Emily grinned, and like most days, Abigail found herself telling her sister all about her life since Emily had left her father's keep, including Abigail's experiences as a newly married laird's lady. They had not yet got around to Emily telling Abigail the full story of how she had ended up married to Lachlan.

"Remember, you had letters to read from me. I got no correspondence from you." Sir Reuben had been unwilling to send a messenger all the way north to the Highlands with nothing more important than a letter. Unlike Lachlan of the Balmoral, the English baron did not have allied clans willing to pass the letters along. "I have hundreds of questions still unanswered."

Abigail did her best to answer them.

They were visiting in the bedchamber Emily and Lachlan were sharing while staying with the Sinclairs. The baby was napping and Abigail's escort waited in the hall, outside the door.

"Your husband is very conscientious of your safety," Emily observed.

"Osgard once told me it was because neither Talorc nor the clan trusted me to be alone. Because I am English."

"You did not believe him, did you?" Emily looked ready to do bodily harm to an old warrior. "It is obvious your clan loves and trusts you."

Abigail nodded in agreement. "Even after finding out about my secret."

"It is so different from Father's keep, is it not?"

"Oh, yes. I feel so free here."

"And valued."

Filled with pleasure at the thought, Abigail smiled. "Yes. For so long the only two people who believed I had value were you and the abbess. Now, I have a whole clan."

It would probably amaze her until the day she died, but she would thank God for it every day, too.

"It's wonderful." Emily started crying again. She'd been doing that a lot.

Abigail laid her hand over Emily's stomach. "Sister, are you sure there is not something you wish to tell me? I do not remember you being so easily led to tears, happy or otherwise."

"It's not certain. I am only a little over a week past when my monthly should have begun. But I can feel a change in my body, odd food cravings and nausea at the idea of meals I usually love. I have not told Lachlan yet, though I imagine he must know." Emily laughed, her delight at the prospect evident. "I did not want him to use it as an excuse to put off our visit."

"When will the baby come?"

"If my calculations are correct, early spring."

"That is such wonderful news."

"Thank you. I did not expect to have two babies so close together. Gail is only eight months old."

"They will be playmates."

"I imagine they will, but I sense this one is a boy."

"I'm sure that will not stop them."

"Oh, Abigail, I am so happy to have you back in my life," Emily said with a hiccupping sigh.

"Me, too." Abigail gave her sister a spontaneous hug. "I wish you could stay longer."

Emily nodded. "But you will come to Balmoral Island for a visit soon, Talorc has promised."

"Yes, and he keeps his promises."

"It is good to be able to trust your husband in such things."

"It is." Abigail let her gaze slide to the sleeping baby and then back to her sister. "Um . . . there is something I have been wishing to discuss with you." The one worry she desperately needed her sister's wisdom in dealing with.

They had already briefly discussed the Una problem and Emily had made no bones about the fact that she thought the other woman should be sent away. Abigail should have been prepared for the protective stance and realized Emily would be no more unbiased than she was, just in a different direction.

She'd brought it up to Guaire and he had suggested she discuss it with her husband, since as laird he had a right to know Una was once again flaunting his directive to accept Abigail as lady of the Sinclairs.

But as frustrating as Una was, she was not Abigail's most pressing concern.

Emily cocked her head at Abigail's prolonged silence. "What is it?"

"You remember what the English priests taught about deafness?"

"The demon thing?" Emily frowned. "Pshaw. We know that isn't true. You haven't been worrying about that old tale, have you?"

"I've been hearing voices in my head," she bluntly admitted.

"Voices? In your head?" Emily asked, not sounding overly concerned. In fact, if it was not stretching the bounds of belief too far, Abigail would have said her sister sounded almost *excited*. "What do you mean?"

"When Talorc and I are making love, I imagine I hear his voice and once I heard the howling of a wolf. Sometimes I think it is just my imagination, because I so desperately want to hear his voice when I can hear nothing else. Only it is so real and, Emily . . . I don't remember what other things sound like. Not the chirping of a bird, the gurgling of a brook, the sound of wind in the trees or even your voice. Yet, I hear his so clearly. And from what I can remember, it is unlike any voice I heard before losing sound."

Emily's brilliant smile made no sense. "You need to tell Talorc, though I'm surprised he has not already noted the situation."

"I did tell him."

Emily's brows furrowed. "What did he say?"

"Nothing."

"Nothing?" She shook her head. "That idiot."

"My husband is not an idiot. He did not judge me. He did confirm he was not worried about it." Which at first had fed her fears Talorc planned to banish her, but then she had seen his acceptance for the gift it was.

"Of course he isn't worried. He knows exactly why you are hearing his voice and that of his wolf in your head." Emily's pansy eyes snapped with annoyance.

"His wolf?" Abigail was more than a little confused. "You mean the big gray wolf that is friend to the clan?"

"That gray wolf is more than friend." Emily jumped up and began pacing the floor.

"You've seen it, too?"

"Only from a distance."

"I've seen it up close twice." She told her sister about the walk in the woods with Niall and then about her near miss with the boar. "The wolf saved my life."

"Of course he did. He is your husband, your mate."

"Emily . . . I am not married to a wolf." She went right from worrying about her own sanity to that of her sister's.

Chapter 18

Perhaps Emily's pregnancy was causing her mind to play tricks on her.

But Emily did not look like she was fantasizing when she said, "Yes, you are."

"Emily—"

"They are werewolves, Abigail."

"Don't tease me. I know I believed Anna's stories of werewolves in the Highlands as if they were gospel and they scared me, but I am no longer a child. And I'm really worried about these voices."

"I'm not teasing you." Emily's violet eyes mirrored her frustration. "Have I ever lied to you?"

"No."

"I am not lying now. There is a special race who live among the clans here in the Highlands."

"The Chrechte."

"So, Talorc told you about them."

"Yes."

"He didn't tell you everything if you do not know they are werewolves."

"Werewolves are only a story," Abigail reminded her sister stubbornly.

"No, they aren't. They are real and Talorc is one. I think it is time I told you the story of how I came to be wed to Lachlan."

Abigail's astonishment grew as her sister told her the story. So did the growing realization that Emily believed every word she said, and if she believed them, they were probably true, which meant so were Anna's stories. Werewolves were real.

If anyone else had claimed such, Abigail would have demanded proof, but this was her sister. The one person in the world who had always loved her and had never lied to her. In addition to her absolute trust in her sister, Abigail couldn't help noticing how details of her sister's story made sense of things that had confused her since meeting Talorc.

"When a werewolf finds his or her true mate, some of them are able to talk to each other in their heads," Emily said. "Lachlan and I can do it."

"Talorc called me his true mate, I thought he meant I was his friend."

Emily didn't laugh, but Abigail would have. What a dolt she had been. Misunderstanding words that explained so much.

"Wolves mate for life and his wolf has mated with you," Emily said with complete assurance. "While it is rare for a Chrechte to mate with a human, it can happen. I'm evidence of that. Our child's presence and my current *condition* is further evidence that mine and Lachlan's is a true mating. I do not understand how I was so blessed, nor how you should share the blessing with Talorc, but it is possible."

Abigail remembered the possessive look of the wolf, both in the forest and then after he had killed for her, and felt faint. "This cannot be true." Though her doubts were more voice than substance now.

"It is. I would never lie to you or tease you about something so important. You know that."

Abigail remembered the way the voice had yelled at her when the wild boar had been coming. "He can talk to me like that all the time or only in moments of great emotion?"

"Lachlan talks to me that way all the time, as I do him. Cait and her husband are true-mated with the gift as well. As far as I know, it is possible to communicate that way all the time for the sacred mates blessed by mindspeak."

"Why didn't Talorc tell me?" Why would he not use their ability to talk in such a special way? How could he deprive her of the sound of his voice when her entire world was silent without it?

"I don't know. He never told me either, when I was here as his intended. Lachlan wasn't the one that told me about the Chrechte's true nature either. Cait did."

"But why hide it?"

Emily gave her a pointed look. "You of all people should know the answer to that."

"Because differences are often seen as threatening."

"Exactly. If their secrets were to be discovered, it is likely the Chrechte would be hunted and destroyed like animals. You know what could have happened to you if people had known of your deafness; how much worse if they discovered someone was capable of turning into a wolf? The Chrechte are mighty warriors but small in number in comparison to their full-human counterparts."

"That does not explain Talorc not telling me."

"No, it doesn't. I do know that the Chrechte protect the secrets of their people very closely. If they are discovered to have betrayed the secret, or someone they tell is found doing so, the sentence is death."

"But you told me," Abigail said, worried for her sister.

"Of course I did. You are my sister and you are mated to a Chrechte warrior. You are no security risk to the people."

"Clearly Talorc disagrees."

"He's not an easily trusting man."

If he loved her, he would trust her, but that wasn't something Abigail was going to mention to her sister. "And I deceived him."

"Yes. Though just as you should understand the Chrechte's need to keep their secrets, he should have understood your need to hide your affliction and not judged you untrustworthy because of it."

"He gets very angry when I call my deafness an affliction," Abigail said, realizing that if she did not change the subject soon, she would break down in grief over the implications of what she had just learned.

"He does?"

"Yes. He says it is not an affliction, just an infirmity and not much of one the way I compensate for it."

"He can be a smart man."

"Yes." It was all Abigail could do to maintain her façade of normalcy for her sister. Her heart was shriveling in her chest at all the conclusions to be drawn from Talorc keeping the secret of the Chrechte from her.

Why was she delivered such demeaning blows each time she thought she had found happiness?

"Are you all right, sister?"

For the first time in her life, Abigail lied to Emily. "Yes. Of course."

"I would like to be a fly on the wall when you break the news to your husband you know all about his wolf."

Abigail could not prevent a grimace from twisting her features.

"He'll be relieved, believe me. Lachlan's wolf needs my acceptance and love as much as his human side. He adores being scratched behind his ears; I bet Talorc does, too."

Abigail forced a laugh and a smile that would even fool her sister. She maintained the façade through her sister's final evening meal among the Sinclairs and leave-taking the next day.

That night for the first time, Abigail begged off making love with Talorc using the excuse of tiredness. Silent tears tracked down her cheeks in the darkness as her husband slept beside her on the furs.

He had deceived her just as she had done him, but still he had cruelly condemned her for keeping her own secrets. He doubted her love for him, but more important, it was clear now that he would never love her.

Not only was she not a Highlander by birth, but she was not a Chrechte. Emily had shared the role her humanity had played in Lachlan's difficulty accepting his feelings for her. And that man was as besotted as any man had ever been in the history of the world.

What chance did Abigail have of overcoming a prejudice so noticeably more ingrained in Talorc?

He had no desire to share his special heritage with her in any way. The wolf, who according to Emily, needed Abigail's love and approval, was withheld from her. Even though they could share the intimate bond of speaking in each other's mind, Talorc held back from doing so with her.

And that was perhaps what hurt the most. Talorc must realize the devastation Abigail had experienced losing sound from her life. To have the chance to hear again, especially her husband's voice, was the most amazing miracle possible.

But he denied it to her because sharing it with her meant sharing his secrets as well. It meant trusting her. Something he would never do for a woman born and raised in the country he reviled. The agony of that knowledge battered at Abigail's already abused heart.

Emily had expressed the wish to be there when Abigail confronted Talorc with her knowledge of the truth.

Only Abigail wasn't sure she had any intention of doing so. She had no desire to have him tell her to her face why he did not believe her worthy to know the truth. Nor did she want to risk Emily getting in trouble with the other Chrechte. No doubt Lachlan would protect her, after all Lachlan of the Balmoral loved his wife, but Abigail did not want to risk causing her sister even the slightest grief.

Emily had never done aught but protect and encourage her. She deserved the same in return.

The next day, Abigail left their "bed" before Talorc woke, having no desire to speak to her husband while her mind and emotions were in such turmoil.

She did not know if she could forgive him for withholding

the sound of his voice from her when he had the power to gift her with it.

Her thoughts in a jumbled mess, she was not paying as close attention as usual traversing the narrow stairway. Her foot landed against the step, but something rolled under her shoe. Losing her footing, she tripped forward. She grabbed desperately for the wall, but the smooth stone did not give her purchase.

Terror gripped her. She was going to fall. Unable to stop her forward momentum, she did her best to throw her weight toward the wall, rather than the empty air, and tuck her head down. She wrapped her arms around it in hopes of preventing a fatal hit as she continued to try to halt her bumping tumble.

She screamed Talorc's name in her head as she landed with a heavy thump at the bottom of the steps that caused her arms to flail involuntarily. Her head knocked against the wall and that was the last she knew.

Abigail awoke on the furs in her bedchamber to an insistent voice demanding her attention. Talorc was leaning over her, his expression fiercely concerned. Or so it seemed. She ignored the voice in her head, knowing it was him calling to her. She turned her head away.

He touched her ear, telling her he wanted to say something.

She refused to look at him. "I fell down the stairs."

He tugged her chin, oh so gently, so she had to meet his gaze. "Do not worry. I am not angry for you walking down the steps alone."

She did not need his assurances. "It was not my fault.

There was something on the steps. It rolled under my shoes and I lost my footing."

"Do not feel you have to make excuses." Talorc shook his head. "Lachlan was right, though it pains me to admit it. The stairs are not safe for a family. I will have a rail installed."

She ignored his reassurance for the important issue at hand. "There was something on the stairs. I felt it under my shoe."

"There wasn't. I found you moments after you fell and nothing was there."

"You found me?"

"Osgard did at first, perhaps a second or two before me, and for all his bluster, he was most concerned."

Talorc frowned and turned his head to glare at someone behind him.

Guaire returned his laird's frown with equanimity. "Osgard has proven time and again that he does not accept our new lady. He knows of her habit to come down the stairs before anyone else in the morning. He is usually the first in the great hall. He could easily have put pebbles on the steps and cleaned them up before you arrived to discover your wife's fallen body."

Abigail did not like the possibility that someone in their clan had tried to hurt her, but she knew *something* had been on the stairs. Before she could say anything, Niall made his presence known.

His glower was twice as ferocious as Talorc's as he stared at Guaire. "You dare accuse our laird's advisor of an act that amounts to treason? He is a loyal Chrechte."

"And because he is Chrechte, he is above reproach, but because I am merely *human*, my opinion counts for nothing? Even though I am seneschal to the holding and care deeply for the safety of my lady?"

The dangerous stillness that came over Talorc and Niall indicated something Guaire had said made them more than angry. It made them dangerous.

Abigail played her friend's words back through her mind and understanding dawned. Guaire had referred to himself as human, not a Highlander, which implied he knew the true difference between the Chrechte and the rest of their clan. And neither Niall nor Talorc had known he was aware of their true nature.

The glare he turned on the two bigger warriors was sulfuric. "Do you think I am blind? I live here with you all."

"That is enough," Talorc bit out with a sideways glance at Abigail.

Guaire's look turned to one of contempt. "By all means, keep your wife, your *sacred mate*, in the dark."

"Leave," Talorc ordered.

"No!" Abigail cried. "He is my friend."

"You countermand my order?" Talorc asked dangerously.

"You withhold enough from me; you will not keep my dearest friend."

"What do I keep from you?" he asked, so clearly certain his secret was safe he was genuinely confused.

That only made her angrier. And as Emily knew, when Abigail got angry, she went silent, not louder. "It is not worth discussing."

He stared at her, clearly nonplussed. "Abigail . . ."

She glared back at him, as mute as she was deaf.

"I have duties to attend to," Guaire said in an obvious bid to end the stalemate between laird and lady. "You need your rest."

Abigail smiled her thanks for his concern. Then she gave Talorc and Niall her meanest look. "You will not hurt him."

Niall jerked back as if hit. "I would not. He is my . . . fellow soldier. I would protect him always."

Guaire looked about as convinced of that as she was of Talorc's love, which was to say, not at all.

"Abigail, what the hell is going on with you?" her husband demanded.

"Mayhap my fall addled my brains," she said with unadulterated sarcasm.

Talorc actually looked relieved by the explanation.

She and Guaire shared a look of pure understanding before the redheaded soldier left the room.

"I would rest," Abigail said, looking at neither her husband nor his loyal soldier.

He brushed her cheek as Emily often did to get her attention. She let her gaze rest on him only because she knew she would not get rid of him if she did not.

"First you will drink some tea I had Una prepare from the recipes in my mother's healing journal."

With her luck, the tea would be poisoned. "No."

"I insist."

"Una hates me." Someone had left pebbles, or something, on the stairs. If not Osgard, then maybe the widow. "I will not drink or eat anything she makes. And don't bother lying to me and pretending someone else did the preparations if it is her. I can read a face as well as lips and I'll know you aren't being honest."

"I would not lie," Talorc said, anger finally kindling in his gaze.

Abigail refused to dignify his ridiculous assertion with an answer. Of course he would lie. Or at least withhold the truth.

When she did not break the silence between them,

Talorc turned to Niall and instructed, "Have one of the undercooks prepare the tisane."

Niall returned ten minutes later with a steaming cup. Abigail had not spoken and had managed to ignore her husband by the simple expedient of closing her eyes and shutting him out.

Talorc was patient with her ill humor and solicitous over that day and the next, but Abigail kept him at a distance. The fact that she had the worst headache of her life made maintaining her cranky attitude easy. Even Sybil's constant harping had never made Abigail's head pound so.

Guaire came to visit Abigail twice a day, but they were never left alone, which propriety might dictate, but she didn't like because it wasn't her virtue Talorc, Niall and Barr were protecting. It was their secrets.

The third morning, Abigail insisted on going to the great hall to break her fast with Talorc and the other soldiers.

Una expressed her concern for Abigail's health, but Abigail was in no mood to play happy families with the widow after her cold treatment and attempts to undermine Abigail's authority with the other clan members who served in the tower. She simply pretended not to notice the woman speaking to her.

The red that covered Una's cheeks said she knew Abigail had not answered on purpose, but she did not attempt to speak to her laird's wife again.

"What was that all about?" Guaire asked while Talorc and Barr were busy planning their day with the soldiers. "I thought you were trying to win her over."

"I've given up." For now anyway. "I just don't have the good humor to deal with her right now."

"She had her hopes of ending her widowed status with Talorc before the king's edict."

That might explain Una's initial coldness, but it did not excuse it. "She said she had been housekeeper for three years. If Talorc had been interested, he would have shown it before now."

"No doubt." Guaire frowned, looking sad and defeated. "She's set her sights on a different warrior now."

"Niall?" Abigail asked intuitively.

"Yes."

Abigail squeezed his hand in silent commiseration.

Guaire's eyes widened and then he mouthed a thank-you before squeezing her hand back.

Niall crossed his arms, drawing Abigail's attention. "If you two are finished holding hands, perhaps you would care to see to your duties, Seneschal."

It looked like she wasn't the only grumpy one around here this morning.

Guaire's expression turned dourer. "I am going to the blacksmith's to check the progress on the tools our clan will take for trade to the gathering. Would you like to come?"

"Yes. I want to tell Magnus thank you for the gardening tool he made for me."

Talorc touched her ear and the familiar gesture combined with the distance she created between them made her wish for something different. She turned her head to face him.

He slid a concerned glance between her and Guaire. "Perhaps you should rest another day." Obviously, he was still worried the seneschal would tell her Talorc's secrets.

If his concern had been for her health, she would have

listened, but as it was, his worry about Guaire telling her what she already knew only made her more determined to accompany him. "I am bruised, not broken. The walk will do me good."

"Do you think he will tell her?" Talorc asked Niall.

"He said he wouldn't. I have never known Guaire to break his word."

"Nor have I." But he couldn't help worrying. Talorc needed to be the one to tell Abigail of his true Chrechte nature, but he had realized when it became clear Guaire was aware of the Chrechte's biggest secret, that if Talorc did not do so soon, she might find out another way.

"Would her sister have told her, do you think?" Barr asked.

"That is far more likely, but if she had done so, I think Abigail would have confronted me with the truth."

Niall snorted. "Or Emily would have when she realized you'd kept her beloved sister in the dark about your wolf."

"She has never been shy about speaking her mind."

"I remember," Barr said with a grin.

"The whole clan remembers her likening me to a goat."

On the way to the lower bailey, Abigail made sure no one else was around before asking Guaire, "You love him, don't you?"

Guaire did not ask who she meant or try to pretend he did not know what she was talking about. He simply gave a defeated sigh and said, "Yes."

"I thought as much."

"I have loved him all my life. I do not remember when

I realized I wanted to kiss him, to touch him as a lover. I only know that I have never wanted another."

"You've never found another man or woman attractive?"

Guaire blushed. "I find many warriors attractive, but the only one who makes me wish to act on those feelings is Niall. I want him so much, I tremble with it. One day, he is bound to notice. And then he will probably kill me."

"Because you are a man?"

"Nay, matings within the Chrechte can be between two men or two women. It does not happen often, but enough that they recognize God's blessing on such love. Niall would be furious to find out how much I love him because I am not Chrechte. He thinks I am weak because—" Abruptly, Guaire stopped talking.

"Because you do not have a wolf nature like he does," she finished for him. "Emily told me the truth of the Chrechte when she was here."

"Talorc believes you are still ignorant."

"I know." It was her turn to feel defeated.

"He is slow to trust, but it will come one day."

"When I am old and gray, perhaps." Abigail sighed. "Tell me more about Niall."

"You do not find my love an abomination?" Guaire asked with a puzzled frown.

"Of course not."

"But the Church teaches it is so. We are not so worried about Rome's edicts here, but I have always been led to believe the English follow her religious edicts without question."

"Some do, some don't." Abigail shrugged. "The Church also teaches that women are last in God's love, even after animals of burden."

Guaire's eyes widened in surprise. "Our priest would never be foolish enough to say such a thing."

"Your clanswomen are fierce."

"Nay, 'tis our warriors that would chase him from our lands for such idiocy."

Abigail smiled. "The Church also teaches a husband has not only the right, but the responsibility to beat his wife."

"Now I know you are joshing me. Not even England's Church would say such a terrible thing."

Abigail wanted to cry at his innocence. "It is the truth. The abbess says that when the Church teaches abuse or hatred, we must consider it carefully in light of Christ's claim that to love God is the greatest commandment and to love others the second greatest, all other laws and prophecies hang on these two."

"Your abbess sounds like a wise woman."

"She is. I do not believe love an abomination any more than I believe God loves me less than my father's oxen."

"Me either. But my love is hopeless."

"Are you sure?" It seemed to her that Niall had strong feelings for Guaire, but she did not know if they were love. So, she did not speculate and raise Guaire's hopes.

"Aye, especially since Una started focusing her attention on Niall."

"He is not attracted to men as you are?"

"I do not know. The Chrechte of our clan are not sexually promiscuous, but Una is a beautiful woman. And 'tis rare enough for a Chrechte warrior to mate with a human, even more so with a male human."

"Una may be beautiful, but she's not nice."

"She's annoying to be sure," Guaire agreed with more vehemence than he might have before the other woman had begun flirting with Niall.

As they came off the path from the motte to the bailey, a pair of soldiers approached them. One wore Sinclair colors, but Abigail did not recognize the colors on the other man's clothing.

After they passed her and Guaire, she turned to the seneschal. "Who was that?"

"A messenger from the king." Guaire had already turned, and tugging Abigail's hand, he retraced their steps up the hill.

Chapter 19

The two soldiers were only a few feet ahead of them, so Abigail refrained from asking Guaire to speculate why a messenger from Scotland's king should be at the Sinclair holding.

When they reached the great hall, she grabbed Guaire's arm. "Wait," she whispered.

He gave her a questioning glance.

"Enter quietly."

"We'd have to be quieter than a spider crawling across the floor for the Chrechte not to notice we are there."

"We can go in the entrance Una uses from the kitchens." She bit her lip, wondering if Guaire would think her awful for wanting to eavesdrop.

"The smell of food will mask our scents."

"Just so." She grinned.

Guaire winked.

They rushed around the tower to the kitchens, ignoring

Una as they walked through her domain. Though Abigail spared a smile for the two women helping to knead bread for that evening's meal.

Unable to hear if she made sound, Abigail stepped as lightly as she could. Guaire stuck close. They reached the entranceway when Guaire held her back.

"We dare not go any farther," he mouthed.

"Can you hear them?" she asked in a barely there whisper.

"Nay, but you can see the messenger's face."

She nodded and turned her attention to the king's soldier.

"The king was most concerned when he learned of the trick the English baron paid on his favored laird."

The trick? Did that mean Scotland's king had learned Sir Hamilton had sent his deaf stepdaughter to Scotland as bride to Talorc? How could he know?

The image of Jolenta's envious countenance swam before Abigail. Her younger sister had been furious such a personage as a laird was wasted on Abigail. What would Talorc do now that the king knew?

She could not tell what her husband said to the messenger, but the man nodded. "Our king has heard your complaint. He will arrange to have your current marriage annulled on the grounds of deception. One way or another, the deaf woman will be taken care of. Sir Hamilton's daughter Jolenta will be sent north to replace her sister. It has already been arranged."

Talorc surged to his feet and shouted something at the messenger. Abigail could only hope he was refusing his king's offer.

"King David was sure you would be pleased by this

offer when he received your message demanding redress for the English baron and his daughter's deception."

Talorc had sent a message to the king telling him of Abigail's secret? He had demanded redress? The nights of making love since then meant nothing. The fact that he had never repeated her words of love or indeed acknowledged the truth of hers made perfect sense now. Talorc had just been biding his time until his king annulled the marriage. Just like Sybil, Talorc had made plans to get rid of Abigail permanently.

Pain lanced through her and she doubled over. Guaire's arms were there, stopping her from falling. She looked up at him, but she could not form the words to tell him what she had heard.

His eyes were filled with compassion, but determination was there, too. "Do not let them see your pain."

She nodded, sucking in air and resolve. She forced herself to stand straight and step away from him.

"We either go back through the kitchen or walk through the great hall. Your choice."

As annoying as she found Una, the other woman would be much easier to hide Abigail's devastation from. She pointed toward the kitchen and Guaire nodded, then led the way. Their pace was much more sedate this time, though they did not dawdle in the kitchen. Thankfully, Una was not there at the moment.

They found her outside. With Niall. Kissing.

Guaire's entire body went rigid with shock, the anguish of what he saw causing him to cover his face.

Niall pushed the widow away, his gaze zeroing in on Guaire with unerring accuracy. He opened his mouth to speak, but Guaire spun away, dragging Abigail with him.

If Niall called after them, she could not hear, but she felt the vibration of the ground as he chased after them. She did not know what Guaire said over his shoulder at the big warrior, but the scarred man did not follow them onto the path to the lower bailey.

Abigail kept walking when she reached the smithy. Not bothering to ask why she had not stopped, Guaire followed. They walked right through the gate, the gatekeeper not detaining them because of Guaire's presence.

They had walked well beyond the wall when Abigail stopped. "Which way?"

"To where?" Guaire asked.

"To my sister's clan. Which way to Balmoral Island?"

"What did the king's messenger say?" Guaire asked, his own desolation dulling his usually bright green gaze.

She told him.

Guaire looked stunned. "Talorc sent a messenger complaining about you to the king?"

"Yes."

"I don't believe it."

"I know what I saw."

"Yes, but . . ."

"The messenger said the king would take care of me one way or another."

Guaire's already pale features leeched of all color. He pointed to the northeast. "Balmoral Island is that way."

Abigail started walking. Guaire fell into step beside her. They stopped to drink from a stream as the sun rose high in the sky.

"Our clan keeps skiffs for crossing the water in a cave at the water's edge," he told her. "We'll have to wait until tomorrow to go to the island though. Walking, we won't reach the water until darkness has already fallen."

"We can stay in the cave with the boats."

"Aye."

They resumed their journey, not stopping to rest until late afternoon. Like all warriors, Guaire carried dried meat in the small bag he kept tied to his belt. They ate that along with berries and greens Abigail foraged. It was no feast, but it renewed their strength to continue their hike through the forest.

Although the moon shone brightly in the sky, it was past dark as Guaire had predicted when they came upon the water.

Abigail stopped and stared, awe superseding the ache of her heart for a magical moment. "It is so vast. And beautiful."

"Aye. During the day, you can see Balmoral Island off in the distance."

"Emily is petrified of water, or at least she used to be. Before her husband taught her to swim. I wonder how she made the crossing the first time?"

"You are not frightened of water?"

"No. Though I used to be terrified of wild beasts."

"Learning your husband is also a wolf changed your heart?"

"Meeting his wolf, if I had but known it at the time." She wrapped her arms around herself, but the chill from her heart would not be warmed. "He came to me while I walked in the forest near the hot springs. It scared me spitless, to tell you the truth, but was amazing all the same. Niall promised me the wolf would not hurt me."

Guaire flinched at the mention of the man he loved.

She laid her hand on his shoulder. "I am sorry."

"Your pain is greater than mine."

"I don't believe that."

Guaire rubbed at his cheeks and Abigail pretended not to notice. "Nothing good could ever come of my love, but so long as he did not find someone else, I let my stupid heart hope."

"Dashed hopes hurt most of all, I think." Hers had left her bleeding still.

"Because they are born of your heart's desires."

She nodded, too choked all at once to speak. Talorc had fulfilled the deepest desires of her heart, or at least she thought he had.

"Will your sister's husband allow me to remain among the Balmoral, do you think?"

"Of course, you would be an asset to any clan."

Guaire smiled sadly. "Thank you."

"You are not going to Balmoral Island. I threatened war on my own king to keep you with me. I'll not let another laird, Chrechte pack leader or not, take you from me."

At the sound of her husband's voice in her head, Abigail spun around. Two huge wolves stood a mere ten feet from her and Guaire.

The redhead had turned when she did. His expression mirrored her shock. "Laird?"

Talorc nodded, though he maintained his wolf's form. The wolf beside him looked like he might be white, but he glowed a pale silver in the moonlight.

Guaire trembled beside Abigail. "Niall?"

The other wolf did not answer as Talorc had done, but padded forward, stopping only when his big head butted against Guaire's side. A look of wonder took over Guaire's features, dissipating the defeated pain that had been so strong only a moment ago.

He reached down and ran his fingers through the wolf's pelt. "Is this okay?" he asked the beast.

Niall barked. Guaire dropped to a crouch. The white wolf rubbed his head against Guaire's cheek and the seneschal buried his head in the beast's fur. The wolf's body shook as if beset by intense emotion, and the man wrapped his arms around the beast's neck.

"He is not afraid of Niall's wolf at all," Talorc's voice was tinged with bleakness.

Abigail used her voice, such that it was, to speak. "If I had known it was you, I wouldn't have been afraid of you either."

"You are so certain of that?" The wolf's eyes . . . Talorc's eyes . . . seemed to look into her heart.

"I have always trusted you with my safety. From the very first moment."

"And yet you ran away."

"You complained about me to your king. You wanted rid of me." Her earlier distress returned, setting grief like a stranglehold around her heart.

"I sent a messenger in a drunken moment of idiocy. I did not want rid of you. Surely I made that clear after I sobered up."

Abigail turned away from him only to find Niall tugging Guaire's plaid off. Shock forced a reaction other than sorrow, at least for that moment.

"Surely he does not mean to mate with him as a wolf?" Abigail asked in her mind of Talorc.

Unwanted pleasure filled her as he answered her. Until that moment she had not been absolutely sure the special form of communication could go both ways. *"Nay, of course not. He is scenting his mate, claiming him so all will know Guaire belongs to Niall."*

And indeed that was what the big wolf was doing. He rubbed his head against every inch of Guaire he could reach. Guaire was laughing, whether because it tickled or he was simply filled with joy, Abigail could not tell, but regardless, her friend appeared quite happy with what the man—werewolf—he loved was doing.

She turned away from the other couple, giving them their privacy. *"Is that why you rub your face against me when we are making love?"* Or used to.

"Yes. I crave scenting you as a wolf."

"But you did not trust me enough to tell me of your true nature, so you could not do it."

"I did not want to love you."

"You got what you wanted."

"Aye, in you I got the deepest, most secret desires of my heart." The words echoing her own thoughts paralyzed her. *"You are my true mate."* He approached her slowly, as if afraid of spooking her. *"I need you to accept me in this form for my wolf to have happiness."*

"What difference does it make if you are going to let your king annul our marriage?"

"I will not. I sent his soldier back with this message: I would consider any attempt to annul our marriage or take you from your clan an act of war."

"You cannot go to war with your own king!"

"It would not be the first time the Highland clans rebelled."

"But we are just one clan."

"I have allies."

"You truly do not wish to be rid of me?" Could it be that easy? No, there was still the matter of trust to settle, but Abigail had realized how much she was willing to work on that when she thought Talorc would be taken from her.

"I would die to protect you, and if necessary, I will kill to keep you."

So, definitely, Talorc did not want their marriage to end.

"You didn't tell me of your true nature." Though he had come after her in his wolf form and was now speaking to her in her mind, he had no doubt intended to tell her the truth. And yet . . . *"You let me believe I was imagining voices in my head. I worried I was going crazy or that the priests might be right and that my mind was afflicted because of my deafness."*

The wolf butted his head against her stomach. *"I am sorry, my angel. I never meant to cause you such grief. None of those thoughts even entered my head. I was afraid to make myself vulnerable to you, and I selfishly acted out of my fear. All that I am belongs to you, and I will never again hold anything back."*

Unable to help herself, she dropped to her knees and wrapped her arms around Talorc's furry neck. *"You hurt me so much."*

"I will never do it again."

She rubbed her cheek against his fur as she finally let tears fall she had not wanted anyone to see. *"Can I trust you?"*

"I pray that you will."

She held on and cried, finding it easier to share her pain with the wolf than if her husband held her as a man. He nuzzled her as she cried, subtly scenting her as he gave her comfort.

Her tears turned to watery laughter. *"I know what you are doing."*

"Aye, the whole clan knows you are a clever woman."

He pulled his head back and licked the tears from her cheeks. *"Now I am kissing you."* The sound of a wolf's chuffing in her mind brought a smile to her lips.

"If you are looking to scent me as Niall scented Guaire, I would like to go to the cave."

A soft shimmer of light ended in Talorc taking his human form. He lifted Abigail in his strong arms. *"I have a better idea."*

As he carried her away from the water, out of the corner of her eye, she saw two naked male bodies entwined. She very consciously did not look in that direction, but she could not help feeling glad for her dear friend and the man she hoped to call friend again one day soon.

Talorc carried her through the forest until they came into a small clearing bathed in moonlight. *"The grass will be more comfortable than the floor of the cave."*

"But . . ."

"No one else is here. Niall and Guaire are back on the beach and too occupied to notice our departure. Once they do note it, they will not come looking."

"You are certain?"

"Yes."

"It is beautiful here."

"Not as beautiful as you."

She shook her head, looking away from him.

"Do not try to hide from me."

"It is easier."

"I will make it easier to love me, I give you my vow."

She spun back to glare at him. *"So now you believe I love you?"*

"Yes."

"Maybe I have changed my mind. Perhaps I want the annulment so I can find a husband who can love me.*"*

"You will never be with another man. You are my true mate."

"But I'm just human. You clearly don't want me for your mate, sacred or otherwise."

"*That is not true; even if I had a choice, I would never want another woman.*"

"*You do have a choice, especially now with your king offering to get rid of me.*"

"*We are sacred mates. I am Chrechte.*"

"*So?*"

"*My wolf will never accept another woman.*"

"*What does that mean?*"

"*You see this?*" He indicated his hard member.

"*Yes.*"

"*With another woman, it would be as limp as milk toast.*"

"*No, you are far too . . . too . . . um . . . virile,*" she said finally.

He shook his head. "*As Chrechte I am not physically capable of mating any but my true mate once my wolf has found her.*"

"*So, it is your wolf that wants to keep me.*"

Chapter 20

A starburst of understanding went off inside Talorc.

He grabbed his precious wife and held her close, looking down into her soft brown gaze, he spoke aloud as well as through their mindspeak. "That is what I told myself. I believed my wolf felt possessive of you, that he wanted to protect you at all costs," he said as the knowledge came over him.

"Are you and your wolf such different beings?" she asked in her soft voice with new tears shimmering in her eyes. "Emily does not speak of Lachlan as if he and his wolf are different beings."

"They are not. My wolf and I are not. We are one in the same, but in my desire to protect myself from making my father's mistakes, I tried to separate my feelings as a laird from those of my wolf. It does not work. I love you with every bit of my wolf's essence, but that is even truer as a man because my wolf cannot share physically in that final consummation of our mating."

"You love me?"

"More than my own life. So much that life is not worth living without you in it."

"You don't mean that. You can't."

"I can. I do. Please, believe me, sweet wife. My own precious angel." He looked at her with nothing less than naked longing. "Do not leave me to the loneliness I knew before you."

"You had a whole clan before I came."

"With not one the true mate of my soul. It took a clever Englishwoman to fill that place inside my heart, to complete the other half of my Chrechte spirit."

"You said I am no longer English."

"You are not."

"I am yours."

"And I am yours."

He said words in her head that she remembered from their mating. "Say them for me, this time speak the vows with truth in your heart."

"I did the first time. I didn't know what I was saying, but in my heart I was giving everything of myself to you."

"But . . ."

"I told you I had changed my plans once we wed. I no longer wanted to be reunited with my sister more than anything. I wanted to stay with you."

"You meant the oaths you gave," he repeated in wonder, needing to take in this truth to heal the wounds in his heart.

"Absolutely."

"That is good because I can never let you go."

"Never."

"You will allow my wolf to scent you now?"

No fear showed in her brown eyes. "Yes."

Dropping to all fours, he let the wolf take him. His already acute senses grew stronger, and the scent of his mate's emotions mixed with those of the forest. She smiled down at him, love and acceptance glowing on her beautiful features.

He tilted his head back and howled in joy, sending the sound through their mindspeak link.

Her smile became a grin."Your wolf is happy."

"I am happy."

"I love you, Talorc," she said inside his head with a conviction her spoken words could not hold.

"You do not fear me in this form?"

"Never."

He chuffed with happiness as he rubbed his head against her. *"Take off your clothes, I need to scent your skin."*

Giggling with clear delight, Abigail undressed.

Though the sight of his wife's nude body would always affect his libido, the most pressing emotion he felt right then was relief. And joy. Finally, he could scent her properly.

He rubbed her belly, leaving his scent behind for all Chrechte to know she was his.

She brushed her hands down the sides of his head, laughter lurking in her gaze. *"Tag, you are it,"* she said with amusement in her mindspeak voice. Then she turned and ran.

He bounded after her, nuzzling her back when he reached her. The playful nature of his wolf asserted itself and he turned in a circle and loped away, saying, *"Your turn."*

He did not go too fast, knowing she ran with the handicap of having only two legs. She caught him at the edge of the clearing, leaping at him. He let her roll him, hearing the wonder-filled laughter in his head. His mate liked to play, and for that he gave thanks. He was not a lighthearted man, more by circumstance than by nature.

But she was showing him that with her, he had a place to let his delight with the good things in life have free rein. They kept the game of tag and gentle tussling up until his body reminded him that there were things he liked to do with his mate even more than playing. He allowed his human form to take him over as he rolled her beneath him.

He slammed his mouth down onto hers and she responded as if she'd been waiting for it. Her mouth was sweet nectar, he could not get enough. His tongue plundered her mouth, but she met every caress of his tongue with one of her own.

Her arms wrapped around his neck, holding on to him so tightly he thought even he would have trouble prying her loose. Not that he wanted to do that.

Not at all. *"I will never let you go,"* he said into her mind.

"Never. You are my husband, my true mate." A wry laugh sounded in his head. *"I thought you saw me as a friend."*

"You are my best and truest friend."

"As you are mine, but one day I will get even with you for letting me prattle on about being friends when you meant we were married in the Chrechte way."

"Duly noted. And one day you will trust me as much as you do your sister."

"I already do."

Soberness filtered through his happiness. *"You were leaving me."*

"I was going to my sister for advice on how to keep you."

Humbled that she would have been willing to fight for him though he had not proved himself worthy of the effort, he broke the kiss to meet her eyes. *"Thank you."* Then he could not help himself adding, *"But if you had talked to me, I would have told you I will always be yours."*

"I was angry. You had withheld your wolf from me and the intimacy of this kind of talking. That hurt so much, to know you could deliberately keep something from me that would be so welcome."

"I am sorry." He hoped she could feel his sincerity because there were no words that could express his profound regret at depriving her of their mindspeak. *"I am ashamed to say I never thought how doing so would hurt you."*

"I did not consider how hurt you would be to find out I had hidden my deafness from you. Love does not always make us brilliant."

"Or brave."

She brushed her fingertip over his lips. *"Knowing you love me gives me all the courage I need."*

"That is as it should be."

"Kiss me."

How could he deny her? He pressed his lips to hers, his body surging with renewed passion with that small caress of mouths. He cupped her breast, kneading it gently and brushing his thumb over her turgid nipple.

She moaned into the kiss as a whimper sounded in his head. How could he have held back from sharing in this intimate communication? He did not know, but he did know that he would never do so again.

Her small hands released their tight clasp behind his neck to rove over his body, and he reveled in every touch.

Needing to be inside her, he rolled them so she was on top. *"Ride me, sweet wife. Please."*

She did not demur but slid down until her silky wet folds met the tip of his granite-hard cock and then engulfed it. Velvet fire enveloped his dick, and Talorc howled in ecstasy.

A feral grin worthy of any Chrechte femwolf creased Abigail's lovely features. She rode him with unfettered passion, freer than she had ever been with him, and he realized that sharing his wolf with her had bridged that final gap between them.

His orgasm built faster than he was ready for, but Abigail was right there with him, screaming out her pleasure in his head while his wolf howled.

In that moment, they truly fulfilled the Chrechte mating promise of being one in body, mind and spirit.

The next morning, Talorc found a small stream for Abigail to bathe in before she dressed and they returned to the beach.

Guaire and Niall were locked in a kiss, their arms wrapped around each other. The beauty of their passion took her breath away. She said as much through mindspeak to Talorc.

"'Tis love."

"Yes."

"I can't help noticing they are both dressed."

"Aye."

"Where did Niall get the plaid?"

"From the cave. We keep some with the boats."

"I'm sure there is one in there for you as well, am I right?"

"Are you saying you do not want to hunt naked with me?"

"How astute of you to take my meaning."

Talorc threw his head back and laughed. Abigail noticed that he sent every sound through mindspeak so she could share in it all with him.

She turned to him, *"I love you so much, Talorc."*

"I love you, my precious angel."

Guaire stepped back from Niall, only to be pulled against the big warrior's side. Burnished streaks appeared across his cheekbones. "Good morning, my lady. Laird."

"Good morning, dear friend. You look happy."

Guaire looked up at Niall, the scarred warrior giving him a far sappier smile than she would have thought him capable of. "I am. Very."

"I am so glad."

"Thank you. You and the laird have worked out your differences?"

"We have. He won't let even his king send me away."

Guaire nodded in approval. "Of course not. You are our lady."

"And you are mated," Talorc said.

The brush of pink turned into a full blush that spread right down Guaire's neck. "We are."

"All this time, he has not been afraid of me," Niall said, directing his words to Talorc.

Talorc's brows drew together in confusion. "His actions . . ."

"He wanted me." Oh, Niall looked proud. "So much so that he trembled in my presence. He always avoided being too near because he feared I would realize his secret desire."

"Secrets keep mates apart," Talorc said with certainty.

Niall nodded, something passing between the two of them that said their communication went deeper than the mere words.

Niall came to kneel in front of Abigail. "I owe you a sincere apology, my own dear lady and friend."

"I am still your friend?"

"Yes. If you will have me." He looked down as if ashamed and then lifted his head so she could read his lips again. "I was jealous."

"Of the time Guaire spent with me," she guessed, finally understanding.

"Yes. I thought he had fallen for you, and though I knew he would never betray his laird, I was furious with envy that he seemed to find in you what he could not see in me—the Chrechte ordained by God to be his mate."

"His love for you never wavered."

"Secrets," Niall said with a poignant expression.

She leaned down and kissed the scarred cheek of her first friend among the Chrechte. "I forgive you and I hope you will forgive me for hiding my own secrets."

"Always."

"Friends?"

"Until death."

They took two days to return to the fortress, Talorc and Niall insisting on hunting to provide food for their mates along the way. Abigail did not mind because it gave her time to talk to Guaire.

"What did Niall say about kissing Una?" she asked as

soon as she thought the two warriors had gotten far enough away.

"He said she kissed him. He let her because he saw me coming out of the kitchen. He thought it might make me jealous. Then he realized how stupid that was, but only too late to stop it. He saw the hurt on my face and it gave him the first hope he'd had since realizing I was his mate."

"When did he realize that?"

"Too long ago." Guaire's entire demeanor was one of frustration. "My fear of revealing myself and his of frightening or overwhelming me kept us apart."

"Perfect love is supposed to cast out fear."

"I suppose it does when you admit it."

"But when you're intent on hiding it—"

"It just causes pain."

Abigail nodded and then said, "Let's make a pact not to regret the past, but rejoice in our present and future."

"Pact." Guaire put his hand out.

Abigail shook it. "Pact."

When they returned to the fortress, Niall made no effort to hide his longtime affection for Guaire. Abigail was delighted to discover that the Highlanders were much more accepting of the love between the two men than her parents or their people would have been. Everyone but Una.

Abigail knew something would have to be done about the other woman, but it would have to wait. Talorc had told her that he had something to show her. She waited for him in the great hall while he and Barr conferred on the soldier's duties for the day.

Finally, everyone else was gone and the only two remaining in the hall were her and Talorc.

He stopped in front of her, looking her up and down and sending tingles everywhere his gaze traveled. "I cannot believe you are my mate. You are so perfect for me."

"I feel the same."

They shared a kiss, but when it started to grow passionate, Talorc pulled back. "Come with me."

"Anywhere."

He smiled, clasping her hand firmly in his. He led her into one of the storage rooms. She looked around in the gloom but did not see anything in particular she could imagine her husband wanting to show her. He lit a torch, though it was hardly dark enough to make that necessary. She understood better when he shut the door and slid a locking bar into place.

How odd to have a lock on the inside of a storage room. She would have asked him about it, but he looked so intent, she hesitated to say anything.

He went to the far wall and pressed something on the shelves holding food stores for the tower. The shelves swung out like a heavy door to reveal an opening in the wall about four feet high and two feet wide.

He transferred the torch to his left hand and put his right one toward her. "Come."

She took his hand and let him lead her through the dark opening. They went down a set of steps into a secret room under the tower. All of its walls and even the ceiling were reinforced with stone.

"What is this place?"

"The Royal Treasure room."

"Royal Treasure?"

Talorc nodded, pulling her toward a smooth stone casket engraved with carvings of wolves along all the sides and the top. "My father was a direct descendant of one of the seven royal Chrechte lineages through his father. When MacAlpin killed all the living princes of our people, he killed those who had inherited royal blood via their mother's lineage, as was our tradition.

"The male lineages were not counted, until holders of the treasure were needed. Then seven men descendant from the seven Chrechte tribes were chosen to be keepers of our last royal gifts. It was this treasure that Tamara's baron lover was trying to take when he tried to burn down our keep and kill our warriors."

"And you are showing it to me?"

"Yes. I trust you with all that I am." He put the torch in a holder and took both her hands. "The only one who knows of the treasury is the protector and his chosen helper. My mother did not know of its existence, nor did my sister Cait. I do not know how Tamara learned of it from my father, but she did. His second-in-command was the only other person who knew about it."

"Niall and Barr's father."

"Yes. When my father told me of the treasure, on his deathbed, I chose to share the knowledge with Niall rather than his older brothers. My wolf chose him as my partner in protecting the treasure as he chose you to be my mate."

"Your own mother did not know about this?"

"No."

"Thank you for telling me."

"All that I am is yours."

"You really mean that."

He nodded. Then he turned to the casket. "Would you like to see it?"

"If you want to show me."

"I do."

He lifted the lid of the marble casket. Inside there were

bones, a large cross like priests carried during mass, a smaller cross on a chain, a modest crown and a sword without even a jeweled handle.

"These are treasures of the heart, not of gold."

He smiled, clearly pleased she understood. "The bones of the right hand of St. Columba, the warrior saint."

"The hand that held his sword and his pen."

"Exactly."

"And the other bones?"

"The skull and right hand of Uven, son of Oengus, the last king over all the Chrechte tribes. The sword and crown are his as well. The cross on the left belonged to Columba, and the one on the right Uven wore into battle."

"Your stepmother was a fool. This treasure may be worth dying to protect, but it is not worth killing to steal. Its value lives in the hearts of the people for whom it signifies history."

"You are an amazing woman, Abigail of the Sinclair. Truly, my secrets are safe in your small hands."

"And my heart is safe in your big ones, though mighty, they are gentle with it."

"Always." Then he saluted like a warrior, right fist over his heart.

She was smiling when she threw herself into his arms to kiss him.

She had found more than a place of security in the world that had been less than friendly since her tenth year; she had found true love and a sacred mate.

No woman could want for more.

Epilogue

Scotland's king did not send a messenger to his favored laird, Talorc of the Sinclairs, in reply to his laird's latest words. He came himself. To meet the woman that inspired such loyalty, he said. Though, it soon became clear he had a secondary motive. He wanted Barr to rule the Donegal clan until young Circin had been trained and reached an age to lead the smaller clan.

Talorc left the choice up to Barr. Barr accepted with the stipulation that Osgard could come with him. The old warrior had admitted to setting both Talorc's horse after Abigail and putting pebbles on the stairs so she would trip. It was clear from his rambling confession that the old man had begun to confuse the present with the past.

He had not intended Abigail serious harm, though both pranks could have resulted in her death. He had wanted to show Talorc what a liability she was to the clan, so he would petition to the king for dissolution of the marriage.

Talorc wanted to kill him, but Abigail pleaded for mercy, and Barr's suggestion was accepted as a workable compromise. Barr left with the four Donegal youths a week after the king.

Una left two days later, after once again countermanding one of Abigail's orders. Talorc overheard this time and took immediate exception, sending the housekeeper back to her family's clan, since the widow had joined the Sinclairs through marriage. Word came a couple of months later that Una had married, taking on a widower with four children under the age of six, and was blissfully happy.

Abigail enjoyed sharing responsibilities with Guaire as seneschal too much to take over Una's position completely, so she promoted one of the other cooks and was well pleased with the results.

But nothing was more pleasing than the gift of each day with her beloved Talorc. Her werewolf was the most amazing and wonderful man that had ever lived, she was sure of it. And she was so very, very grateful that she was his mate. She did not understand it, but miracles were by their nature incomprehensible.

She only knew that far from being cursed as others might claim because of her deafness, she was blessed with this rare gift of life and love.

Turn the page for a preview of
the first book in the

CHILDREN OF THE MOON SERIES

Moon Awakening
by Lucy Monroe

Available now from Berkley Sensation!

Chapter 1

"And so the werewolf carried the lass off and neither was ever heard from again." Joan's sepulcher tones faded as the dark shadows in the kitchen reached out to wrap around the two young women listening so avidly to her every word.

Emily Hamilton tried to imagine being carried off into the wilds by a werewolf, or being carried off anywhere for that matter, but couldn't. She was nineteen, well past the age when most ladies were married, or even dowered into a convent. She would spend her life as her stepmother's drudge.

She sighed. Not even a werewolf would risk Sybil's wrath to carry Emily off.

"Are there truly werewolves in the Highlands?" her younger stepsister, Abigail, asked in careful Gaelic.

Joan shook her head, nary a wisp of her gray hair peeking from the housekeeper's wimple she wore. "Nay, lass.

Though if ever there were a place such monsters might thrive, it would be that harsh and hilly land."

"I thought you said the Highlands were beautiful," Emily inserted, her own Gaelic more natural than Abigail's.

But that was hardly a surprise. Her younger sister speaking at all was the result of Abigail's tenacity. When the fever had almost taken her life three years before, it *had* taken her hearing. It had also destroyed what existed of family harmony in Emily's home.

Deafness was considered a sign of the damned by some and a curse by most.

Sybil made it clear that she would have preferred her daughter had died rather than be so afflicted. Overnight, Abigail had gone from being an asset her stepmother counted on to advance her own place in the world to a problem best avoided. It was left to Emily to coax her younger stepsister back to health and into living amidst the household again.

Out of fear that Abigail would be rejected by the rest of the keep like she had been by her own mother, Emily had done her best to hide her sister's affliction. The younger girl had helped, working hard to learn to read lips and continue speaking as if she heard the voices around her.

So far, the deception had succeeded. Few people within the keep knew of the fifteen-year-old's inability to hear.

"It's a beautiful place, or so my mother always told me . . . but a harder land to live in. Och . . . The clans are so wild, even the women know how to fight."

Emily thought it sounded like a magical place.

An hour later, the rest of the family and the servants were in bed. Everyone, that was, except her father and stepmother. They were in the great hall talking. Emily was usually the last of the family to go to bed and she burned with curiosity to know what was important enough to keep her parents from their slumber.

She stopped at the top of the stairs leading to the great hall and moved into the shadows. Eavesdropping might not be ladylike, but it was a good way to satisfy her curiosity and her need to stay informed of her father and stepmother's plans. Too many others depended on her to protect them from Sybil's machinations and her father's cold indifference to their welfare.

"Surely, Reuben, you cannot expect to send Jolenta!" her stepmother cried.

"The king's order is quite explicit, madam. We are to send a daughter of marriageable age to this laird in the Highlands."

Emily ducked behind a small table, making herself as diminutive as possible. It was not difficult. Much to her personal chagrin, she was not precisely tall. It was a fact tossed at her by Sybil often. She had no "regal bearing," as befitting the daughter of a landholding baron. She supposed there was nothing regal about hiding behind a table, no matter how tall she might have been. And that was that.

"Jolenta is far too young to be married," stormed Sybil.

"She has fourteen years. Emily's mother was a year younger when I married her."

Sybil, Emily knew, hated any mention of her husband's first wife, and responded with acid. "And a baby can be betrothed in the cradle. Many girls are wed when they are a mere twelve years, but almost as many die in childbirth. You could not wish such a fate for our delicate flower surely?"

Her father made a noncommittal sound.

"You might as well suggest we send little Margery as send my dear Jolenta."

In her hiding place, Emily had to smile. Margery was a mere six years. Even the Church refused to recognize marriages contracted between parties under the age of twelve.

"If Jolenta is of an age to marry, then surely Abigail at fifteen is also. This will doubtless be her only opportunity," Sybil said callously.

Bile rose in Emily's throat. She'd always known the other woman was cold, but such a suggestion was monstrous and her father had to know it.

"The girl is deaf."

Emily nodded in agreement and inched out of her hiding place so she could see her parents. They were sitting at the head table almost directly under where she stood and were too intent on each other to look up and see her.

Sybil said, "No one knows except the family and a few servants who would not dare to reveal our secret."

But Abigail could not hope to hide such an affliction from a husband, which was exactly what her father said.

"By the time he realizes she is so flawed, he will have consummated the marriage. Then he will have no recourse," Sybil said dismissively. "He's a Scotsman after all. Everyone knows they are barbarians, especially the Highland clans."

"And you are not concerned about what he will do to her when he realizes?" Sir Reuben asked.

Emily had to bite her lip to stop from screaming at the selfish woman when Sybil simply shrugged delicately.

"I have no desire to end up at war with one of the Highland clans over this."

"Don't be foolish. The laird is hardly going to travel this distance to take his anger out on you."

"So, I am foolish?" Sir Reuben asked in a dangerous tone.

"Only if you let old-womanish fears guide you in this decision," Sybil replied, showing how little her lord intimidated her.

"Aren't you the one who recommended I send the bare contingent of knights to assist my overlord in his last request for warriors?"

"We could hardly leave our own estates inadequately guarded."

"But his anger over my stinginess has led to this request."

"I was right though, wasn't I? He did not sanction you."

"You do not consider the loss of a daughter a sanction?"

"They must marry sometime and it is not as if we do not have a gaggle of them."

"But only one of whom you consider utterly dispensable."

"The others could still make advantageous matches."

"Even Emily?"

Her stepmother's scoffing laughter was all the answer her father got to that small taunt.

"I will send word to the king that he can expect my daughter to travel north to Laird Sinclair's holding within the month along with her dowry."

"Not Jolenta?" Sybil asked, her voice quavering.

Sir Reuben sighed with disgust. "Not Jolenta."

He meant to send Abigail. Horrified, Emily shouted, "No!"

Both Sir Reuben and Sybil started and turned their heads toward her like two buzzards caught picking over a carcass.

She flew down the stairs. "You mustn't send Abigail to such a cursed fate!"

Sybil's mouth pursed with distaste. "Were you eavesdropping again?"

"Yes. And I'm glad I did." She turned to her father, her heart in her throat. "You can't think to send Abigail so far away to a husband who might believe her affliction is a sign from God that she is unclean."

"Perhaps it is such a sign," Sybil inserted, but Emily ignored her.

"Please, Father. Do not do this."

"Your stepmother has pointed out that it may well be Abigail's only chance at marriage. Would you deny it to her?"

"Yes, if it means sending her to a barbaric Scotsman who will be furious when he realizes how you have tricked him." As her father's face hardened, Emily forced herself to rein in her temper. She did not wish to lose the battle before she'd begun because her demeanor offended her father. She lowered her eyes, though it was hard to do. "Please, Father. Do not be offended, but I believe Sybil is wrong. I do not think a proud leader of a Scottish clan would take such deception in stride and be content to spend his fury on his hapless wife."

The fact that either of her parents thought that an acceptable alternative was more than she could bear.

"You believe the clan leader would declare war?"

"Yes."

"What does she know?" Sybil scoffed. "She knows nothing of the world."

"I have heard the tales of these fierce people, Father."

"Tales told to frighten foolish children," Sybil said.

"So my daughter is foolish as well?" Sir Reuben asked, proving he had not forgotten his wife's earlier insult.

Sybil's hands fisted at her sides as if she realized she'd made an error in speaking so plainly now that they both knew the conversation had been overheard. Her father's pride might accept such intransigence from his wife in private, but he would not tolerate others—even a lowly daughter—seeing him in a light that could make him appear weak.

Emily was determined to use that to her advantage. "Father, you are one of the wisest of the king's barons. Everyone knows that."

"Too wise to risk war with a barbaric people simply to placate an overmanaging wife?"

Emily knew better than to answer, so she remained silent while Sybil gasped in outrage.

"Who would you have me send in her place?"

"Jolenta?" she asked.

"No!" Sybil cried and then she grasped her husband's sleeve. "Consider, my dearest lord, the betrothed of Baron de Coucy's heir died of a fever not a month past. The baron will be looking for a new bride to contract very soon. His mother has already made it clear she finds Jolenta pleasing."

The younger girl had spent the last two years at Court, an honor Emily had never been extended.

"I thought you said she was too young to wed."

"A barbaric Scotsman, but not the son of a powerful baron."

"Then who would you have me send in accord to the king's order?"

"Abigail . . ."

"No, please, Father . . ."

"I do not fancy a war over the disposal of one of my daughters."

Emily winced at her father's comment. Silence had

fallen between her parents and she feared its outcome if she said nothing. Yet terror at her own thoughts and what they would mean for the sister she would leave behind as well as for herself filled her.

She took a deep breath and then forced herself to say, "Send me."

"*You?* You think, my lord, that the Scotsman will not go to war over you sending such an undisciplined girl? She's sure to mortally offend him her first week as his wife."

"You said it yourself, they are barbarians. He would hardly appreciate a true English lady."

Old pain seared Emily's heart. Her father had no higher opinion of her than her stepmother. She had known that particular truth since her own mother's death, when he had berated a small girl crying over her mother's grave with the knowledge she was not the son he had craved. If she had been, her mother would not have died trying to give birth to another.

Emily knew the cruel words for the lie they were . . . now. But until she had seen Sybil grow large with child twice more after giving her father the heir he sought, she had believed them. And felt unworthy because of them.

But she no longer believed that to be born female made her unworthy. Six years of correspondence with a powerful abbess had healed her of that affliction. She reminded herself of that fact as she raised her gaze to meet her father's.

It was as if he had been waiting for her to do so. "Think you that you will fare better than Abigail in the wilds of Scotland?"

"Yes."

"I think perhaps you are right." He turned to his wife. "It is decided. I will send Emily in answer to my overlord's demand."

"And Abigail?" Emily asked.

"She will remain here, under my protection."

The large black wolf sniffed the air, his powerful body coiled to spring into instant motion if needed.

Away from his own territory, even in the company of his companions, the situation was wrought with danger. He had not brought an attack force and the clan he had come to spy on had a full contingent of wolf warriors. Some of them were even as mighty as his own.

That meant treading carefully.

He made his way silently through the forest, knowing his two companions followed, though he could not hear them. The presence of all three went undetected by man or beast and that was as it should be.

His father had started teaching him to mask his scent from the night of his first change, and he had perfected the art. Other werewolves and even wild animals could come close enough to touch him in the dark and never know he was there. He had chosen two warriors just as skilled to accompany him.

Though he stopped often to sniff the wind, it was not his ultrasensitive nose that caught the first signal that his brother Ulf had been right. Rather, his ears picked up a sound no human could have heard at such a distance. From the clan's holding beyond the trees and across the expanse of heather-filled grass, he heard the unmistakable sound of the lass's laugh.

The femwolf, Susannah, was here.

Her soft human voice spoke, though even his superior hearing was not up to deciphering the words. She did not sound as if she was in distress, but that did not alter the facts or how he must respond to them.

Clan law . . . ancient clan law, known by most Celts and every Chrechte warrior that had joined them two centuries before . . . had been broken. A Balmoral woman had been taken to mate without the consent of the clan chief.

Lachlan, Laird of the Balmoral and pack leader to the Chrechte contingent among them, would not tolerate the insult.

Ulf had been right about what had happened to the fem-wolf who had disappeared during the last full moon hunt. He had also been right when he said the Sinclairs must be made to pay. No Highland chief would tolerate such insolence leveled against his clan and himself as a person. It implied the Sinclairs thought he was too weak to enforce clan law, that his warriors did not protect their women.

England would be his ally before he would allow such a view of his clan to stand unchallenged. However, it was not a declaration of war that would give a message of the greatest impact to the other Highland clans, but well-planned revenge. As he had told Ulf when his brother had suggested mounting an immediate attack on the Sinclair holding.

Riding an exhausted horse and feeling less than wonderful herself, Emily surveyed her new home with both curiosity and trepidation.

The journey from her father's barony had been a long one and arduous upon reaching the Highlands. Shortly after reaching Sinclair land, an envoy of warriors arrived to finish escorting her to their keep.

Emily had been both disappointed and relieved to discover that her husband-to-be had not accompanied them. Part of her wanted the first meeting over, but an even bigger part was content to put it off indefinitely.

The Sinclair warriors had refused to allow the English soldiers any farther onto Sinclair land. They had taken over her escort and Emily found them poor company indeed. They did not speak unless asked a question and then they answered in monosyllables if possible. Would her husband-to-be do the same?

Perhaps she would feel better if people would stop staring at her so. No one smiled, not even the children. Some adults openly glared at her. She turned to her nearest escort. "Some of the clan seem hostile. Why is that?"

"They know you are English."

Apparently that was supposed to explain it all because he stopped talking and even her curiosity was not up to questioning the soldier further.

So the clan knew she was English? That must mean they were expecting her.

For those in any doubt, her dress would have given her away, she supposed. She'd donned the dark blue tunic over her clean white shift with stylish wide sleeves three days ago. It was now as creased and bedraggled as the rest of her, but even if it had remained pristine, it was nothing like the garb of the Highlanders.

They all wore plaids, even the children. The colors were muted green, blue and black. It was a striking combination. She'd said something to that effect to one of her escorts upon first meeting—admittedly in an effort to pretend she wasn't noticing the fact that their lower legs were as naked as a baby being washed. He had growled that of course it was pleasing; they were the Sinclair colors.

She'd stopped trying to make small talk soon thereafter.

She turned her interest from the less-than-welcoming people to the Sinclair castle. The construction surprised her. She wasn't sure what she had expected, but something so much like her own father's home was not it. The ground had been raised to a hill with a moat around it. The keep, which looked like a single high tower was built on top of the hill with a wall all around. The timber wall extended down the hill to surround the bailey as well.

She hadn't imagined anything so grand in the Highlands. Perhaps her husband-to-be was not such a barbarian after all. Perhaps he would even have a kind heart and allow her to send for Abigail to come live with them. That was her most fervent hope.

Her escort led her across the drawbridge toward the keep.

A group of soldiers on the steps of the keep caught her eye. They all stood with arms folded and scowling at her approach. One soldier, who stood in the middle and was taller than all of the rest, scowled most fiercely. She tried to avoid looking at him because the dislike, nay *hatred*, emanating off of him was frightening.

She hoped he was not one of her husband-to-be's close advisors. She scanned the crowd to find her future husband, their laird. Her escort had led her almost to the scowling soldiers before she realized that one of them must be him. Her only excuse for being so slow to realize it was her deep desire for it to be otherwise.

Please don't let it be the angry man in the center, she prayed fervently, crossing herself for good measure.

When the soldier in the middle stepped forward, she offered up a last desperate plea. But she knew it had been in vain when, without acknowledging her, he waved for her escort to follow him.

"Where do you want the Englishwoman?" called the soldier nearest her.

Her future husband merely shrugged and continued

inside. For the life of her, she couldn't think of any good excuse for his behavior. Even if he was a barbarian as Sybil claimed.

She could only be glad that Abigail had not been sent in her place. God alone knew what kind of horrible things he might have done to her gentle sister. Or perhaps it was the devil himself who knew.

She banished the wicked thought, but could not dismiss as easily the sense of doom settling over her.

Enter the rich world of historical romance with Berkley Books.

Lynn Kurland

Patricia Potter

Betina Krahn

Jodi Thomas

Anne Gracie

Love is timeless.
penguin.com

Discover
Romance

berkleyjoveauthors.com
See what's coming
up next from your
favorite romance
authors and
explore all
the latest
Berkley,
Jove, and
Sensation
selections.

Fall in love

- See what's new
- Find author appearances
- Win fantastic prizes
- Get reading recommendations
- Chat with authors and other fans
- Read interviews with authors you love

berkleyjoveauthors.com